Book 4 in the Amber Ridge Series

unbroken

NYSSA KATHRYN

An NW Partners Book
Cover by Deranged Doctor Design
Developmentally and Copy Edited by Kelli Collins
Line Edited by Jessica Snyder
Proofread by Amanda Cuff and Jen Katemi
Cover Photography by Briquelle Kayanne Photography

❀ Created with Vellum

This time, she comes first. No matter the cost.

Life with her husband had become an endless waiting game: waiting for him to return from missions, waiting for a baby that never came, waiting for his mother to accept her. So after years of IVF, loneliness, and endless heartbreak, Indie Reed made the impossible choice—she left her husband. But a year later, shortly after returning her unsigned divorce papers, Colt comes home... and Indie needs to decide if she's strong enough to let him in again.

One mistake cost Colt Reed the most important thing in his life: his wife. Now he's left the Marines for one reason—to get her back. It wasn't a sacrifice; it was a decision. Because one year without her felt like a lifetime. He didn't choose her when he should have. Didn't notice how his job was affecting her...how she spiraled deeper into depression with each failed round of IVF...or how his own family was treating her. Now, he won't stop fighting until Indie understands she's his only priority.

But as Indie and Colt begin to rebuild what's broken, not only does his mother turn out to be more of an obstacle than he ever imagined...but the deadbeat father he hasn't seen in more than twenty-five years suddenly returns. And it's far from a happy reunion.

ACKNOWLEDGMENTS

Thank you to my entire team for helping me drag this book over the finish line—Kelly, Jessica, Amanda and Jen, you're all amazing and so important for every book baby I release.

Thank you to my amazing ARC team. You are my final eyes before my story is released out into the world and your reviews push me to write the next book.

And, of course, thank you to my amazing husband for giving me the time, space and energy to write. And our two daughters—you are amazing, and I can't wait to see the women you become.

PROLOGUE

 ne Year Ago

WHERE WAS HE? He was supposed to be here. He was late. An hour late.

Indie Reed tapped the screen of her phone for what had to be the twentieth time. It was almost five. So close to when that call from the nurse was coming.

Most IVF nurses didn't call at five. They liked the morning. She'd had to fight for the later call. And she *had* fought. Because it was the only time Colt could be here.

Her gaze moved from her phone to the street through her living room window. Still nothing.

Why? He knew how important this was. He should be answering her calls. Actually, no, if he was going to be late, he should be calling *her*.

She breathed in a lungful of air, a tremble starting to skitter through her fingers.

She felt sick. The kind that didn't just crawl around her belly.

She felt it everywhere. In her mouth. Her limbs. Deep in her body.

If the nurse gave her bad news and he wasn't here, she wasn't sure what would happen. Would she crumble? Break? Or would her body just go numb?

Six years. Six years of trying and failing to have a baby, each one harder than the last. She hadn't known the world of infertility could be so dark. She hadn't known *a lot* six years ago.

And now? Now she was struggling. Hell, struggling didn't even touch the surface of the hole that had begun to form in her chest. The hole that kept getting bigger and bigger. Some days, she wondered how big it could get before she completely hollowed out.

This was their last embryo. After six years of trying, four years of that being IVF, she wasn't sure she was strong enough to go through another round. The hormones, the injections, the procedures. And the hope...the hope that built with every round, only to be squashed by those two words: not pregnant.

No. This time, it was going to work. She was pregnant. She had to be. She'd intentionally not tested this round, needing to wait for the results of the blood test.

She closed her eyes, the thuds of her heartbeat so strong that she felt them throughout her entire body.

Where was he? She tried to be understanding of his commitments to the military. He was a Marine. Most of the time, his life wasn't his own. But right now, he was supposed to be here.

His plane had arrived into Bozeman two hours ago and the drive to Amber Ridge was only an hour.

She hit his name on her cell again and pressed it to her ear.

Pick up. Please, pick up. Tell me you're close, Colt.

The click of someone answering lit hope in her chest.

"Indie. It's Sylvia."

The hope crashed and burned at the sound of her mother-in-law's voice. "Sylvia. Why are you answering Colt's phone? Is he with you?"

"We're at the hospital. He'd just gotten to Amber Ridge when I started getting chest pains. I called him in a panic because I thought I was having a heart attack. Thank God I wasn't! He's just talking to my doctor in the hall."

Air thickened in Indie's lungs, making her next breath so hard her chest squeezed.

He was with his mother. Sylvia knew what time Colt was getting in. She'd also known how important this call was.

She'd done this on purpose. She'd done similar things before.

But that wasn't what hurt the most. It was that Colt had gone to her. Colt *always* went to her.

"He's not going to make it..." The words were barely a whisper from her lips, the heaviness trying to drag her to the floor.

"Oh, the call from the clinic. I'm sorry. I completely forgot. He won't be long."

It didn't matter how long he took—the nurse was calling any second now. "I need to go."

She hung up and, like clockwork, her phone started ringing, the name of the fertility clinic on the screen.

For a moment she just stood there, her heart rate speeding up and stumbling over itself. The fear that came with each beat slipped out to other parts of her body.

Alone. She had to do this alone. She had to be strong.

With shaking fingers, she hit the answer key. "Indie speaking."

"Hi, Indie, it's Nurse Raven from Amber Ridge Fertility Center. How are you?"

There was something about the nurse's voice...slow, each word deliberate.

Suddenly, Indie wanted to run. To hang up and be as far from this call as possible. Because even though a second ago she'd told herself to be strong, she didn't feel strong right now. She felt like she was standing on the edge of a cliff, and the next words had the power to tip her over the edge.

"I'm okay," Indie said softly. A lie. Possibly the biggest she'd ever told. Nothing about this was okay or fair or made a bit of sense. "Just waiting for you to call."

There was a small pause. "I'm sorry. Unfortunately, the results of your blood test came back negative. You're not pregnant."

Not pregnant. The words slipped beneath her skin, so familiar, yet still so much power to hurt.

There was no baby. Six years of trying. A million needles and tests and heartache, and she was *still* exactly where she'd started.

How many times could she create space in her heart for someone who never arrived?

The nurse continued talking, but the woman's words started to blur as a buzzing sounded between her ears. When her body felt too heavy, she dropped to the couch, her head falling between her knees in an attempt to breathe. To try to stop the devastation, the hopelessness, from swallowing her whole.

It was never going to happen. She was never going to get pregnant and hold her baby in her arms. She was never going to hear their little laugh or see what color their eyes were. She'd never feel those chubby fingers wrap around her own.

A sob broke out of her throat and tears burned her eyes. All those timelines she'd grieved, and this was just another. But it felt more final.

At some point, the phone slipped from her fingers and she just cried. Loud, ugly tears as the pain bled out of her.

Time passed, but she couldn't move. And when the front door opened, she didn't immediately look up. She knew exactly who it was.

"Indie?"

Slowly, she forced her gaze up.

Colt's face paled. He moved toward her, fast steps that closed the distance between them.

But she shook her head. "Stop."

He halted, confusion mixing with the concern in his dark eyes. "Indie—"

"You weren't here. I needed you, and you weren't here."

Agony twisted his features. "I know. My mom called me, hysterical that she was having a heart attack. I meant to call you when I reached the hospital but my phone died. I'd just plugged it in when Mom answered your call."

Of *course* she'd said she was having a heart attack. If she'd used the same "chest pains" excuse as last time, Colt wouldn't have gone to her before the IVF clinic called. But a heart attack? Yeah, that worked.

He stepped closer. "I'm here now. And I need to make sure you're okay—"

"I'm not." The words cut into the air like a knife. Her voice almost cracked, but she forced it to remain steady. "I haven't been okay for a long time."

"I know." Two whispered words from him. "Trying to have a baby has been challenging—"

"Challenging? Colt...it's destroying me. I've been stuck in this place of trying to have a baby for six years, and I'm losing hope. I'm losing strength. I'm losing my ability to see any light in this world. And today, I needed you!"

"How can I fix this?"

Fix it? As if this was a broken chair that needed a nail or some glue. Or a cracked shard of glass in a window.

This wasn't fixable. She was broken. *They* were broken. And in a couple of days, he'd go back to the Marine Corps and she'd still be here, alone, wondering how on earth she was supposed to get through another day.

It wasn't his fault that he had to go back to work.

"I can't do this anymore." The whispered words tumbled from somewhere deep inside her, and the second they were out, she wanted to tug them back. But she physically couldn't bring herself to do it. Because *something* did need to change. Otherwise, she wouldn't make it.

An expression crossed his face. Confusion...panic. It looked so out of a place on the man who usually carried the world on his shoulders. "What do you mean, you can't do this anymore?"

"It's too hard. Every day is too hard." *Had been* too hard for so long.

"Indie—"

"I can't breathe, Colt." Her voice broke and she couldn't inhale a full breath. "Some days get so dark I wonder if I'll ever see light again. Between infertility, wondering if you're going to return after your missions, and dealing with your mother, *I'm drowning.*"

"My mother?"

"My head is underwater," she whispered. "I just...I need something to change. I need a break."

"From me?"

"From *everything*. From the world I've created for myself. I need to figure out how not to feel broken."

* * *

COLT'S WORLD TILTED. No, it fucking spun off its axis, and he had no idea how to pull it back into place.

He stepped forward, craving her touch. "Indie. I'm sorry I wasn't here when you needed me. But you can't end this marriage. I love you. And you love me."

A single tear slid down her cheek, and it gutted him. Everything about this moment made him feel like there was no version of him that could get out of this whole.

Another step forward, the need to touch her suffocating him. "Please...let me be here for you. Let me make this right." He reached out a hand.

"Don't—please."

He stopped, the agony in her voice weaving inside him. He

was so used to having answers. Being decisive. In his line of work, you had to be if you wanted to survive. But this? He had no fucking clue what to do.

This pain in Indie's eyes wasn't new. He'd known she was hurting. Known she'd been struggling for a while. Infertility was hard. But when had it gotten *this* bad? When had she become this despondent, this deep in her grief?

He'd missed it. Yes, he worked a job that demanded a lot of him. Yes, he was away a lot, but Indie was his *wife*. He should have seen how bad things had gotten.

"Don't ask me to leave," he whispered. "Fight for us. Fight for *me*."

Another tear slid down her cheek. "I've *been* fighting, Colt. I've been fighting for so long, and now I'm just tired." Her breathing hitched. "I need it to end."

It? Meaning the pain? Or them?

It didn't matter. Either way, she wanted him to leave. To step out of their house and accept this *break*. But he couldn't. His feet wouldn't fucking move.

"I *can't* lose you," he pushed, the shake in his voice something he'd never heard before.

"You already have. Because I'm not the Indie you married. I think I lost a little bit more of myself after each round of trying. I don't know how many more pieces I can lose before I just disappear."

"Then we'll stop trying. We'll take a break from *that*, not us."

Her breathing grew faster. So fast, she pressed a hand to her chest. "No. I need you to leave. I need..." Her chest heaved.

"Let me be here for you."

She shook her head. "I need space to *breathe*." When he didn't move, her voice grew louder, desperation coating each word. "Please, Colt, let me breathe without you here. Let me figure out how to save myself."

The urge to tug her into his arms consumed him, pulling at his limbs.

But he fought it. Fuck, he fought it. Because every time he got closer, the ache in her eyes deepened. The tears became thicker and the panic more intense.

He couldn't fix this. Not right now.

And he loved her. Shit, he loved her so much he would tear his own damn heart out of his chest if it meant saving hers.

So he stepped back, the move feeling unnatural.

"Okay, Cricket. I'll go. But this isn't over. I'll be back. We *will* survive this."

It took every ounce of his strength to turn. To walk out of the house they'd bought together and pull the door closed behind him, feeling like he was leaving his wife in the middle of a hurricane.

He didn't leave the porch right away though. He couldn't. Instead, he waited.

Then he heard it.

Indie's crying.

The sound was loud, and it destroyed something inside him. Made him feel like a fraction of the man he thought he was.

He pressed his forehead to the door, wanting to go back in. To break down the door that separated them, and hold her. Keep all the fractured pieces of her together.

He didn't. He forced himself to go to his car. But again, he didn't leave. He lifted his phone and texted Clara, Indie's cousin and best friend.

Ten minutes later, Clara pulled up in front of the house and ran up the walk. He waited until she'd stepped inside before finally turning on his engine.

That's when he made the decision. He had one more year until his contract was up—then he was coming home, and he was fixing his marriage.

CHAPTER 1

*L*ate...very late.

Indie shot a glance at her watch and groaned, then sped her steps to a sprint through the trees toward her car. Well, *her* version of a sprint. She definitely wasn't winning any awards for her speed. But then, the camera bag weighed her down, so it wasn't entirely her fault.

Trees whirled past her, the smell of pine thick in the air. At least the rain had held off for her shoot, even if the session had run over. But to be fair, the sun had been stubborn, and she'd needed to wait for it to poke through the trees in just the right way so she could get *the shot*...and it had been *so* worth it.

She exited the forest into the parking lot, where she quickly unlocked her car and climbed in.

She turned the key. The engine didn't start.

Dammit.

She tried again. Still nothing.

"Come on, come on, come on." Third try and the engine finally kicked over. "Thank God."

A week ago, she wouldn't have had this problem. But a week ago, she'd had her super reliable Subaru Crosstrek that never broke down. Now she had this hunk-of-junk Honda Accord that had been built before she was born...literally.

But it had been cheap. And that Subaru money was needed.

She checked the time on her dashboard as she drove. Half an hour. It should be enough time to quickly drop everything at the house, change, and make it to the fertility clinic in time for her appointment. Plus, they always ran late. Or at least, they *had*. She hadn't been back in over a year.

Nerves fluttered in her belly. Nerves that she was doing the wrong thing. That she'd regret this. And maybe she would. Maybe this would all end in heartache...again.

But she was in a better place now. She'd been to therapy, healed so much of herself, and gotten a ton of acupuncture from Clara. She hadn't climbed her way out of the darkness—she'd clawed her way out by her fingertips. She wouldn't fall into that dark place again.

One year. It had been one year of healing...and one year of being separated from Colt.

Her heart thumped at the memory of Colt's text messages over the last twelve months. The phone calls she hadn't answered. The visits she hadn't been home for.

But she'd had to focus on herself. So much of her had been scared that seeing him again might put her right back where she'd started. It would bring back all the failed IVF attempts.

And not a lot else had changed, either. His mother was still his mother. He'd still been in the military.

But now he's out, a voice whispered in her head.

Not just out, he was here in Amber Ridge. He'd been back home in Montana for almost a month.

She'd booked this meeting at the fertility clinic before she'd known he was coming home. She was almost thirty-five, with a ticking clock when it came to her fertility.

Even after telling herself she'd never do IVF again, she felt like she owed it to herself to give it one final go.

But could she actually go through the process again? This time with a sperm donor?

Time would tell.

She was halfway home when her phone rang, Clara's name flashing on the screen. She put her cousin on speaker. "Hey, can you hear me?"

"You're muffled. Are you using your car's Bluetooth?"

She cringed. Crap. She hadn't told Clara she'd sold her car. She hadn't told anyone. They'd ask questions and probably work out that she was having money problems, something she absolutely did not want, because then everyone would step in offering help. And she was not taking money from family.

"No. You're on speaker." She cleared her throat. "Is everything okay?"

"Yeah, I just wanted to check on you before your appointment."

Those nerves took off in her belly again.

"Are you doing okay?" Clara asked softly.

"Yeah, I'm doing okay. I mean…it's just an information appointment to find out about the process of using a sperm donor. I'm not committing to anything."

"It's still a big deal. I know I've already offered, but I'm more than happy to come with you."

Indie was shaking her head before Clara had finished speaking. "No. You've been through so much this year."

"Indie, I'm fine now."

It had been less than a month since Clara had been chased down and shot at. "I'm okay to go by myself. But I appreciate the offer."

"Fine, but if you change your mind—"

"You'll be the first to know."

"Good."

There was a long pause, and Indie could almost hear her cousin thinking. "Say it."

"Say what?"

"Whatever you're trying to work up the courage to say."

Clara sighed. "I was just going to ask if you'd seen him yet."

She sucked in a breath of air. "I haven't seen him." Although, that probably had everything to do with her sudden need to become a recluse.

"Is that because, in an effort to avoid him, you haven't been going out?"

Dammit. Her cousin knew her too well. "I'm not answering that question. Have *you* seen him?"

There were two seconds of silence that gave Clara away before she answered the question. "He was in Rob's Diner last week."

"Last week? And you're only just telling me now?"

"And I saw him on Sunday night at CJs. And maybe this morning, when I was walking to Sassy Stems."

Indie's fingers tightened around the wheel. "You can tell me when you see him."

"I know, but I don't want to make you sad."

Did she look sad every time someone brought up Colt? "We're separated. I sent him divorce papers. We have to learn to coexist in this town."

Divorce papers. The words sounded big and heavy. They'd felt right to send at the time. She needed to move on. It was the final step in her healing.

But now that he was home? Maybe not so much.

"Uh-huh." Why did her cousin say it like she didn't believe it?

"Did you talk to him?"

"He came over and said hi at the diner. He asked how I was doing. Then he asked how you were doing."

Her heart gave a little kick. "And what did you say?"

"That you were amazing. Thriving, actually."

Indie almost snorted. Was selling her car to fund a round of IVF with donor sperm "thriving"? Probably not.

She turned onto her street. "Thank you for saying that. And thank you for checking in." She pulled into her driveway and turned off the engine.

"I'm always on your side, Indie."

"How are you and Holden?"

"This morning, he brought me an almond croissant and sweet tea in bed. Sometimes I have to pinch myself that I got so lucky."

"Good. You deserve to be happy." After everything Clara had been through, and the cancer she'd fought, she had earned every second of happiness she got.

"Thanks, Indie. You do too."

Maybe she'd find her way back to happy one day. She wasn't deep in the grips of depression anymore. But she could definitely be doing better. "Thanks. Chat soon?"

"I want an immediate update after your appointment."

Indie laughed. "Done."

The smile was still on her face as she climbed out of her car. God, she was lucky to have Clara. Her cousin had supported her a lot over the past year, just as her aunt Pam had. Without them, she wasn't sure she'd have gotten through.

Exactly why she didn't want to tell them about her money problems. They'd swoop in and save her, and they'd already saved her enough.

She grabbed her camera bag from the back and crossed to the door of her single-story ranch-style home. It was beautiful. A house she and Colt had bought together, just like the house they owned in California.

She'd assumed he'd keep the one in California and she'd keep this one, but now that he was in Amber Ridge, she wasn't sure what was going to happen.

Unlike her, Colt came from money. Old money. His mother was very well off, and as an only child, Colt had received a large trust fund from his maternal grandparents, whereas Indie wasn't even booking photo shoots.

And the worst part was, she had no idea why. A couple of years ago, her business was thriving. So freaking thriving, she'd had to turn down jobs. Now? She was lucky to get a couple bookings a month.

It was frustrating.

She unlocked her front door and stepped into her house—only to stop.

The hall light was on. She never left the hall light on. She never left *anything* on. She was almost overly obsessive about turning everything off because electricity was expensive.

Quietly, she slipped her camera bag to the floor and opened a drawer in the hallway table. Under the false bottom, she lifted her pistol. Then, slowly, she inched into the living room.

"Hello?"

She was just nearing the kitchen when a figure stepped in front of the island.

Her heart stopped.

Colt.

His familiar dark eyes bore into her, and he seemed to take up all the space. He was tall at six three, and right now he looked every one of those inches.

Suddenly, she couldn't move. She couldn't breathe. All the walls she'd built to protect herself started to crumble. It felt like no time had passed at all. Like the year of no kisses, no late-night conversations, just disappeared. He looked exactly the same, and her heart ached to cross the space between them and wrap her arms around him. To let him hold her.

Her fingers tightened around the grip of the gun. "What are you doing here?"

"Hey, Cricket. I've missed you."

Her heart squeezed. She hadn't heard that nickname in so long. He'd said he used it because she was small but fierce...but she didn't feel so fierce anymore.

"What are you doing in my house?"

One side of his mouth lifted, and yeah, she knew exactly what he was thinking. That it wasn't her house, it was *their* house. Their *home*. The home they'd chosen together. The home they'd wanted to raise a family in.

"I couldn't stay away any longer." He stepped toward her.

Air soared into her lungs. She'd been avoiding as many public spaces as possible because she knew that the second she saw him, she'd feel exactly what she was feeling right now. An impossibly heavy yearning. The feeling of close never quite being close enough.

He took another step toward her. "Can you put the pistol down, Cricket?"

Shit. She hadn't even realized she was still pointing it.

She lowered the gun. "Fine. But you don't touch me."

His brows flickered, and he seemed to consider that for a moment. "I'm just here to talk."

Talk? They'd never been good at just talking. Touching was their love language. It had been since high school.

"About what?" But she knew exactly what.

"Us."

How many times had she played over this conversation in her head? A million times. And every one of them had ended differently. "You didn't sign the divorce papers."

"Did you expect me to?"

No. The word was a whisper in her mind.

"You wouldn't answer my calls," he said softly. "You wouldn't respond to my texts. I had to resort to checking in with other people to make sure you were okay."

She frowned—but then it hit her. "Aunt Pam."

"And your brother. I hate that I couldn't be here to check on you myself."

"I'm okay."

"You look good." His gaze moved over her body, and she barely held back the shiver.

She'd always liked his eyes on her. They felt intimate and familiar.

He ran his fingers through his hair, and that's when she saw the ring on his finger. His wedding ring. He still wore it.

"You're out," she said quietly.

"I am."

"You loved your job."

"And look what it cost me."

Her breath hitched. "That wasn't why you lost me."

"It was part of the reason."

Thousands of women married Marines. She should have been able to cope with having a husband with those kinds of commitments. But that, in combination with the infertility and his mother...it had been too much.

Weak. The word had flickered in her head more than once over the last year.

"That doesn't make you weak."

Indie flinched at his words. He'd always had this freaky ability to know exactly what she was thinking. It was just one of the reasons she'd believed nothing could break them. Until something had.

CHAPTER 2

*C*olt shoved his hands into his pockets. It was his only
defense to stop from reaching out and touching her.

A year. A whole fucking year of no Indie, and he was still
supposed to keep distance between them. To not get close to
those moss-green eyes. To not feel that soft skin of hers.

Fucking torture.

"You haven't touched our shared bank account," he said.

Her brows rose like the very idea was crazy to her. "We've
been separated for a year. Did you expect me to?"

There were a lot of things he'd expected in the last year. To be
separated from his wife at this point wasn't one of them. "You're
still my wife."

Her eyes flared.

Every unanswered call had killed him. Every time he'd come
home to Amber Ridge and she refused to see him made him want
to say to hell with his military commitments.

"Have dinner with me." The words were out before he could
stop them.

For a single second, longing flashed in her eyes. She *wanted* to
have dinner with him.

But then she blinked. "Crap, what's the time?" She pulled her phone from her pocket. "I'm late."

"For what?"

She didn't answer his question, just spun and ran to the hallway table, where she put her pistol away before sprinting into her bedroom. The door closed with a definitive click.

His back teeth ground together. He needed to talk to her. He'd given her time to get used to the idea of him being back in Amber Ridge, but they needed to figure this out. He was home to stay, and she was his *wife*, dammit.

He stopped in the hall and stared at a photo of Indie and Clara. He ran his finger over the wooden frame. A frame he'd hung. Only, it had held a different picture then.

One of him and Indie on their wedding day.

Was the wedding photo behind this one? Or had she taken it out? Put it somewhere she wouldn't see it so she wouldn't have to think about him or them or their marriage?

The bedroom door opened. Indie had changed out of her dark jeans and vest, and now she wore nice slacks and a blouse.

She pulled on sandals by the door.

"You look nice." That didn't even touch the surface of how she looked. She'd always been the most beautiful woman in any room.

Her shoulders tensed. "Thanks. We'll have to chat another time."

"Tomorrow?"

She lifted her purse from the hall table. "I can't tomorrow."

"Sunday?"

"I'll have to check if I'm free." Once her shoes were on, she stepped through her door.

He followed behind her, frowning at the beat-up Honda. The fuck? "Where's your Subaru?"

"I sold it."

"And bought this piece of shit?"

"It's perfectly safe."

Like hell it was. It looked older than *him*.

"Can you lock up after yourself?" she asked. "I'll see you later."

She wrapped her fingers around the handle of her car door, but before she could open it, he reached out and gently gripped her arm. "Cricket."

She stopped. And God, just the feel of her skin beneath his fingertips was a reminder of how much he'd been starved of her over the last twelve months. Every day had been a battle. And not a battle he'd often won.

She didn't pull away, but the muscles in her arm flexed.

Long seconds passed before she finally turned, and the hesitancy in her eyes hit him like a physical gut punch. Once upon a time, she would have thrown herself into his arms. That time had passed.

"What, Colt?"

"I can't leave without knowing when we're going to talk." Because the idea that they *wouldn't* talk, that they'd keep living in the same town without any contact, was unbearable.

Her gaze flickered between his eyes. "Where are you staying?"

"For now, I'm at Mom's."

A sudden hardness shuttered her features. "I'll message you."

His mind shot back to the night they'd broken up. She'd mentioned his mother as part of the reason they'd broken up, and he'd never understood it. But damn, he'd thought about it a lot. "Is everything—"

"I really need to go, Colt."

She went to turn, but he stepped closer. "Promise me you'll text."

She glanced over her shoulder, and her mouth was so close to his that all he had to do was lower his head and he'd touch her lips with his own.

"I'll text," she whispered.

Everything in him screamed to lower his head. Kiss her. Taste her.

But he forced himself back. He had to earn back her trust, and that would take time. He had to fix what he'd broken. "I'll talk to you soon, Cricket."

She nodded quickly before sliding behind the wheel. Her engine didn't start on the first try. But then, the thing was a fucking rust bucket, of course it didn't.

They had money. And despite what she thought, his money *was* her money. She shouldn't be driving that car. She wouldn't be driving it for long. No damn way.

He stormed across the street to his Audi RS 5 and slammed the door after him.

He drove faster than he should have to his mother's house. He was even frustrated about that. He'd planned to rent a place until he could mend things with Indie, but his mother's health wasn't great. She suffered from panic attacks, high blood pressure, and severe asthma, so he worried about her living alone.

Sometimes the panic attacks got so severe that she thought she was having a heart attack. When he was young, the panic attacks had been about his deadbeat father, who'd disappeared when Colt was eight. Leaving him and his mother was the best thing that man had ever done for both of them. Now, the panic attacks had just become a part of his mother's life.

He pulled into her driveway, and he was about to get out when his phone rang.

Noah, Indie's brother.

Colt put the cell to his ear. "Hey. Are you back?"

"About to get on my flight to Bozeman now."

Just like Colt, Noah had been a Marine, but while Colt had been stationed at Camp Pendleton most recently, Noah had been at the Marine Corps Air Station in Cherry Point, North Carolina. They'd never lost contact though. The man was a year older than Colt and had been a friend for as long as he'd been dating Indie.

"How does it feel to be coming home?" Colt asked.

"Good and bad. It hit me the hardest when I stepped off base for the last time."

"I know that feeling. I've been out for a month, and I still can't believe it."

"Ever regret it?"

"No." His answer was instant. "I spent a year without my wife. Hardest damn thing I've ever done. Never again."

"Have you seen her?"

His fingers tightened around the cell. "Just now."

"Uh-oh. What happened?"

Had the anger in his voice given him away? Not anger toward Indie. Toward himself for losing her. "She didn't want to talk. Ran out saying she had an appointment."

"Maybe she did."

"I'm sure she did. But I'm also sure that if she wanted to cancel for the husband she hasn't seen in a year, she would have."

"Give it time. You guys went through a lot. She wasn't in a great place a year ago. Even six months ago, she was still struggling to find herself again."

He leaned his head back and closed his eyes, hating hearing that. Hating that he wasn't there for her.

"Plane's boarding. I'll see you soon."

Colt nodded even though his friend couldn't see him. "Meeting Friday at the adventure park, right?"

"Yeah, looking forward to it."

Colt hung up and climbed out of his Audi.

His gaze ran over the old Victorian mansion where he'd grown up. The intricate brickwork. The wraparound porch. It was a combination of heritage and luxury, and it fit his mother perfectly.

For most people her age, it would be too big to take care of, but what Sylvia Reed couldn't do herself, she employed people to do. Cleaners. Gardeners. Hell, sometimes she even hired a cook.

NYSSA KATHRYN

He stepped inside, the strong smell of coffee and baked goods hanging in the air. The grand staircase and wide hall sat in front of him. He strode through the living and formal dining room to find his mother in the kitchen.

She turned from the cast-iron stove, a wide smile curving her lips. "Darling, you're home."

He crossed the space between them and pressed a kiss to her head. "Hey, Mom. Baking?"

"Huckleberry scones for bridge club." She frowned. "You left before I could make you coffee."

"I stopped at Rob's Diner. Their coffee's still shit, by the way."

"Oh, you should try The Tea House. Mrs. Gerald makes a divine latte."

"We have a tea house in Amber Ridge?"

"Shocking, I know. But they're not just good at coffee. Their pie is to die for."

Interesting. He'd always thought nothing changed in the small town of Amber Ridge, but maybe he was wrong

"Did you go anywhere else?" his mother asked.

"I saw Indie."

She paused for a moment before turning. "Really? Was this the first time seeing her since…"

"Being back, yeah."

His mother frowned, concern in her eyes. "How did it go?"

"Not the way I was hoping." But kind of the way he'd expected.

His mother gave a small nod.

"I'm going to head to the park and take a walk." He needed to get outside. Clear his head. He touched his mother's arm as he passed, only to stop and turn. "Mom?"

"Yes, honey?" She smiled at him. A warm, familiar smile he knew well.

"I know I asked you this when Indie and I first separated, but nothing ever happened between you two, did it?"

His mother tilted her head. "What do you mean?"

"It always appeared you had a good relationship, but—"

"We did. At least, *I* always liked *her.*"

It was the same answer she'd given him a year ago. He'd pushed, needing to know if there was more, but his mother had been adamant there wasn't. And he'd never known her to be a liar.

But then, he hadn't known Indie to be one, either.

So what the hell was going on?

"You'd tell me if something happened between you, wouldn't you?"

"Of course."

He scrubbed a hand over his face. "Okay." It wasn't okay, but what the hell else was he supposed to say? "Have a good day, Mom."

He needed to get to the bottom of it—and he needed to get to the bottom of it soon. *Someone* was going to tell him what was going on.

CHAPTER 3

*I*ndie's fingers were tight around the wheel as she drove to The Tea House. She should be thinking about Noah. Her brother was home, and she was about to see him for the first time in months.

Instead, that damn IVF appointment still played on her mind. It had been days, and she was *still* thinking about it. A month ago, she'd been so sure she wanted to give it one last try. Okay, *sure* was an overstatement, but she'd been interested in the information. Then Colt strolled back into her life and the idea of having a baby who wasn't genetically Colt's just felt wrong.

The second she'd gotten home, she'd plonked the folder of sperm donors onto her kitchen table, which was exactly where it had sat ever since. She hadn't touched it once.

Why did having a baby have to be so hard? For her at least. Why couldn't she have been one of those women who just decided they wanted a baby and a month later, she was pregnant?

Because everyone has their hard, and this is yours, a voice whispered in her head.

She needed to shove all the IVF and Colt stuff to the back of her mind for now and focus on Noah.

While she'd never been close to her sister, she and Noah were best friends. Maybe because they were the closest in age, with him only a year older. Or maybe because Bonnie was three years her junior, yet had always found a way to act even younger.

Of course, Bonnie wasn't in Amber Ridge any longer. Not after what happened to her boyfriend, then their parents a few weeks later.

Indie's heart clattered against her ribs. Thirteen years since the car accident that had killed her parents. And thirteen years since Bonnie had up and left town, not caring about everyone she left behind.

She'd tried to keep in contact for a while, but Bonnie never responded, so she'd stopped. And even though they hadn't been close, it hurt. It all hurt.

She pulled into The Tea House parking lot, took a deep breath, then climbed from her car. That's when she saw him.

Noah.

He was across the lot, getting out of his truck. He looked exactly the same as always. Tall, with sandy-blond hair and bright blue eyes.

A smile she couldn't stop stretched her mouth, and she ran toward him, sprinting across the lot before leaping at him. He caught her easily, his strong arms wrapping around her, and she breathed her brother in.

"Hey." His deep, familiar voice hit her in the chest.

She buried her face into his shoulder. "I've missed you!"

"Can't be as much as I've missed you, sis." His arms tightened around her.

When they finally separated, she wiped tears from her eyes. "You're home."

"I'm home."

"For good?"

"I hope so. I've got nowhere else to be."

She linked her arm through his as they walked toward The Tea House.

"So why are we at a tea house instead of Rob's Diner?" Noah asked.

"Because the diner coffee sucks, whereas Mrs. Gerald's will make you want to order ten on the spot."

"Good coffee? In Amber Ridge?"

"You've missed a bit, big brother." They stepped inside and found a booth, and she couldn't take her eyes off her brother. "I can't believe you got out."

"I gave a lot of my life to the Marines. It was time."

Mrs. Gerald stopped at the table. "Hi, Indie. Your usual chai spiced latte?"

"Yes, please, with a side of rhubarb pie." She looked across at Noah. "Mrs. Gerald, this is my brother, Noah. He's just got out of the Marines."

Noah smiled up at her. "It's nice to meet you, ma'am."

"Oh gosh, no ma'am. It makes me feel old. It's nice to meet you too, son. And thank you for your service."

Noah dipped his head.

"What can I get you?" she asked.

"Just a strong black, please."

"You got it."

"If you think you're sharing my pie, you have another thing coming," Indie said the second Mrs. Gerald left their table.

"I know better than to try to take dessert from you."

"Good." She grinned at him, but that grin waned when a familiar expression crossed his face. The one that said he was about to ask a personal question. "What?"

"How are you doing?"

She wanted to lie. To tell her brother she was fine. It was easy over the phone. He couldn't see her face, and she could hang up before he asked too many questions. Right now, he'd see right through her.

"I'm better than I was a year ago. The break from IVF has done me good."

Noah frowned. "What about the break from Colt?"

Again, she could lie, but with Noah there was no point. "It's been hard. But being with him was hard too. Before we separated, I was just in such a bad place and that bled into our marriage."

"I'm glad you're doing better."

"Me too." She'd kept her brother updated on everything over the last year. Apart from Clara and Aunt Pam, he was her closest person.

He cocked his head. "You saw him the other day."

It wasn't a question. But it kind of was. "I did. It hit me pretty hard. But I'm glad I had a month to get used to the idea of him being in town first."

"What are you going to do?"

"Is burying my head in the sand an option?"

He didn't even crack a smile. "You've never shied away from tough situations, Indie."

"I don't know what I'm going to do. I'm scared." The last two words dropped into the air like a small explosion. She hadn't really allowed herself to feel that fear until Colt stood in her kitchen. It was why she hadn't searched him out.

"Scared of what?"

"To return to where I was a year ago." Her heart beat faster, the memory of that darkness making nausea coil in her belly.

Noah leaned forward. "Indie, things are different now. Colt's not returning to his special operations team. He's here. And so am I. Plus, you're taking a break from IVF. I don't think you'll find yourself in that dark place again, but if you did, you have people to help you."

"I had people last time. I had Aunt Pam and Clara. And I still didn't realize how bad things had gotten until that night."

She didn't need to say which one—they both knew. The one

when she'd been told her last embryo didn't take. The one when she'd ended things with Colt and her entire world felt like it was imploding.

She shook her head. "Let's talk about something else. Tell me about the adventure park."

"Indie—"

"I'm okay. Really. Now please, I want to know about your new work venture."

He sighed. "I'm actually meeting Colt there this afternoon."

Her belly gave a little kick. "You are?"

"Yes. Randy, our contractor, is meeting us. We're going to do some of the work ourselves, but we want to get it done quickly and outsourcing is faster."

"That sounds good." Crap. Her voice was too high-pitched, and if the slight frown on Noah's face was anything to go by, he heard it.

"If you're not okay with this—"

"I am." Maybe if she repeated that enough times, she'd convince herself it was true. But what right did she have to tell her brother not to open a business with her husband? None. If they wanted to do it, it was their choice.

"This was Colt's idea," he said quietly. "I didn't have any other plans in terms of work, so I said yes. But say the word and I—"

"You're doing it. It's done. Plus, ziplining, bouldering, and mountain bike riding are all your favorite things. It's perfect for you. Just because Colt and I are separated doesn't mean the two of you need to separate. Besides, it's a small town. I need to get used to Colt being around." Even if it did feel ridiculously hard.

Mrs. Gerald stopped at their booth and set down their coffees and a slice of pie.

Holy Hannah, the pie looked good. But first, coffee.

She sipped the hot liquid, not even caring that it burned her tongue, because it was *that* good.

Noah sipped his drink. "Shit. That's really good."

"Told you."

He eyed her pie.

"Fine. One taste." She pushed her plate across the table.

He spooned some into his mouth before groaning. "Shit, when did this place open and where was it while we were kids?"

"Apparently, it's been open for years, but Mrs. Gerald made really bad coffee and sold mostly loose-leaf tea. Aspen helped her make it great."

"Aspen, as in Jesse's woman?"

"Yeah. Have you seen Jesse, Becket, or Clara yet?"

"No, but Aunt Pam has insisted I attend Sunday night dinner."

She chuckled. "Yeah, that's still mandatory."

"We're lucky to have her. After Mom and Dad died and Bonnie left, at least you still had them."

"We *both* had them."

"Yeah, but I was away in the military. You were here."

"They're our family."

"They are." His brows flickered. "You haven't spoken to Bonnie?"

That familiar ache coursed through her belly. The same one she got whenever she thought about Bonnie. "I message her every so often. I don't get a response."

He shook his head. "I wish she'd just come home and stop blaming herself for everything."

Indie swallowed. She agreed. But she also felt angry. Angry that Bonnie had run when they'd needed each other most. It only made everything hurt worse.

But she shouldn't have expected anything else from her younger sister. Bonnie had always thought about Bonnie first.

"I don't know if she'll ever come back while the White family is here," Indie said quietly, referring to Bonnie's deceased boyfriend's family. "I'm going to the bathroom."

She slid out of the booth and crossed the café to step into the restroom. On her way back, she spotted Ivory Hanks, who was one of her regular photography clients.

"Ivory."

The middle-aged woman straightened and turned, eyes widening slightly. "Indie. Hi."

"Hey. I haven't seen you in a while. How's Penelope?" Ivory had the most adorable Shih Tzu named Penelope, who was in all her annual photos.

"Penelope's good." The woman nodded, maybe too vigorously. "She's at doggy daycare right now."

"I've heard great things about Sky's place. We're getting close to your annual photos if you want to book them in soon."

Another widening of Ivory's eyes. "Um…I'm not sure we'll get any photos this year."

"Oh…is everything all right?" Ivory had been her longest-running client. In fact, a lot of her business in the early days had been through Ivory's recommendations.

Another vigorous nod. "Yes. It's fine. Everything's fine. I just don't know if we'll have time. We're going away."

"We can always plan the shoot around your trip."

"Maybe. I'll call you. I've got to go. It was nice seeing you."

"You too."

Indie was still frowning as she slid back into the booth.

"What's wrong?" Noah asked.

"Ivory's a client and she was acting…strange. She said she won't be booking her annual shoot. She's not the first regular to say that."

"Why?"

"I don't know."

"Is everything okay with the business?"

"It's been…slow. But I'm sure it'll bounce back." At least, she prayed it would. Her photography business was her entire income. "It *will* bounce back. Now tell me about your last few months as a Marine."

Over the next hour, she listened to her brother's military stories and filled her belly with pie and chai spiced latte. She smiled and laughed more in that hour than she had in a long time.

When it was time to go, she stood, only to step straight into a wide chest. She gasped and stumbled back. "I'm sorry, I..."

She stopped at the sight of the older man's face. He had to be in his sixties. Maybe older. But it was his eyes that she couldn't look away from. Dark eyes, almost black. They were so familiar.

Had she met him before?

The man had a scar on the right side of his jaw, and he was tall. Really tall.

Annoyance flared through those dark eyes. "You make a habit of walking into people?"

Her brows rose. "No."

"Is there a problem here?" Noah asked, voice hard as he came to stand beside her.

"No problem," the man said, not taking his eyes off her. "Next time, watch where you're going." Then he left The Tea House.

If someone could give off a bad vibe in one conversation, then that man did exactly that.

"Do you know him?" Noah asked, still watching the man through the window.

"No. But he looked kind of familiar."

"I thought that too."

Noah slipped an arm around her back and led her outside.

"Is this your car?" he asked, a look of what could only be described as concern on his face as he stared at it.

"It is."

"What happened to the Subaru?"

"I sold it."

"And bought *this*? Why?"

Shit. You'd think she'd have rehearsed an answer by now. "I just did."

His eyes narrowed. "Do you need money, Indie?"

Double shit. "No." Well, yes, but no way in hell was she taking any from her big brother. She was an adult. She'd figure this out herself.

Before he could respond, she wrapped her arms around him in a big bear hug. "It's so good to have you back."

"Indie—"

"Just say it back, Noah."

There was an exaggerated sigh before he wrapped his arms around her. "It's good to *be* back."

She pulled away. "Good luck meeting with your contractor."

"Thanks. We've had a few phone calls, so I'm not concerned. You can come check it out if you want."

With Colt there? That was a big fat no. Not right now, at least. She needed to warm up to the idea of seeing him first. "I've got some photos to edit."

"Okay. I'll call you."

She smiled, and Noah squeezed her arm before she slid into the car. And even though her life kind of felt like a mess with Colt being back, the IVF stuff, and her money issues, it was still nice to have her big brother home in Amber Ridge.

At least one thing was good.

CHAPTER 4

*C*olt climbed out of his Audi, the cool mountain air
hitting him in the face.

Fuck, it was good to be home.

And it was even better to be back here at the old adventure
park where he'd spent so much of his childhood. The second he'd
found out it was up for sale, he bought it. What the hell else was
he supposed to do with the trust fund his grandparents had
given him?

He crossed the parking lot to the old log cabin. Or more accurately, the pile of logs that now only faintly resembled the cabin it
used to be. The place was supposed to have a reception area, an
office, and a kitchenette...but right now, it was falling apart.

He looked past the cabin to the trees. There was no fencing
around the property; there never had been.

Two hundred acres of rough landscape that had once been a
thriving adventure park. Rock climbing and bouldering. Hiking
and mountain bike trails. An old zip line course. Even cabin
rentals around a camping site.

How long would it take to get the place back to the way it had
been?

A truck pulled into the parking lot and Noah climbed out. "Well, if it isn't Colt Reed."

Colt crossed the distance between them and pulled his old friend into a hug. "It's been too long, brother."

"You're not wrong." Noah stepped back. "How have you been?"

"Better now that I'm home."

Noah nodded slowly. He knew exactly how hard this year had been for Colt without Indie. "Good. Hopefully it keeps getting better." He looked at the cabin. "We've got our work cut out for us."

"Nothing we can't handle."

Noah chuckled, his gaze going to the truck beside Colt's Audi. "Randy's already here?"

"His truck is. Haven't seen him. I just got here."

A rustling noise sounded in the trees a second before an older man stepped out, his hair whitening and his gut hanging over his trousers. "Colt, Noah, you made it."

Colt stepped forward and shook his hand. "It's good to see you, Randy."

"You too."

Noah did the same. "What do you think?"

Randy blew out a long breath. "Trails are completely overgrown. Cabins look like knockdowns. The zip line course needs a complete rebuild."

"Can you do it?" Colt asked.

One side of Randy's mouth lifted. "Son, my team can do anything. Just depends how much time and money you got."

"We're in no rush," Noah said. "And we'll put in some labor, too."

"That will help." Randy frowned at him. "I don't mean to be nosy, but this land would have been expensive. Add in the renovations..."

He was asking how they were paying for it, without asking how they were paying for it.

"We got it cheap," Colt said. "And we can afford it."

He'd barely touched the money in his trust fund. He'd never had reason to touch it...until now.

Randy nodded, looking like he had more questions. Instead, he turned to study the old office. "Come on. I'll walk you through it all. We'll start at this pile of firewood."

Over the next few hours, they assessed the old adventure park, and Randy was right—the paths were so overgrown, the three of them could barely move from one area to the next. There was graffiti all over the granite cliffs that were used for rock climbing and bouldering. The equipment sheds were falling apart.

It was going to take a lot of work. But it would be worth it. Because he wanted this. He wanted to see a new round of kids speeding down the zip lines and riding their mountain bikes down the trails.

The sun was just starting to set as they approached the cabins. Four in total, built around a communal firepit. As Noah and Randy talked, Colt stepped onto one of the old porches. The wood creaked beneath his feet.

He tried the door, and it opened. Then he frowned. It looked cleaner than it should. There was a living area to the left, with a small kitchen to the right and doors at the back of the cabin, which led to a bathroom and bedroom.

He stepped into the kitchen and ran his finger along the countertop.

No dust.

Someone had been in here recently.

A creak sounded behind the closed bedroom door. Colt quickly crossed the space and pulled it open to see a bed with an old mattress...but that wasn't what had him pausing.

It was the open window.

He crossed to the window and scanned the tree area outside. Nothing. At least, nothing that he could see.

The thud of footsteps behind him had Colt turning to see Noah and Randy stepping into the room.

"Someone's been staying here," Colt said quietly. "I think they snuck out when they heard me come in."

Randy didn't seem fazed. "Probably Milo."

Colt frowned. "Who's Milo?"

"He's a drunk. He has a home, but he gets kicked out almost every night. We find him squatting in rundown or out-of-the-way places around town."

"I assume you call the sheriff," Noah said.

"Nope. He eventually leaves. Good guy, just doesn't know how to limit his liquor." Randy snapped his notebook closed. "I think I've got everything. I read in an email there's an old hunting shed on the west side. Are we doing anything with that?"

Noah shook his head. "It's a mile into the forest above the bouldering cliff. Access isn't great, so we're leaving it for now."

"Easy. I'll put the quote and timeline together and get back to you."

"When would you be able to start?" Colt asked.

"We're just finishing a big job now, so if you give me the go-ahead, pretty much right away."

Noah smiled. "This feels too easy, Randy."

The older man chuckled. "Wait until we start. So many problems will pop up you'll be begging me for easy."

They headed back outside. When they reached the cars, it was evening and officially dark.

Colt shook Randy's hand. "Looking forward to working with you."

Randy laughed again. "You say that now. Just wait."

When Randy left, Colt turned to Noah. "We really doing this?"

"I'm more excited than I was before. I love getting my hands dirty."

He did too. But then, he'd never been scared off by a bit of hard work. And right now, he needed a distraction from Indie. "Guess we're reopening the Wilderness Adventure Park."

"You sure you don't mind putting the money in for the startup?"

Colt grinned. "What the hell else am I going to do with that trust fund?"

"Gamble? Buy a private jet? An island?"

"Not really my thing." He squeezed Noah's shoulder. "I'll see you in the morning."

He headed back to his car. He was about to start the engine when his phone rang. His muscles locked when he saw the name on the screen.

Indie.

* * *

"I DON'T THINK they're in here," Clara called, voice sounding far away.

But she couldn't be *that* far. The freestanding shed on the back of her property was only six by six. Although, there were a hell of a lot of boxes in here. Boxes of stuff she'd shared with Colt. Photobooks. Bed sheets. Little trinkets that he'd given her.

"I didn't think they were either, but we checked every inch of the house," Indie said, rummaging through one of the stacked boxes. "I thought I put the rings in a box, sealed it up in my closet, but they weren't there. Maybe I accidently put them in here."

But she really hoped she hadn't. They were far too expensive for that.

"We've been looking for an hour, and I'm scared that rat's going to come back." There was a small pause. "Maybe this is the universe telling you that you should keep them. He gave them to you."

Indie's heart gave a little thump. Okay, it wasn't little. It was a huge, gigantic thud that rattled her ribs. Of *course*, she had to give the wedding and engagement ring back...they were Colt's. "They were his grandmother's. They should stay in his family." She huffed when she got to the bottom of the box.

They weren't here. They weren't inside. They weren't anywhere.

Clara rounded the boxes, finally coming into view. "I don't think we're going to find them this evening."

Indie eyed the boxes they hadn't been through yet. There were a lot. Too many for one evening. "You're right. I'll look again tomorrow."

Clara's brow furrowed. "Indie, I say this with love, but if he wouldn't sign the divorce papers, what makes you think he'll take the rings back?"

"It doesn't feel right to keep them." They stepped out of the shed, and she locked the door. "There are so many things we need to discuss. The rings. This house and our home in California." She needed to adult up and just do it.

Clara nodded slowly. "Yes, but it doesn't need to be immediately. You can leave it for a while. Give yourselves time to adjust to both of you living in the same town."

When they entered the back door, Indie's gaze immediately went to the folder from the IVF clinic. Before her sudden need to search for the rings, she and Clara had spent the afternoon eating Thai while looking through the information.

Clara lifted the folder. "You know you're not going through with this, don't you?"

It was true. None of it was sitting well with her.

She lifted her half-drunk glass of wine. "I thought I *might* go through with it, before I saw Colt. I just so badly want to become pregnant. And I know there are other ways to become a mother. I just need to really make sure I've exhausted this way first."

"You *will* be a mother."

Unexpected tears built in her eyes. "You never think it will be you, you know. You see people struggle with infertility but that's *them*...until it isn't."

Clara squeezed her hand.

"Then," Indie continued, "you commit to IVF and you think, this is it. Because it's supposed to be what gets you your baby... and then it doesn't."

"It got your hopes up."

"Every round, we did something different, and I told myself, 'This is the one.'" She swiped a tear from her cheek. "I'd start calculating due dates and planning where the bassinet would go. And every time I'd either test or just eventually get that call that we weren't pregnant, it hurt. It hurt *so much*."

"Come here." Clara pulled her into a hug, and Indie let more tears fall. Tears of sorrow for every failed round. For the baby she craved with everything she had but never got.

It was only the ringing of a phone that had them separating.

Clara lifted her cell. "It's Holden. He's here to pick me up, but I can tell him—"

"No. I'm fine. He's here to take you home; go be with him." She swiped the last of the wetness from her cheeks.

Clara looked at her, worried. "Are you sure?"

"Of course. I'm sorry I got upset."

"You *never* need to apologize with me. Okay? Besides, crying's good for you."

"I love you."

"Back at you, cuz."

They hugged one more time before Clara left. She knew Holden would be at the door, but she didn't go out there. He didn't need to see her puffy red eyes.

After tipping the rest of the wine down the drain, she turned off the lights, then went to her bedroom to change into an oversized T-shirt that she wore to bed...one of *Colt's* old T-shirts. She'd stolen it back in senior year. It was that old. So old that the material had gone stretchy and sections were almost see-through.

She lifted her phone and scrolled down to Colt's number. Her finger hovered over his name. She wasn't sure why. Maybe because sometimes she just craved his voice. The ability to speak to him about everything and anything.

And she *could* call him now. He wasn't deployed somewhere dangerous with his Marine unit. He was here, in Amber Ridge.

But could she take the risk? Sure, he was out of the military, but his mother was still right where she'd always been. And what if Indie needed him, like she had that last time, and he chose Sylvia over her again?

She shook her head, about to close her bedroom door and spend the evening watching reruns of *The Rookie*, when something sounded from the kitchen.

Her heart jumped. What was that? The scrunch of plastic?

Slowly, she stepped out of her bedroom and listened.

Nothing.

She shook her head. Of *course* it was nothing. Because there was nothing wrong. All the doors were locked.

She turned to step back into the bedroom, when she heard the same crinkling sound again, but this time louder.

Her heart sped up and she clicked the name that was still up on her phone. The name that had always signified safety. The name of the person she absolutely should *not* be calling.

"Indie?"

"Colt...someone's in my house."

CHAPTER 5

$\mathcal{C}$olt pressed his foot to the floor as he sped to Indie's. Thank God he wasn't far.

Someone was in her house. Who? Why?

When he got his hands on the asshole, they were a dead man.

He turned right onto her street and parked behind her car in the driveway. Before getting out, he opened the glove box and took out his Glock. Then he was running. Sprinting to her front door.

He grabbed the handle. Locked. Dammit. Quickly, he found his key.

The second he stepped inside, quiet fell over him. Quiet and darkness.

First he checked the living, dining, and kitchen areas to the right. Nothing immediately drew his attention. Didn't mean no one was here though. He tried the bedroom door, but it was locked.

"Cricket? It's me."

For a second there was silence. Then the soft pad of footsteps before the lock clicked. He stepped inside to see Indie wearing an old T-shirt of his, face pale.

Relief hit him so hard in the midsection, air whooshed out of him.

She was okay.

He scanned her body, searching for injuries. There were none. None that he could see, anyway.

He cupped her cheek. "Are you okay?"

She nodded quickly, even though she looked far from okay. "The noises are coming from the kitchen."

"*Are coming*? You've heard more?"

She nodded, the move jerky.

"Stay here. I'm going to find them."

"Okay." He went to step away but stopped when she touched his arm. "Colt...be careful."

"I'm always careful, Cricket. Lock the door after me."

He cracked open the bedroom door and aimed his Glock. In the hall, he pulled the door closed behind him with a soft click. Noiselessly, he stepped into the living room. The darkness might be a problem for some, but he was so used to it that it was almost an advantage. How many missions had he done in the dead of night? Too many.

He was just looking behind the couch when the crinkling of plastic sounded.

The pantry. What the fuck was someone doing in there? Hiding? Getting ready to jump him?

With silent steps, he inched into the kitchen. The door to the pantry was ajar. Another crackle noise cut through the quiet.

Three more steps and he grabbed the handle. In one quick motion, he whipped the door open and aimed the Glock.

Nothing.

The fuck?

The rustling sound came from nearby. Frowning, he holstered his Glock and lifted an oddly heavy box of cereal from a shelf. There was his culprit.

A rat. A *big* one.

He chuckled, closing the box so the animal couldn't escape. He didn't release the rat near the back door, instead going to the far corner of the yard before lowering it to the grass. The rodent scurried away.

"I'm glad it was you, buddy. Didn't really feel like shooting anyone tonight."

He'd just stepped back into the house when Indie entered the kitchen, pistol in hand.

Her gaze darted around the room before returning to him. "Where is he?"

"*He* was a rat."

She frowned. "A rat?"

"Yes, ma'am."

She visibly exhaled, and she lowered the pistol to the counter before scrubbing a hand over her face. "I'm so sorry. I freaked out."

"Hey, it was a big rat. You had every reason to call for backup."

Her lips stretched into a smile, and even though it was small and tentative, it was the first smile she'd sent his way in over a year, and fuck, it made him breathless.

"Thank you," she sighed.

"You can call me anytime, day or night, rat or intruder or even just to talk. You know that."

Even the fact that she'd called him tonight surprised the hell out of him. She could have called her brother. Or she could have called either of her cousins, Jesse or Becket. But she'd called *him*.

Was it because even after everything she'd said, she knew it wasn't over between them?

She cleared her throat. "Do you want some coffee?"

"Sure." He never drank coffee at night. But if taking her up on her offer meant he got more time with her, then he'd drink an entire fucking pot of it.

As she moved toward her pod machine, he watched the curve

43

of her bare thighs stretching from beneath the T-shirt. *His* T-shirt.

Did she realize she wasn't wearing pants? Or was she so used to him that she didn't care?

Either way, the sight of all that smooth skin made his cock turn to stone. He forced his gaze away, only to catch sight of a folder on the counter.

Amber Ridge Fertility Center.

Why was *that* there?

"Is this one of the old folders from when we were doing IVF?" He lifted it and opened the folder, just as Indie turned.

She gasped. "No, wait…"

It was too late. He frowned at the first page. At the big bold heading that read: "Sperm Donors."

What the hell?

He turned over to the next page…and sure enough, there was a whole damn bio of information on a guy.

Indie rushed forward and pulled the folder from his fingers. "You weren't supposed to see that."

"You're doing IVF with a sperm donor?" Jesus, saying the words out loud tasted like acid on his tongue.

"No. I went to an information session at the clinic the other day, just to explore the option."

"Having a baby with a man who isn't your husband is an *option* for you?" She was *his* wife, and she was thinking about having another man's baby?

Fuck no.

Her mouth opened and closed. "Colt, we're separated. And I still want a baby."

"Separated but still married, Cricket."

"I'm almost thirty-five. I want to be a mother."

"Well, let's make a baby then." His words came out too loud. Too angry. But he couldn't stop them.

She scrubbed her hands over her face again. "We tried. We tried for so long that it destroyed us."

"It *didn't* destroy us."

"It destroyed *me!*" She looked back at him. "The physical and mental toll it took on me...I can't even explain it. It broke me. I felt *broken*. And I thought maybe if I tried by myself, it might be different. Easier."

He couldn't stop himself. He closed the space between them and gripped her waist. "I know it was hard. And I'm so damn sorry I couldn't be here as much as you needed me. But I'm here now. And if you want to do another round of IVF, I'll do it with you and hold your hand every step of the way. I have nowhere I'd rather be. I would do *anything* for you, Cricket."

Tears pooled in her eyes. "I've missed you."

Her eyes widened like she hadn't meant to say those words out loud.

"You have no idea. I told myself I was okay, but the second I saw you, I remembered what okay was supposed to feel like."

Her breath hitched. Then suddenly, her hands moved up his chest—and she pulled his head down and kissed him.

And the second her lips touched his, he could breathe for the first time in over a year.

* * *

INDIE WAS KISSING COLT. She hadn't kissed him in over a year, yet everything about him felt so achingly familiar. His soft lips against hers. The power in his arms as they wrapped around her. It was the kind of familiar she wanted to fall into. Let it envelop her. Sweep her away to that place that was for just the two of them.

Her lips separated and he dove in, his tongue tangling with hers, claiming her.

His kisses had *always* felt like more of a claim. Like he knew she was his and he was telling her with his entire body. There was never any hesitation. And right now, it felt like he was trying to take every moment they'd lost over the last year and make up for each one. Hold her tighter. Explore her deeper.

She groaned at the taste of him—it always reminded her of the rain. Soft and grounding. Rich. But there was also sweetness there. It was all so infinitely unique to Colt.

She wove her fingers through his hair. Soft locks that were in such contradiction to the hardness of the rest of him.

He spun them and lifted her to the island. Then he was between her thighs, the thin material of her shirt bunched around her waist. And she felt him right there, hard and long, pressing to her core, making desire flare in her lower belly.

It was as though that year of distance just disappeared. The unsent text messages. The unspoken words and lost touches... All of it just gone. And she was in her husband's arms. The man she'd loved since she was a teenager.

His mouth skimmed down her cheek, then her neck. Every kiss like fire against her skin, leaving a burning trail.

When his head reached her chest, her breath caught. Then he was cupping her breast before his lips wrapped around her pebbled nipple through her shirt.

She opened her mouth to cry out, but the air was so thick, no sound came out. She latched onto his hair, tugging and pulling, trying to keep herself still even though her entire body wanted to move and writhe against him.

When his teeth grazed the bud, she threw her head back and gasped. He'd always known exactly how to touch her to make her wild.

She wrapped her legs around him and hauled his hips closer. She was so deep in her lust for Colt that she didn't feel the cool air against her chest until he switched to her other breast, this time taking her bare nipple between his lips.

And suddenly she was lost, unsure how to find her way back

to reality. How to touch her feet to the ground again or see anything outside of her husband.

She was just reaching for the button of his jeans when he lifted his head and touched his forehead to hers.

"Indie...we should stop."

Everything was such a haze that she had to play his words over in her head a couple of times to make sense of them. "Stop?"

"I don't want to rush this. I want you, all of you, body and soul. And I want to do that properly. Slowly. I want to earn back your trust."

Even though he was right there, not having his mouth on her skin felt like a bucket of cold water on her head. And bit by bit, reality began to slip back in.

Oh God... She'd just made out with Colt. She'd gone on and on about how they were separated...and the second time seeing him, she was ready to jump back into bed with the man.

What was wrong with her?

She pushed against his chest and he stepped back. His eyes stayed on her as she slid off the counter and made sure her shirt covered her body. "You're right. Of course you're right. I'm s—"

"Don't say you're sorry. I'm sure as hell not. I love you, Cricket. And touching you, making love to you, is the most natural thing in the world."

She met his intense black gaze and almost couldn't breathe.

"You're my wife," he said slowly, like she needed measured words to understand. "And we *will* work our way back to where we were. Eventually."

She couldn't respond. She didn't have words. Because he'd said it like a vow. Like she was still his and that was all there was to it.

He scanned the room. "Are you okay?"

Okay? Was hot and bothered with a pulsing need in her belly *okay*?

"Yes," she lied.

"Do you want me to stay?"

She forced herself to shake her head. They both knew exactly what would happen if he did that. And he was right. They couldn't just fall into old ways. They had to be better.

He stepped forward, causing her heart to crash against her ribs. Slowly, he pressed a gentle kiss to her forehead, one that made a million butterflies take off in her belly.

"Lock up after me." The words were soft, then he crossed to the door. He spared her one more intense glance over his shoulder before he stepped out.

Her knees suddenly felt so weak that she almost slid to the floor.

She didn't. She forced her knees to lock and followed his path to the door, where she flicked the lock. Then she pressed her temple to the wood, wondering what the hell she was going to do next.

CHAPTER 6

"*Y*ou *kissed?*"

Indie tugged the cell from her ear. Too loud...too freaking loud.

Before responding, she glanced around the grocery store to make sure no one was within listening distance. This town was too small. "Yes. We kissed. Well, I kissed him. And it was a *great* kiss. But then, Colt's kisses were always amazing. We never lacked in that department."

Which was strange. Often when couples struggled with infertility, intimacy became almost like a chore. It was scheduled in and something you *had* to do rather than wanted to do. But with Colt, it had never been like that.

"Okay, so how did the kiss end?" Clara asked. "Or did you—"

"No." Indie lifted a carton of milk and set it in her basket. "We didn't, and that was thanks to Colt's self-restraint. *I* was a second away from ripping off my panties and doing it right there and then."

She scrunched her eyes closed in chagrin. Apparently, one year without sex and she'd become a desperate woman. Desperate for Colt, at least.

"Did he say why he stopped it?" Clara asked.

"Because he doesn't want to rush us. He wants me body and soul, and he wants to earn my trust back slowly."

Clara sighed. "Oh, Colt…"

She frowned at the price of eggs. When had they become so expensive?

She mentally calculated the money in her bank, because yes, she *was* living paycheck to paycheck. She hadn't touched the money from the sale of her Subaru yet. It was meant for IVF, but based on how the Honda was doing, she might just need to buy it back. Or at least get something similar.

"So what's the next move?" Clara asked, sounding far too excited. "Has he texted yet?"

"No, he hasn't." And yes, she'd been pathetically checking every chance she got. Heck, she'd looked at her phone every hour, all day, *expecting* a text. Which was dumb. He was probably giving her space because it was *she* who'd left *him*. "But to be fair, I haven't messaged him either."

"You should."

She nibbled her bottom lip as she grabbed a loaf of bread. "Maybe. Things *are* different now. Colt's home. We're not doing IVF. And even though he's living with his mother, things might be different with her." Ha, and pigs could fly.

"Exactly."

Like the very mention of the woman had conjured her up, Sylvia Reed stepped into the aisle.

Indie barely held in the groan as she met her mother-in-law's eyes.

"What's wrong?" Clara asked.

Okay. Maybe she hadn't held in the groan. "Sylvia's here. And she's walking straight toward me."

This time, Clara groaned. "I'm sorry. But maybe this is your chance to see if she's changed at all."

In the couple weeks since she'd last seen the woman? Doubtful.

"Chat later, Clara." She hung up as Sylvia stopped in front of her. "Hi, Sylvia."

"Indie. It's so nice to see you. How are you?"

Even when Sylvia was nice, there was something...off about her. Like her question was almost condescending. "I'm good, thank you. How are *you*?"

"Well, now that my boy's home, I'm happier than I've been in a long time."

Yeah, Indie was sure she was. Sylvia had always had this strange dependence on Colt. Maybe because his father had left when he was eight, and then it was just the two of them. She'd once read that when boy moms didn't get what they needed from their partner, they sometimes sought emotional fulfillment from their sons, and Indie had always wondered if that was what was going on with Sylvia.

"It's nice that he's home," Indie said politely. "If you'll excuse—"

"Have you two spent any time together?"

Wasn't Colt living with her? Wouldn't *he* have told her? "We've seen each other a couple of times."

Sylvia's lips thinned, and something passed through her eyes. Fear maybe? Or annoyance? It was hard to tell. "I'm sure you have a lot to catch up on. Did you date while you were separated? Or was that just Colt?"

Indie flinched, and she couldn't even hide it. "Colt dated?"

No...he wouldn't do that. He was the one insisting that she was his. That they were still married.

But she hadn't answered his calls over the last twelve months. And she'd sent him freaking divorce papers.

"He did," Sylvia said easily, like the words weren't daggers in Indie's chest. "Only briefly, since he was based in California, but he actually came up a lot in the last year. You know Audrey? She makes those pretty bracelets, and stores sell them for her around town."

Nausea crawled up her throat. Of course she knew Audrey. They'd gone to high school together, and she was beautiful. And kind. And probably wouldn't fall into a pit of depression after a few rounds of failed IVF.

Sylvia frowned and looked at the ceiling as if she was thinking. "There was another girl, too...a woman in California who was staying with him when I visited. Savannah, maybe?"

Two? No. That couldn't be true. Colt wouldn't have dated two different women while she'd been simultaneously in love with him and trying to work through the hardest battle of her life due to depression.

Why did her heart race though? Because Colt was cute and if women found out he was available they'd be all over him? "I need to go, Sylvia."

"Oh, dear, you've gone pale. I'm sorry. I thought since you separated from him that you wouldn't—" She stopped, her gaze catching on something behind Indie. Suddenly, it was the older woman's face that lost all color.

Indie turned slightly and spotted a man. A familiar man. It was the guy she'd run into at The Tea House, when she'd caught up with Noah. The one with the black eyes and the scar.

And he was looking straight at Sylvia.

Indie turned back to Colt's mother, and if possible, she'd lost even more color. "Do you know him?"

Sylvia's mouth opened and closed, something akin to fear crossing her features. "I...I need to go." She spun and rushed out of the aisle, walking faster than Indie had ever seen her move before.

Frowning, Indie shot another glance over her shoulder to see the man still watching Sylvia. Then he shifted his focus to Indie, and a shudder coursed down her spine before he walked away.

Who was he? If Sylvia knew him, did Colt?

She hurried to the front of the store and paid for her groceries before heading to her car. She'd just slipped behind the wheel when her phone dinged with a text.

Colt: Hey, Cricket. How are you today?

And suddenly she remembered everything Sylvia had said before that guy had appeared, about Colt dating other women. It probably wasn't true. It *wasn't* true. Sylvia knew how to lie, and she was forever trying to put a wedge between Indie and Colt.

Still, the insecure part of Indie, the part that had always wondered if Colt would have been happier with someone stronger than her, made doubt flicker in her mind.

* * *

COLT USED a crowbar to pull up another old wooden board from the deck. He'd been working on this log cabin all day, and he wasn't close to getting rid of the rotten wood.

Fortunately, he wasn't in a rush. He and Noah wanted to do this right and that would take time.

Cool evening air ran over his skin as he threw the board onto the pile beside the cabin. His phone lay a few yards away.

Two texts. He'd sent Indie two texts this afternoon, and she hadn't responded to either one.

He moved on to the next board.

Why? After last night, he'd been so sure they were on the same page again. That she wanted to get their marriage back on track as much as he did.

Had that not been the case?

No. He'd felt it in her. She'd been right there with him the entire time.

His phone rang, and his heart did one of those loud fucking thuds at the possibility that it was Indie.

He lifted his cell, only to swallow the disappointment before hitting speaker. "Hey, Mom."

"Colt, are you okay?"

He frowned. His mother's voice was high and her words so fast they tumbled into one another. "Yeah, I'm fine. I'm working at the park. Are *you* okay?"

"I'm fine."

Not true. She sounded as far from fine as you could get.

"When will you be home?"

He checked his watch. "I'm not sure. Probably late, based on the progress I'm making." Or lack thereof.

"You need to eat, Colt."

"I'll order food. Unless you need me home for some reason?"

There was a small pause before his mother responded. "No. That's okay. But you'll let me know if anything's wrong, won't you?"

"What would be wrong?"

"Nothing." That came far too quickly. "Stay safe, honey."

She hung up, and Colt frowned at his cell. What the hell was that?

He was just shoving his phone into his pocket when footsteps sounded. He turned as Noah stepped out of the trees, closely followed by his cousins, Jesse and Becket.

A smile spread across Colt's face as he stepped off the deck. "Hey. I didn't see you guys get here."

"We came from the other side." Jesse pulled him into a hug. "It's good to see you, buddy."

"You too." He turned to Becket and took his outstretched hand. "It's been a while."

Becket chuckled. "You're not wrong. Finally got out, I see."

"I did. Decided I needed a new challenge." Or a couple of new challenges, if he included his marriage.

"I was just showing them around," Noah said.

Becket whistled. "You got a lot of work on your hands."

"Fortunately, I'm not afraid of getting my hands dirty."

Jesse shoved his hands into his pockets. "Heard you're staying with your mom?"

"It's just short term. I heard *you* guys are partnered up now."

Becket's smile widened. "Sky finally realized I'm not the neighbor from hell."

Jesse scoffed. "Not sure about that. But yeah, I'm with Aspen. We're happy."

"That's good." It really was. They were great guys who deserved to be happy.

They spent the next twenty minutes catching up on things before Jesse and Becket headed back to their cars through the forest.

Colt turned back to the deck, but he could feel Noah's eyes on him.

"What's going on?" Noah finally asked.

Was it that obvious? "What makes you think something's going on?"

"You've got your I-hate-the-world expression on your face. You were trying to hide it while the guys were here, but I saw."

He lifted the pry bar and started working on the next rotten board. "It involves your sister."

"So you think you can't tell me."

"I *know* I can't tell you."

"Because you had sex?"

The muscles in his back tightened. "No. We kissed."

"Okay, that's good. Why the scowl?"

"I *thought* it was good. Now she's not answering my texts, and I'm worried that..."

"Worried that what?"

He pulled the board up and threw it on the pile before looking back at Noah. "She had a folder from the IVF clinic in her kitchen."

"Why would she—"

"It had information on sperm donors."

Noah's head reared back. "What the fuck?"

His thoughts too. He scrubbed a hand over his face. "She said she wasn't going to go through with it. But it was there, and now she's not answering my texts, and the thought of her being pregnant with another man's baby... Fuck, I can't even think about it."

"Of course you can't. She's your wife."

"She is. And I love her so damn much. I want her to be happy. And if being happy means she needs to be permanently separated from me, then I'd accept it. It would kill me, but I'd let her go. But she *loves* me. I know she does. I feel it whenever we're together. And I know I can make her happy."

"So don't stop fighting."

"I—" A sound in the trees had his head whipping around. Like the crunch of leaves beneath feet. "You hear that?"

Noah stepped forward. "Yeah."

"Think it's a wild animal?"

"Maybe. Or maybe that semi-homeless guy Randy was talking about."

Colt stepped toward the tree line. There it was again—but this time, fast footsteps moving *away* from them.

He jogged toward the forest, only to stop a few yards in when he spotted the slight imprint of footsteps in the dirt. He crouched. "Someone was definitely here."

Noah came to stand beside him. "We could go after him. Together, we'd stand a good chance of catching him."

Colt studied the trees around them. "I've got enough going on. Randy said this Milo guy is harmless, and those cabins will be done and locked soon enough. Hopefully, he moves on."

CHAPTER 7

*I*ndie scrubbed a hand over her face as she left her bedroom. She was tired. Really freaking tired. It appeared that sleep was not her friend at the moment, and that was all thanks to one man—Colt.

Damn him and his ability to invade her mind at every hour of the day.

What she needed was coffee. A huge, gigantic mug of coffee. And it had better help her focus on the photos she needed to edit.

She couldn't get him out of her head. In her dreams, they always started happily married, but then things changed. Sometimes he returned to the military. Sometimes he chose his mother over her when she was in some kind of desperate situation.

But last night, he'd started dating another woman. Audrey. And it exacerbated every insecure part of her and made toxic, invasive thoughts creep in. That maybe Audrey would have been able to give Colt a baby. Or if she couldn't, maybe she would have been able to handle the IVF and the mother-in-law and the military commitments without feeling like the world was closing in on her.

Her heart squeezed.

Of course she knew Sylvia had said it to get a reaction out of her, and even if it was a lie, which it more than likely was, it *had* gotten a reaction out of her.

She stopped at the coffee-pod holder. Empty.

No. She was not mentally or emotionally equipped to deal with the day without caffeine.

She dropped her head into her hands, but the second she closed her eyes, that dream flashed back to her. Of Colt with his arm around Audrey...and Audrey's big pregnant belly.

Tears suddenly filled her eyes.

Her doctors had always said their infertility was unexplained. Which seemed ridiculous to her. If she couldn't get pregnant, then something had to be wrong, and it was the doctors' job to work out *what*.

But they never had. And that was one of the hardest parts of the whole thing. Because with the absence of any medical reason for her infertility, she'd started to blame herself. In her head, it had become *her* fault that she couldn't have a baby. That she couldn't give Colt a child.

She squeezed her eyes shut to try to stop the tears, but one still slipped out. She scrubbed it off her cheek.

The knock on the front door had her straightening. She wasn't expecting anyone, and she was not in the mood for company.

She moved to the door and looked through the peephole. Her chest rose on a sharp inhale when she saw the person on the other side.

Nope. Absolutely not. No part of her felt up to seeing him right now. Not after her dream last night. And not without caffeine in her system.

Maybe if she stayed really quiet—

"Indie, I know you're in there. Please. I just want to talk."

Her nose wrinkled. Well, that plan wasn't going to work. She could simply not open the door. But Colt had a key, and there was no question in her mind that he'd use it if he was worried about her. And she *had* been avoiding him for the past four days, so he could definitely be worried by now.

With a deep inhale, she opened the door and was immediately hit by Colt's dark, intense eyes. By the way he towered over her looking so strong and fierce and protective.

And his smell. How did he always smell so dang good? A warm, cedarwood kind of scent.

"Hey." Her voice was quiet. Probably too quiet.

His brows flickered. "What's wrong?"

"Nothing." She walked to the kitchen, taking the moment turned away from him to gather herself. She opened the fridge and pulled out two bottles of water. "I don't have any coffee, sorry."

She closed the door and turned to see Colt had followed her. He was close. *Really* close. He lifted a hand and tucked a stray lock of hair behind her ear. "You're pale."

She gasped at the light touch. "I didn't sleep well."

"Why not?"

Because of you. The words whispered in her head. But they weren't entirely true. It was also because of her, and his mother, and the insecurities that remained buried deep inside.

"A few reasons." It was the best she could give him right now.

He watched her for another moment before gently saying, "Come here."

He tucked her into his chest. For a second, she was frozen, the sudden feel of his arms around her like a shock to her system. Then she melted into him, letting his strength, his familiar scent, chase away everything that had been haunting her that morning.

She wrapped her arms around him and breathed him in. God, he was so achingly familiar.

He'd known how desperately she needed a hug. Because Colt knew her better than anyone else in the world.

It was only when they finally separated that she realized her tears had wet his shirt. "Oh God. I'm sorry."

"You never need to apologize." He gave her a steady look. "Want to talk about it?"

She shook her head. Absolutely not.

He seemed to consider that for a moment. "Okay. But you *do* need coffee."

Despite everything, she laughed. She *really* needed coffee. "I do. But unfortunately, I'm all out."

"Lucky for you, there are these great places that sell coffee. And not just the beans—they combine it with milk and put it in a cup."

She playfully hit his shoulder. "Okay, funny guy, but that would require leaving the house, and I planned to be a hermit in my photo-editing cave today."

"Take a break from the cave and come get a coffee with me." When she nibbled her bottom lip, he cocked his head. "Please."

Did he know that she could never say no to his please? "Okay. But can we walk? I need the fresh air."

"You got it."

It was only a ten-minute walk to The Tea House. A perk of Amber Ridge being the size of a shoe.

She grabbed her phone and pushed it into her back jeans pocket before stepping outside. Colt was there, waiting. He touched a hand to the small of her back. And even though she should probably have stepped away, she didn't. She let the warmth of his palm heat her entire back.

Three minutes into the walk, she asked, "Aren't you going to push?"

"Push what?"

"Me...for an answer. I just cried into your chest and said it was because I was tired." Which was true. But why was she tired? Something she was sure Colt would like a specific answer to.

"I'd like to know. But it's your choice if you share." He shot a glance down at her. "I have another question for you, though."

Oh God. "What?"

"How are you out of coffee?"

Her brows shot up. "That's your question?"

"Yeah. You used to buy those pods in bulk as if every store within a sixty-mile radius was about to sell out."

She cringed. It was true. She'd done so many sunrise shoots back then that she'd relied on coffee to get her going in the morning. She still relied on it, but pods were expensive. A problem she wasn't going to share with Colt.

She lifted a shoulder. "Maybe I've changed in the last year."

His brows flickered, and he was looking at her like he was wondering if that was true. In a lot of ways, it was. She felt better within herself. Her head was finally above water. But nothing had changed about the way she felt about Colt.

A couple minutes of silence passed. It was a nice silence. The kind that felt comfortable. But then, silence with Colt had always been comfortable, and neither of them had ever felt the need to fill it with unnecessary words or questions. It was the kind of quiet that she could sit in for a long time. And honestly, she would choose silence with Colt over any kind of noise with anyone else.

"So," he finally said, breaking that quiet. "I've been wondering what these sperm donors are like."

Jesus, she did *not* want to talk about that. "Colt—"

"I mean, how do they sell themselves?"

"Sell themselves?"

"Yeah. Do any of them make you think they have golden sperm?"

"Colt—"

"Well, if you're going to inseminate yourself with someone's sperm, you'd *hope* it was golden."

She rolled her eyes. "I told you, I'm not doing that."

NYSSA KATHRYN

"Why aren't you?"

Because of you.

The silent words hummed in her head. And they were true. It was why it had never really been an option. Just something she'd wanted to explore because she *did* want a baby, and she and Colt were separated.

But...she couldn't. Not without Colt.

"It's just not for me." She kicked a rock down the sidewalk. "Even if it was, I don't think I could go through with all the injections and hormones and procedures again. Maybe I'm just not meant to carry my own baby." The words hurt. So much that her chest felt tight once they were out.

"Hey. This isn't the end of your journey to becoming a mother, Cricket. Don't lose hope."

She swallowed, wanting to believe him. "I ran into your mom in the store the other day."

"You did?"

"Mm-hmm. She didn't tell you?"

"No. But I haven't seen much of her these last few days. She's been a bit off."

"Off how?" And did it have something to do with the man in the grocery store?

"Just acting strange. She's been checking in a lot, but really short conversations. She said something about Ben visiting."

Indie looked up at Colt. "Ben, as in your mom's security guy?" At least, that's what Sylvia called him, but he was more part of the family than an employee. Plus, he was getting a bit old to be security. He visited Sylvia often, staying with her for stretches of time. Colt had known him since he was eight.

Colt nodded, almost like he was stuck in his head. "Yeah. What did she say when you ran into her?"

Sylvia's words played over in her head again.

Did you date while you were separated? Or was that just Colt?

She wrapped her arms around her waist. "Actually, she told me you dated over the last year."

He grabbed her arm, stopping her on the sidewalk. "*What?*"

"Yeah. Audrey from high school and a woman named Savannah in California." Both names left a sour taste in her mouth. They shouldn't. Audrey was lovely, and this Savannah person was probably no different.

"She said that?" Colt growled.

"I didn't believe it." But obviously her subconscious did if she was dreaming about it. "But I did break up with you, so if you wanted to date other women—"

"I *did not* want to date other women—which is exactly why I didn't. It's not even remotely true."

Of course not. It was another way for Sylvia to hurt her.

"My mother's friends with Audrey's mother," Colt said, stepping closer. "When she was moving into her house, her mom asked me to help. I did. There was Burt's pizza as a thank you, and that was it."

Her tummy did a strange roll at the thought of Colt eating pizza alone with Audrey.

"Cricket."

She looked up.

"Did you hear me mention Burt's pizza?"

A small smile played at her lips. "Your idea or hers?"

"It was the only place that was open. And it was as terrible as always. And Savannah's a Marine. She was at my place when my mom got there—once. And I told Mom we were discussing a job. I don't know why she'd say otherwise."

She wrung her hands together. "I'm glad. Not about the pizza. I would've been surprised if it had been good. But that you didn't date."

"Did you?"

"Date?"

"Yeah." Something flickered over Colt's face. Uncertainty? Maybe some fear?

"No. Even if I wanted to, which I didn't, I wasn't in the mental place for that." Hell, she'd barely been living.

He looked at her so intensely that, for a moment, she didn't breathe. She had to force the air into her lungs as she turned and started walking again. Colt met her step for step.

They were almost at The Tea House when a guy stepped out of the café. He had a bag strung over his shoulder.

Indie immediately stopped. His head was down, but she could see who it was.

"That's him," she whispered.

"Who?"

"That guy was in the grocery store when I saw your mom. I don't know who he is, but your mom went really pale and almost ran out of there."

The man lifted his head, and Colt went very still beside her.

But only for a second—then he moved quickly, grabbing Indie's arm and tugging her behind him.

"What the fuck are you doing here?" Colt suddenly growled. And that rage...it tore through every word.

The man lifted a brow as he stepped closer. "Well, that's not a nice way to greet your father."

* * *

FURY COURSED through Colt's veins. Fury that Gordon Sharp *dared* to ever show his face in this town again. That the asshole was standing so fucking close to Indie.

"It takes more than some DNA to make a father," Colt said, voice low and dangerous. "I'm going to ask you again. What are you doing here?"

Twenty-six years. It had been twenty-six damn years since he'd set eyes on his father, and the asshole looked every one of those years, plus more. The smoking and drugs must have finally caught up with him.

Gordon lifted his hands. "Hey, you may not like me, but I'm still the man who raised you. You're still a Sharp."

"Wrong on both counts. You didn't raise me, and my last name changed the second you left town."

There was a small narrowing of his eyes. Yeah, the asshole didn't like that. Good.

Gordon tilted his head to look around him at Indie. "You his?"

"Don't talk to her. Don't even *look* at her."

There was a small lift of the corners of Gordon's lips. "She the girlfriend?"

"She's none of your business. Last chance to tell me why you're here."

He chuckled, his gaze going to the street before flicking back to Colt. "I'm here to see *you*, son. To see your mother. It's way overdue."

"The fuck you are."

"Don't believe me?"

"I believe that you've only ever cared about one person—you. So if you're here, that means you want something. Tell me what it is so I can say no and you can fuck off back to wherever the hell you've been the last twenty-six years."

"Jesus. You're a different person than the kid I left."

"Than the eight-year-old you tried to control with fear? Yeah, I am. And I will knock you to the fucking ground if I have to. You won't even see it coming."

Indie touched his back, and he pushed her farther behind him. Even with him in between them, she was too damn close to the asshole.

Gordon's eyes narrowed, then he made a mistake…he looked behind Colt at Indie. *Again.* "I might have better luck talking to your pretty lady than you. What do you think, honey?"

Colt moved so fast, the asshole didn't see him coming. He

grabbed Gordon by the collar of his shirt and shoved him hard against the wall. Then he got close—really fucking close. "You talk to her again, and I will *kill* you. Do you understand?"

"Colt! Don't."

Indie's startled voice was loud behind him, but he barely heard it, all his focus on his father. On the cascade of memories of the things this man did to his mother. Of him not giving a shit about anyone but himself.

"You belong in prison," Colt growled.

"And yet, here I am."

Indie touched his arm this time. "Colt...don't do anything you'll regret."

He'd regret doing nothing even more.

"Colt." A new voice sounded. Jesse's. "Everything okay?"

"Not even close," Colt said quietly.

His father lifted a brow. He almost looked amused. "What're you gonna do, son? Hit me in front of the sheriff? Do it. It might make you feel better."

That was the thing. It wouldn't.

"Colt." This time, *Jesse* touched his arm. "Step back, man."

Colt lowered his head and got so close he could see every fucking pore on his father's face. "Leave Amber Ridge. You don't want to stick around and see what I'll do."

His father's lips twitched. "Is that a threat?"

"It's a warning."

CHAPTER 8

*A*nger still coiled in Colt's gut, trying to consume him. Heating the air he breathed. Making him want to simultaneously hit something and yell.

His father was *here*, in Amber Ridge, after over twenty-six years away.

Why?

Memories of the worst moments of his life flashed in his head. Of his father's violence when he'd been high on whatever drug he was taking. Toward him. Toward his mother. But also the danger his father had put them in when he pissed off the wrong people. When he took money that wasn't his.

He tightened his fingers around the wheel and drove faster.

Jesse and Indie had wanted answers. He hadn't been able to give them any. Not right then. He'd barely been able to talk. Instead, he'd watched his father walk away while using every scrap of self-restraint he had to not go after him. Then apologized to Indie before leaving her with Jesse.

His father was the one secret he'd kept from Indie. She knew the basics—that he'd left when Colt was eight. That he hadn't kept in touch.

She didn't know *why* he'd left. That his mother had changed the locks. Cut him off from any family money. Hired Ben.

Why he hadn't told her, he wasn't sure. Maybe because after his father left, he and his mother *never* spoke about the man, not even to each other. Or maybe a part of him was ashamed of the scum he'd come from.

He pulled up in front of his mother's house to see a van with Secure Safe Systems printed on the side.

His eyes narrowed at the men installing new locks on the front door.

And suddenly his anger shifted from his father to his mother. She knew. She'd known for *days* that his father was in town, and she hadn't said anything.

He climbed out of the Audi and stormed inside. He checked the kitchen and living room. Upstairs, he checked his mother's bedroom.

Nothing. Where was she?

Then he looked out the window.

She was trimming her hydrangeas. He shouldn't be surprised. The garden was where she retreated when things got hard. It was where both of them had spent almost the entire first eight years of his life while his parents were still married and Gordon lived with them.

His mother turned her head when he stepped outside. "Colt, you're home."

That was it? She wasn't going to mention the new locks on the doors or the new security system being installed? Or hell, the fact that she'd seen his *father*, a man who'd tormented them both for years?

She turned back to her hydrangeas. "Shouldn't you be at the park? I'm sure there's so much work to do there."

"What are the security guys doing out front?" He wanted her to tell him herself.

"Oh, just upgrading a few things. It was time."

Frustration squeezed his insides. Then he saw it...his mother's pistol. She'd clearly tried to hide it behind a potted plant, but he saw the grip poking out.

"You weren't planning to tell me, were you?"

"Tell you what?"

His jaw clenched as he tried to holster his anger. "That you saw him."

He didn't need to say the name. She knew.

She paused, the muscles in her back visibly tensing before she slowly straightened and turned. "How did you know?"

"Well, first Indie saw him, and she told me that you spotted him in the grocery store."

His mother's brows flickered. "Indie doesn't even know what your father looks like."

"You're right. But *I* do. So I knew exactly who I was looking at when he walked out of The Tea House this morning."

Her mother's chest rose, fear and panic swirling in her gray eyes. "You saw him?"

"I did. And I wanted to kill him, Mom. I wanted to murder him right then and there."

She paled. "You didn't—"

"No. But I could have. You should have told me."

She swallowed. "I didn't want to alarm you."

"Alarm me? You don't think it was pretty damn alarming to run into him while I was walking with my wife to get coffee?"

His mother's mouth opened and closed. "It's not a big deal. He's returned a couple of times over the years, and I always call Ben to shadow me and scare him away."

Colt gaped at her. "He's come back before?"

"Yes. But like I said, Ben makes him leave."

"Goddammit, Mom. This is information I need to have!"

"Why? You were working a dangerous job, and you're my son. Your only responsibility is to make sure you come home to me alive. Why would I make you worry about this too?"

"Because he's my *father* and he used to hurt us, so I should be here to protect you."

"*No.*" She stood and stepped forward, a new hardness on her face. "That's my job. You're my son, and my entire job is to protect you."

"That's not—"

"Don't tell me it's not true." She closed the rest of the space between them. "You are my child. And I let you see far too much, far too young. I will never forgive myself for the time those men broke into our house, looking for your father, and the danger it put you in. Not to mention your father's drug-induced rages. The guilt lives with me every day. I will spend my life protecting you. Yes, my idea of protection might differ from yours, but I won't stop. I can't."

Tears shone in his mother's eyes, making him drop his forehead into his hand before scrubbing his face. He didn't agree. But this argument was getting him nowhere.

"I don't want you going out alone," he said, when he lifted his head.

"I won't. Ben will be with me."

"Good. Is he staying here?"

"No. He knows you're here, so he's at a hotel. But he gets here early each morning. He just left for a little bit, otherwise you would have caught him on your way in."

It didn't make him feel better. None of this did.

His mother swallowed. "How was Indie?"

Colt frowned. She wanted to talk about Indie after all that? "She's fine. She said you told her I'd been dating."

"Oh...was I not supposed to mention Audrey? I'm sorry."

"I didn't *date* Audrey."

"You didn't?"

"No. I helped her move. And you know that."

"Oh. Okay. I'm sorry. I must have misinterpreted things." His mother tilted her head. "How about we have her over for a meal this weekend so I can apologize in person?"

"Mom, I don't think—"

"It's a good time? Of course it is. I'm not letting your father dictate my life. Trust me, he'll disappear soon, just like he always does. We can't put our lives on hold. So...lunch or dinner soon?"

"I'll ask Indie."

"Good." She patted his arm and went back to her garden as if nothing had happened.

But Colt could barely see through the rage. His father was back. And while his mother might not think it was a big deal, to him it felt like the floor had been ripped from beneath his feet and he was falling, with no way of getting back up.

* * *

INDIE LEANED her hip against the kitchen counter, her gaze flicking to her phone. It was late. She should be in bed. But all she could think about was Colt. The anger in his eyes when he'd grabbed his father. The way he'd watched his dad leave, like he was prepared to kill the man if he came back.

It had been a huge ordeal, and since then, nothing. She hadn't heard from him.

She nibbled her bottom lip. Should she text him? Call?

All Colt had ever shared about his father was that he'd left when Colt was eight. He'd made it sound like no big deal. Like the man had left no imprint on his life.

But after today, she didn't believe that at all.

She lifted her phone and opened a text to Colt. She wrote something, then deleted it. Then she wrote something again. She deleted it a second time.

Crap. She scrunched her eyes.

Why was it so hard to message him? Because they were separated? Because they'd barely spoken in the last year?

The ringing of her phone shot her eyes open. But it wasn't Colt's name on the screen.

Noah.

She answered the call. "Hey."

"Hey, Indie. Jesse told me about the altercation outside The Tea House this morning. Are you okay?"

"I'm fine. But I can't get it out of my head. Has Colt ever mentioned his father to you?" Her heart picked up speed, scared that Noah would say yes. Scared of the possibility that Colt had shared more with her brother than he had with her.

"No. All I know is he left when Colt was young."

So, it wasn't just her. "Have you spoken to him today?"

"He was at the park, but he had his headphones on and was hammering the shit out of the overgrown branches along the trails. I left him alone."

She nodded, even though her brother couldn't see her.

"Indie...if you see that man again, I want you to walk in the other direction. Don't interact with him. Especially if you're alone. Okay?"

All the fine hairs on her arms stood up at the prospect of meeting Colt's father alone. Even if that interaction between him and Colt hadn't taken place, she would still know the guy was bad news. There was just something about him...a darkness.

"I won't." She pulled at a thread on her T-shirt. "You know, I thought he looked familiar that first time I saw him. Now I realize...he looks like Colt. But he also doesn't."

"If Colt doesn't like him, he must hate that."

Yeah, she wouldn't be saying that to him anytime soon.

"Do you want me to come over?" Noah asked gently.

She smiled, warmth filling her belly. It was so nice to have her protective big brother home. Jesse and Becket were like that too. Hell, Jesse had already texted and called to check in, but it was different with Noah. "Thanks, but I'll be okay. How's the new place?"

"Full of boxes and half-eaten takeout containers. But I'm getting there."

"Well, if you need help, just call. I'm cheap labor with just the cost of a pizza."

"Burt's pizza?"

She scoffed. "God, no. We'll make the pizza."

"I thought you were about to tell me his pizzas have gotten better since I've been gone."

"The opposite. Worse. Much worse. Clara found three black hairs on her last pizza."

"That's kind of gross."

"Not kind of, it *is* gross. But Burt's like the big happy uncle you want at every party, so I still buy a pizza every so often."

"Lucky bastard."

She chuckled. "Seriously though, let me know if you want some company while you unpack."

"Thanks, Indie. I will."

She hung up, and before she could talk herself out of it, she typed out a text. Three simple words.

Indie: Are you okay?

She was about to set the phone down when dots popped up.

Colt: Yeah, I'm all right. Are you? I'm sorry about this morning.

Indie: I'm okay. Confused, but okay. What haven't you told me?

Colt: A lot.

Her pulse picked up, and she didn't know how to feel about that. She knew she didn't have the right to feel angry, when she hadn't shared everything either. She'd kept every passive-aggressive comment his mother had made over the years from him. She'd kept the hurt to herself. The anxiety at the prospect of seeing her. So how could she be angry that Colt had kept a part of his past hidden?

Her phone suddenly rang. She picked it straight up. "Colt—"

"He was a drug addict."

She closed her eyes and let that information sink in. "I'm sorry."

"He would drink and do drugs. And then he'd get mean. Hit my mom. Try to hit me."

Pain gripped her heart. It squeezed so tightly that she almost grabbed her chest. "Try?"

"My mom would get in front of me, to shield me. I fucking *hate* those memories."

And Colt had seen it all. Sadness and grief and agony swirled inside her.

It explained so much. Why Colt never saw the parts of his mother that she saw. Why he never heard the unkindness in her voice. He was forever trying to make up for his childhood.

Because not protecting her from his father would have hurt Colt. And more than that, his mother had taken the brunt of his fathers cruelty to protect him.

"It took Mom a long time to cut him off. Too long. She put the accounts in her name so he wouldn't have access to any money. She tried to get him help. Instead of accepting that help, he stole drugs and money from the wrong people."

Her stomach dropped, because she knew what was coming next.

"They broke in. I hid in the library. That's the day she finally kicked him out."

Her heart broke for the child version of Colt. "Why didn't you tell me?" she whispered.

"Because I was a coward. It hurts to talk about. To think about. And I hate admitting that his blood runs through my veins. So when I told you my father left, and you accepted it, I took the easy way out and left it at that."

"Your past, even if it's painful, is a huge part of what makes you who you are, Colt. My past, with my parents' death and sister leaving, is painful too, but I shared that. You left out this big part of yourself."

"I know." Regret weaved into his words. "I'm sorry."

She pushed off the kitchen counter and moved to the living room window. "What are you going to do?"

"I'm going to find him."

"No." The response was instant, and a complete reflection of the panic that flared in her chest.

"I need to make him leave town," Colt pushed.

"You told him you wanted him gone today. If you have that conversation again, in private, without any witnesses..." She didn't finish her sentence, because she didn't need to. The anger she'd seen in Colt this morning was something she'd never witnessed before. That man had been capable of things that could get him into a lot of trouble.

"Indie—"

"I don't want you to find him, Colt."

"What am I supposed to do then?"

"Tell Jesse what you told me. Maybe he or his guys can scare him away. Maybe they can keep an eye on him and catch him doing something he shouldn't."

"I can't—"

"You can. For me. Please? Promise me you won't go searching for him."

Silence. It hung over the line and felt thick and heavy.

Her voice lowered. "Colt...*please*. I can't lose you."

No, technically they weren't back together. But he was here. They could find their way back to each other.

Colt sighed. "I'll do my best. But if *he* finds *me*—"

"You call Jesse."

Another pause. "You know I'd do anything for you, right?"

"Is that you agreeing?"

"Yeah, Cricket, that's me agreeing."

The relief almost made her light-headed. "Thank you."

"Now, can I ask you to do something for me?"

Nerves fluttered in her belly. "Sure."

"Have dinner at my mom's this weekend."

She scrunched her nose. That was the last thing she wanted to do. In fact, she'd rather bathe in a pool of lava than have dinner with Sylvia Reed.

A polite "no thank you" was on the tip of her tongue, when she stopped herself.

Now that she knew what Sylvia had gone through with Colt's dad, she had new sympathy for the woman. It didn't excuse her behavior, but it explained some of it. "Can I think about it?"

"Of course. No rush."

"Thank you."

"Keep your doors locked for me, okay?"

"Always."

She hung up, her skin still tingling from hearing his voice. Maybe dinner with Sylvia wouldn't be so bad.

Or maybe she'd be her normal self, and Colt would see everything he'd missed for so many years.

CHAPTER 9

*C*olt pulled into the Amber Ridge Sheriff's Station parking lot.

He should be at the park helping Noah and Randy's team. But he'd barely slept last night, thoughts of his father being so close to Indie yesterday toying with him. And according to his mother, the asshole had been back multiple times over the years.

He was frustrated and angry and a million other things.

He turned off the engine and climbed out.

Every time that bastard returned, his mother should have told him. How many times had he returned while Colt was away in the Marines? He had no idea because his mother wouldn't give him any details. She got all vague and claimed she didn't remember.

She did. After what that man had put her through, she would've catalogued every single visit.

Before getting out of his car, he pulled out his cell and called Ben. He still hadn't crossed paths with the guy.

Ben answered on the third ring. "Colt, is everything okay?"

"I need to know the details of my mother's security and what you're doing about Gordon."

There was a small pause. "She told you."

"No. I saw him for myself. She *should* have told me."

Ben sighed. "Yeah, she should have. I've been telling her that every time he makes an appearance."

"How many?"

"Every two or three years."

Jesus fucking Christ. "Has he ever touched her?"

"Once or twice. Nothing serious. He always wants money."

He'd touched her. More than once. And Colt hadn't been here to protect her.

"She doesn't give him any," Ben continued. "She calls me. I get here. Scare him away and tail her to make sure he doesn't get close. Although, this time, I can't find him. I've checked all the usual motels. I'm going to check the Airbnbs this week."

"What can I do to help?"

"Nothing. You stay away from him, Colt. The main reason your mother didn't want you knowing was because she was afraid of what you'd do."

Afraid he'd kill the guy? He wouldn't. Or at least, he was pretty sure he wouldn't. "You're going to protect her, right?"

"With my life."

"Good." Ben and his mother had always been close. He was the one his mother had called the night those men had shown up, asking for money. He'd been the one to inform Gordon that he wasn't welcome in the house anymore. Ben was more of a father than his own dad had ever been. "I need you to keep me updated."

"You'll know everything I know."

"Thanks. And Ben...thank you for looking after my mom."

"Always."

He hung up. Colt had always had this suspicion that Ben was secretly in love with his mother. Why nothing had ever happened between them, he wasn't sure.

Inside the station, a middle-aged woman smiled from the front desk. "Hi. Can I help you?"

"I have an appointment with—"

"Colt."

He looked up to see Jesse stepping out of the hall, coffee in hand.

Colt dipped his head. "Hey."

"Come in." Jesse indicated toward the office to the right.

Colt followed the other man in and closed the door behind him. "Nice office."

"Thanks. Comes with a side of arrests and a shit ton of paperwork."

Colt chuckled as he sat opposite the desk. "Good to know."

"How's the park going?"

"We're getting there. Randy's team is making quick progress."

"When do you think you'll open?"

"Not sure yet. Hopefully in a couple of months."

Jesse's brows lifted. "That soon?"

"I'm pretty keen to try that zip line."

Jesse grinned. "Shit, I haven't been on that since I was a kid."

"Great memories."

"You're not wrong." Jesse leaned forward. "Now, tell me about your dad."

That familiar tightness wrapped its fingers around his chest. "His name is Gordon Sharp. He left town when I was eight. He was into drugs, and I'm pretty sure he was also an alcoholic. When my mom cut him off, he got in with some bad people who he owed money to. Mom had to kick him out and hire security."

Jesse's jaw visibly clenched. "Is your mom safe?"

"She still has that security, but I'd like your team to keep an eye out for Gordon."

"I've already given a description to my deputies. I wish I could do more, like a background check, but for that I'd need—"

"Cause. I know. That's why I'm here, telling you what I can about him so that you know he's dangerous, and that danger follows him." He pulled a photo out of his wallet. He wasn't even sure why his mother had this old picture, but she did. He slid it across the desk. "This photo was taken about thirty years ago, but it's all I have."

"Thanks. This will still help my deputies." Jesse lifted the photo before looking back at Colt, almost assessing. "Do I need to be worried about *you*?"

Did everyone think he'd kill the guy? "No. You don't need to worry about me. As long as he leaves Indie and my mother alone."

Jesse's brows rose. "What about Indie?"

Colt's jaw clicked. "I asked her to be careful. To call me at the first sign of trouble and not go places alone."

"Do you think he'd touch her?"

A vein throbbed in Colt's temple. "To maintain his addiction, he's probably capable of anything."

* * *

INDIE FOCUSED on the couple through the lens. Bo and Georgia stood by the cliff's edge, their fingers intertwined. They looked at each other like they were the only two people in the world.

Beautiful. And so fixated on the other person they probably didn't even realize rain was about to come in.

She snapped the photo, then a couple more, trying to capture the emotion.

When Bo lowered his head and kissed Georgia, Indie zoomed out, trying to get both the kiss and the mountains behind the couple in the frame.

Her favorite types of shoots were families, but engagement sessions were a close second. There was just something about a couple who had their entire future in front of them that made the photos come out almost dreamy.

Back when she'd started, newborn shoots had been the highlight of her weeks, but the longer she'd struggled with IVF, the harder those became.

Bo whispered something in Georgia's ear, and she tipped her head back and laughed. Indie focused on the expression on Bo's face. The way he watched Georgia.

Devotion…that's what it was.

A drop of rain hit Indie's cheek. She lowered the camera. "Okay, guys, I think we just snuck the shoot in before the rain."

Bo and Georgia stepped away from each other, but Bo kept an arm curved around his fiancée's waist.

"You got everything you needed?" Georgia asked.

"I did. You've got some gorgeous photos here."

She beamed at Indie. "Thank you so much."

"You're welcome. I'll edit them and have them back to you in the next week or so."

Bo dipped his head. "Thanks, Indie."

Georgia lifted her bag, and they were about to pass her when she stopped. "I just want you to know that I never believed any of the rumors."

Indie frowned. "Rumors?"

"Yeah, you know, the ones about money and your business. I knew it was all ridiculous." She squeezed Indie's arm. "Can't wait to see the edits."

The couple walked away, but Indie remained exactly where she was. There'd been rumors involving her business and money? What rumors? And was that why bookings had been so low this past year?

Her heart started to beat faster, confusion and anger and frustration simmering inside her.

Who would start—

No.

Sylvia wouldn't be *that* evil…would she? She wouldn't really go so far as to try to ruin Indie's business. Sylvia knew it was her only source of income.

Why not? The question whispered in her head.

She had to find out.

She crouched and started packing up her equipment when a rustling noise came from behind her. She looked over her shoulder and frowned, watching as wind blew the branches of the trees.

Colt's phone call from that morning came back to her. The one where he'd asked her to remain with people because he was concerned about his father. Shit. She'd completely forgotten.

But she was fine. She was alone.

She turned back to her equipment and had just set her camera in the case when what sounded like a branch snapping echoed behind her.

This time, she shot to her feet and turned. "Hello? Is anyone there?"

Quiet surrounded her. But it did nothing to calm the beating of her heart behind her ribs.

She swallowed and was about to lift her equipment bag when the ringing of her cell made her jump.

Oh, good God, Indie, it's just a call.

She pulled her cell out to see Colt's name on the screen.

"Colt?"

"Hey. Are you okay? You sound breathless."

"Yeah, I'm just packing up."

"So you finished your shoot?"

"Yeah." She left out the part where the couple had already gone, because that would probably just make him mad. She frowned at the sound of an engine. "Where are you?"

"I actually just arrived at the lookout point parking lot."

"You did?"

"Yeah. In case the couple left and you're alone. *Are* you alone?"

How did he know? She sighed. "I am. But I'm heading back now. Sorry, I got distracted." She lifted her bag and was about to head back when she noticed something shiny on the ground, near the spot where Georgia and Bo had been standing.

"Indie, you need to be careful. My dad's seen us together."

She moved toward the cliff edge, bending over and lifting a silver bracelet. Georgia must have dropped it.

"I parked," Colt said quickly. "I'm coming toward you now."

"I'll meet you partway. I'm walking back—" Another branch snapped behind her, this one sounding closer. She gasped and spun—but she moved so fast that her foot slipped and she stumbled back, screaming as she went over the cliff.

CHAPTER 10

*I*ndie's scream pierced the phone line, making Colt's heart jackhammer in his chest.

"Indie?"

No answer.

He slammed the car door closed and ran, sprinting through the trees. He knew exactly where Indie liked to take photos. It was the same place he'd proposed to her—right on the edge of a cliff.

Why had she screamed? Was it his father? Was the asshole there? Had he hurt her?

Air whipped at his face, his feet sinking into the wet earth with each step. He ignored the cool rain hitting his skin and forced his body to move.

When he finally reached the break in the trees, his gaze went straight to Indie's camera bag near the edge of the clearing.

She wasn't here. Where was she?

Then he saw her fingers, just a hint of them poking over the edge.

Fear wrapped around his throat, trying to choke him. He

lunged forward and dropped to his knees to see Indie hanging over the edge, barely holding on.

Fuck.

He grabbed her wrist and, in one powerful tug, pulled her up to the surface.

She collapsed into his arms. "Colt! Thank God!"

She wrapped her arms tightly around him, and he just held her, completely unmoving. Fear paralyzed him. Made his limbs feel nailed to the ground.

"You're okay," he breathed, like he needed those words to be out in the world. As if that could cement them as truth.

"I'm okay," she repeated.

After what felt like endless minutes, he forced himself to lean back, but he still gripped her shoulders, unable to let go. "What happened?"

"I thought I heard something, and I spun around too quickly." Her chest heaved with panicked breaths that were just beginning to slow. "I slipped."

"What did you hear?"

"I don't know. The shuffle of movement. The crack of a branch."

Colt's fear twisted into something else. Something darker, that made every muscle in his body twitch as he turned his head and scanned the area.

It looked like they were alone. But there were a hell of a lot of places to hide in this forest.

Indie shook her head, raindrops hitting her face. "It's raining and windy. I doubt there was actually anyone here. I should get my camera to the car before it gets too wet."

"I want to call Jesse."

"Why?"

"I want his deputies to do a search of the area—"

"No, it was probably an animal."

"Indie."

She started pushing to her feet, and he helped her up. "I was clumsy. I don't want to waste my cousin's time."

His jaw clenched. "It's not a waste of time. It's making sure my father isn't stalking you."

"Your father doesn't even know me."

"He saw you with me. He saw *me* being protective of you. He knows you're important to me. He could use that against me."

"He doesn't even know I'm here."

In the small town of Amber Ridge, it wouldn't be hard to find that information.

She reached to lift the camera bag, but he grabbed it first. Then he gripped her hand and tugged her behind him as he moved. His gaze never stopped scanning the forest around them while they made their way back to the parking lot. He had a bad fucking feeling in his gut, and it had everything to do with that asshole being back in town.

And Indie had just slipped over a cliff—a fucking *cliff*. If he hadn't been there to pull her up…

No. He couldn't think about that.

When he reached her car, he put her camera bag in the back before turning to her. "Are you okay to drive?"

She nodded, but her fingers continued to tremble in his hold. "Indie—"

"I'm okay." She stepped closer. "I'm a bit rattled because I slipped, but you pulled me up. I'm okay to drive. I'll see you tomorrow."

He could have laughed. "I'm following you home."

"You don't need—"

"I'm following you home, Cricket."

She sighed. "Fine."

She stretched up to her toes and kissed him before sliding behind the wheel.

Colt fisted his hands to stop from pulling her back. When he reached his Audi, he'd already heard Indie try to start her engine two times.

Her car...another damn problem. He needed to get her a new one, and he needed to do it fast. But he already knew Indie wouldn't accept it willingly...not yet.

On the way to her house, he called both Jesse and Ben just to update them on what had happened. Ben said he'd check the area, but Colt already knew he wouldn't find anything. If it was his father, the man would be long gone.

* * *

INDIE TOOK one hand off the wheel and squeezed it into a fist. She needed to get rid of the tremble. Colt was already losing his mind. She couldn't let him see how shaken she really was.

She'd slipped off the edge of a cliff. She could have died. If Colt hadn't been there, she would have. With the rain and wind, a couple more seconds and she wouldn't have been able to hold on any longer.

She swallowed hard, begging her beating heart to slow.

Had there been someone in the trees? She'd said no, but she thought she'd heard someone. And yes, it could have been a wild animal. Or maybe she was just trying to convince herself it was an animal because the idea of Colt being right, that his father *had* followed her out there, made a chill sweep over her skin.

She pulled into her driveway and her gaze went straight to Colt in her rearview mirror. He was already out of his car, his shoulders bunched, jaw clearly tense.

The guy looked every bit the former spec ops soldier he was. And he looked angry.

He came to her door. When he opened it, the hinge groaned. "We're getting rid of this pile of metal."

"No, *I'm* getting rid of it." She reached behind her for her camera bag and climbed out, rain dribbling on her shoulders.

"But until I do, this *pile of metal*, as you put it, is perfectly capable of getting me from point A to point B."

Was it nearing the end of its life? Yes. But it was still getting her places.

He took the camera bag from her hold. "What if you finish a shoot in the mountains—it's dark, wet, you have no signal, and your car stops working?"

Talk about worst-case scenarios. But...it was true. "A lot of things would have to go wrong for that to happen."

"Yeah. A lot *could* go wrong."

She slotted her key into her door and stepped inside. "I'll get a new car soon."

Colt set the camera bag onto the hall table. "Why isn't your heat on?" he asked, obviously noting how cold it was in the house.

"I don't leave it on when I'm not home."

"You used to. If I recall correctly, you said you keep the heat on so that the house feels like a warm hug when you get home."

Oh God, she *had* said that. "I guess with maturity comes the knowledge that I was just throwing money out the window."

His brows lowered, and he did that thing where he studied her far too closely.

Crap.

She quickly walked to the linen closet off the hall and grabbed two towels before handing one to Colt.

"Thanks." His deep rumble of a voice rippled over her skin. "Are you okay?"

She stopped at the kitchen counter and used the towel to dry her arms and face. Her clothes were damp, and yeah, she was wishing she'd kept the heat on. "I'm fine."

"Not convincing, Cricket."

He closed the space between them until he was close. Too close.

She crossed to the fridge and opened the door, then pulled

out bottles of water. When she turned, it was to find Colt not looking at *her*. He was looking at the now closed refrigerator doors.

He switched his attention back to her. "You have hardly any food."

Double crap.

His frown deepened. "You sold your car and bought something that barely runs. You don't leave the heat on because you're worried about the bill. You have almost no food in your house, and you haven't been doing many photo shoots. You're having money problems."

"I'm fine." The words were a reflex. She moved to step past him, but he gripped her arm.

"Cricket, you have money in our shared accounts. Use it."

"No."

Frustration cut across his expression. "*Why?*"

"Because that's *your* money. Your family money, and the money you earned as a Marine. It's not mine to use."

"It will always be yours to use because you're my wife, and it's my job to make sure you have what you need."

"I *do* have what I need."

"You barely have food, heat, or transport! Let me take care of you."

"Colt. I'm okay."

He didn't look like he believed her. Another step forward. "I want to stay here in case my father makes an appearance."

"No." She shook her head as if to emphasize just how much of a no it was.

"Why not?"

"Because we're not ready for that. A couple months ago I was signing our divorce papers."

"I never wanted that. And neither did you."

It was true. But no way was she admitting that out loud right now.

When he touched her hip, she pressed a hand to his chest, intending to push him away, but she realized his shirt was soaked. "Hang on, I have some of your old shirts. I'll grab you one."

She walked away, speeding out of the kitchen and into her bedroom. In the bottom dresser, she pulled out one of his shirts.

"You kept them in there."

She jumped. Jesus Christ, he moved quietly. "Yeah. I boxed a lot of stuff and took other things to your mom's, but I kept this drawer. I'm not sure why."

Lie. She knew exactly why. Because the thought of removing the last bit of Colt from the home hurt. And she'd already been hurting too much.

When she handed him the shirt, their fingers touched, and a bolt of electricity shot down her arm.

She wasn't sure what she expected, but the second he tugged off his wet shirt, air stalled in her lungs. Good God. The man was just as sculpted as the last time she'd seen him. Maybe more.

The urge to touch him was so intense that she actually shoved her hands behind her back to stop herself.

When she looked back up at his eyes, it was to see him watching her, desire aimed back at her. A desire that matched her own.

"When you look at me like that, going slow is the last thing on my mind," he whispered.

Hers too. But slow was smart, wasn't it? A year ago, she'd been a shell of the person she was today. She had to make sure she was safe in this relationship. That he would choose her over anything else.

She took a quick step back and cleared her throat. "Thank you for saving me today, Colt."

"I'll always save you, Cricket. And these conversations…about me staying close and money…aren't over." He tugged the shirt over his head. But before leaving, he stepped forward and pressed a kiss to her forehead.

And she felt that kiss everywhere. In her toes. Her blood. Even her bones.

"Lock up after me." His warm breath brushed over her skin.

Then he walked out, but she didn't move for a full minute after he'd left. All she could do was breathe.

CHAPTER 11

$\mathcal{T}$he music was loud in CJ's bar and the crowd thick. Colt didn't want to be here. Hell, he didn't want to be anywhere other than with Indie, but she was having a night with Clara, and he said he'd give her the time she needed, so that's what he had to do.

In the last week, they'd talked every day. It felt good. Right. But it also wasn't enough. He wanted to hold his wife. Kiss her. Remind her multiple times a day what she meant to him.

"You okay?" Noah asked, lifting the beer to his mouth.

"No. And I won't be until my father gets the hell out of Amber Ridge."

"Hey, this is supposed to be a night off from all that. You've been exhausting yourself, pulling twelve-hour days at the park. You need a break."

"He could be a threat to my mother *and* my wife. Hell, he could be a threat to you, as my friend and business partner."

"I can take care of myself. And your mother has security, and Indie is making sure she doesn't go anywhere alone. So far, there hasn't been any trouble."

"I still think he was at her shoot last week." He drank more of his beer. "Distract me. How are you doing, being back?"

There was a flicker of a frown across Noah's brow. "Good."

Colt studied him. His voice. His features. Was there something he wasn't sharing? "You sure?"

"Of course. I've got my own place that Holden's helping me fix up. I finally emptied the last box of shit. Life's good." He swung the beer back. "You and Indie still making progress on your relationship?"

Was he changing the subject because he didn't want to talk about himself? "I brought her coffee this morning. She kept the kitchen island between us the entire time, like she was scared I'd touch her."

"She just needs time. She went through a pretty rough patch. She wants things to be different this time."

"And they will be. I'll make sure of it." He knew he couldn't promise that she'd never go through the same thing again, when it came to pregnancy. But he was committed to doing everything in his power to make sure she was safe and happy, not just today or tomorrow, but forever. "You know she's having money problems?"

"She tell you that?"

"No. I figured it out."

"I know she hasn't been booking a lot of shoots, but I assumed she was still doing okay. But now that I think about it, she *has* been cutting costs. And what the hell's with that car?"

"You mean that piece of shit she's driving around?"

Noah's jaw clenched. "I don't like it either."

"She has money. *Our* money. But—"

"She won't touch it. I'm not surprised. She sees it as yours."

"It's both of ours. I wish she'd use it."

"I agree with you. I—" Noah stopped, looking at something behind Colt. "Is that Randy and his crew?"

Colt turned, spotting Randy and his guys standing around the pool table.

When Randy met their gazes, his mouth cracked into a wide grin, and he waved them over.

"Guess we're joining them," Noah said with a chuckle.

They wove through the crowd to the pool table.

"Hey, we didn't know you guys were coming here tonight," Colt said, as he shook Randy's hand.

"It's Waldo's birthday."

Waldo, a young guy in his early twenties, waved his hands. "Hey! It's my birthday!"

Randy shook his head. "He's had a few to drink."

"True." Waldo grinned, joining them. "But doesn't mean I'll show up to work hungover tomorrow. Cross my heart."

Colt didn't believe him for a second. The guy already looked plastered.

"Maybe you can just take the day off," Noah said with a chuckle.

"Maybe. Or maybe I'll just go camp in one of those cabins tonight with Milo, aka Sky Jerky."

Colt frowned. "Sky Jerky?"

"He's been leaving a lot of Big Sky Jerky wrappers lying around," Randy said. "The old guy's getting messy."

"Have you seen him?" Colt asked.

"Nah, but Milo's good at evading people so he's not forced to leave before he's ready."

"He'll get out of there once we start doing the cabins," Waldo said, before laughing. "Or he won't, and we'll just gut and renovate the place around him."

The guys continued to talk, but Colt's mind went back to the same place it always went...Indie.

His hand twitched to pull out his phone and text her. He wanted to know what she was doing with Clara. To make sure she was okay.

It felt wrong to be anywhere in Amber Ridge and *not* be with her. They'd dated since high school. He barely knew how to exist in this town without her.

Fuck it.

He pulled his cell from his pocket and typed out a text.

Colt: Hey. Just checking that you're okay.

He'd just hit send when Waldo whistled. "Well, well, who are those pretty ladies? Guess it really *is* my birthday."

Colt turned his head—and his cock turned to stone.

Indie. She stepped into the bar with Clara by her side, wearing a floral wrap dress with a fringed hem. The dress emphasized her ample breasts, and the ankle boots with the heels drew his gaze to her shapely legs.

"Wonder if the girl in the flower dress is single. She's not wearing a wedding ring."

Colt's body tensed at Waldo's question. "She's *not* single," he growled.

"You know her?"

"She's my wife." He downed the rest of his beer before setting the bottle on a nearby table and moving across the bar.

* * *

INDIE WATCHED the wind move through the trees from the passenger seat of the car.

"Are you thinking about him?" Clara asked, breaking the silence.

Of course she was. She was always thinking about him, whether she wanted to or not. "Maybe. This morning, I tried to use the kitchen counter as a barrier between us."

Because any time he touched her at all, she turned into a freaking mess. Her heart rate shot up. Her skin tingled. And she was about ready to fling off her clothes and drag him to bed.

Yeah, she really did feel that desperate.

"Why?" Clara asked gently. "You told me the kiss was good."

"It was better than good." A million miles ahead of good.

"Okay. And you've decided not to go through IVF without him. You're not doing IVF *at all*. So that stress, plus the stress of him being in the military, isn't there. It's just—"

"His mother." She turned to look at Clara. "You know she asked me to come over for dinner on Sunday night?"

"When?"

"Well, *she* didn't ask me. She asked Colt to ask me."

"Uh-huh, she's trying to play the good mom in front of Colt."

"Maybe. After finding out about Colt's dad though, I kind of feel sorry for her. Not enough to forgive her for all the unkind things she's said, but...I don't know. Her husband was a drug-addict alcoholic who used to hurt her."

Clara's eyes softened. "Being married to a man like him would have been awful."

"And with a young kid? She needed to protect her son from his own father. And despite everything, she *does* love Colt."

"But if she loves Colt as much as she says she does, and Colt loves you, then she should welcome you."

"Unless she thinks I'm not good for her son."

Clara glanced at her, then back to the road. "That's ridiculous. You started dating in high school, and he hasn't looked at another woman since. Sylvia should love Colt enough to love you too."

"Maybe to her, I'm unlovable."

Clara scoffed as she pulled into the parking lot beside CJ's. "No, you're not. Maybe *she's* unhinged."

Indie climbed out of Clara's Volkswagen. "She liked me for the first few years. Or at least, I think she did. It was after we got married and started trying for a baby that she got cold."

Which had kind of felt like a kick in the gut. Because that was when the fertility struggles had begun, and she'd needed support. She certainly hadn't gotten it from Sylvia.

"Maybe we should buy her something," Clara said, as they headed toward the entrance of the bar. "Soften her up."

Indie snorted. "That woman has a hell of a lot more money than me. I doubt there's anything I could buy her that she'd want."

"Actually, I've been wanting to talk to you about that."

Oh geez, first Colt, now Clara. "I'm fine."

"I know. You've told me. But if you're not, I want you to let me or my mom help you."

"I am *not* taking your money, or Aunt Pam's money." Absolutely not. Even the thought made Indie feel sick.

"Well, you can't keep driving that thing you call a car. Every time you get in it, I don't know if I'll see you alive again."

"I'm going to replace it."

"Good. But—"

"Nope. You've said what you needed to say. I appreciate it, but I'm okay. Now, we're stepping inside the bar, and we're going to drink and have a good time." Then, as if to prove it, she gripped Clara's wrist and dragged her inside.

She'd only gotten two steps beyond the door when she saw him.

Colt. He was with a group of people, one of them being her brother.

Good God, this town really was the size of a shoe. She smiled at them before directing Clara to a table.

Clara grinned. A big-ass grin that made Indie's jaw tense.

"Say it," Indie said.

"It's like the universe wants you two to be together and happy."

"Maybe. Or maybe the universe is out to get me."

"Nope. I'm right. And your destiny is walking up to us right now."

She turned just as Colt stopped at the table.

"Hey."

Sexy voice. Sexy tight shirt over his too-hot-to-look-at muscles. Life really was unfair. "Hey yourself."

"I didn't know you were coming out tonight."

She lifted a shoulder. "Last-minute decision. But I'm not alone. I brought Clara."

Noah arrived at the table next and bumped Clara's hip. "Hey, cousin."

"Well, if it isn't Noah Hayes." She bumped his hip back.

"Can I get you a huckleberry martini?" Colt asked her, voice low.

Her heart gave a little thump that he remembered her order. But of course he remembered it. He knew her better than anyone else in this world.

Noah smiled at Clara. "Want me to get you an apple juice?"

She grinned at him. "Aw, you remember that I don't drink!"

"Of course I do—you're my favorite cousin."

Clara rolled her eyes. "Bet you say that to my brothers too."

"Uh-huh, but I only mean it with you."

Clara chuckled and started talking to Noah about her brothers, as Colt lowered his lips to Indie's ear. "Dance with me."

Her heart did one of those skip-a-beat things. She looked up and immediately regretted it, because his lips were right there, and man oh man, they looked kissable. "We shouldn't."

"Says who?"

"The laws of attraction in combination with us moving very slowly together."

"Indie Reed…is that you admitting that you're attracted to me?"

"You will never catch me saying those words out loud—your head will get far too big."

The corners of his lips lifted before he lowered his head even farther, his mouth brushing her ear as he whispered again, "Dance with me."

A small shudder coursed down her spine. And when he took her hand, she completely forgot that she shouldn't be following him. She forgot about going slow and being careful and just went where he took her.

When they reached the dance floor, he held her against him, so close that there was nothing to breathe in but him. Nothing to feel but his arms around her.

And suddenly she was thrown back in time. To before infertility had darkened their lives. Before the stress of everything had dragged them down. To when it had just been them.

She allowed herself to lean into him and borrow some of his strength.

He lowered his mouth to her ear again. "You feel good too."

Too? Had she said he felt good out loud? Or was he just doing that reading-her-mind thing?

She swallowed. "Who are the group of guys?"

"Randy's construction team. They're doing the work for the park."

"And you're drinking with them?"

"It was a coincidence. Noah and I didn't know they'd be here. If the young guy who's had too many drinks comes over to you, send him away. Or better yet, send him to *me*."

She frowned. "Why?"

"He thinks you're...pretty."

She almost laughed at the near anger in his voice. "Do *you* think I'm pretty?"

"No. I think you're gorgeous."

Air caught in her lungs. Colt had always had a way of making her feel like the most beautiful woman in any room she walked into.

"Where's your wedding and engagement ring, Cricket?"

She jolted. Crap. "Stored away safe." It wasn't a lie. She just wasn't sure exactly *where* they were stored.

He nodded, but the thinning of his lips said he didn't like that she didn't wear it. While he always had his on.

"I'm glad you didn't date while we were separated," she said quietly, needing a change of subject.

"It was never going to happen. Just like signing those divorce papers."

Had she ever expected him to sign them? She wasn't sure. She actually wasn't sure how *she'd* signed them.

She looked away and spotted another couple watching her on the dance floor. A married couple she'd photographed a few years ago.

She smiled at them, but they both quickly looked away.

Strange.

She looked back at Colt. "Have you heard any rumors around town about me?"

"What kind of rumors?"

"Involving me and…money. Maybe something to do with my photography business?"

"No. Who told you there was a rumor?"

"A client made a comment." She shook her head. "It's probably nothing."

But the realistic part of her knew that wasn't true. Because rumors would explain everything. Why business had been so bad. Why clients were acting strange around her.

She needed to know who started them, particularly if it was Sylvia.

Colt's arms tightened around her. And when his thumb grazed her side, her skin burned like it was on fire.

"So…where did we land on that dinner at Mom's?" he asked.

She looked back up at him. If she wanted to give this marriage another go—and she really did—then she needed to work things out with Sylvia. She needed to figure out why the other woman disliked her and if that was ever going to change.

"I'll go to dinner at your mom's."

He gave her a sweet smile. "Yeah?"

"Yeah."

"Good." He lowered his head and touched his temple to her head. "You make me happy, Indie."

Her eyes shuttered, and she just let herself feel the intensity of the moment. The warmth that his arms around her brought...and not just a physical warmth. The peace she felt when she laid her cheek against his heart. She hadn't felt peace in so long.

When the music eventually sped up, she stepped away from Colt, but there was resistance in his hold.

She cleared his throat. "I might go get a drink."

"I'll come with you."

"No. It's okay. I won't be long." She needed a second to breathe without him. And maybe to cool down a little.

Colt's brows lowered, and for a moment she thought he wasn't going to let her go. But then he nodded. "Don't take long."

"I wouldn't dream of it."

She headed to the bar, and the second she got there, she sucked in a deep breath.

Yep. The space was definitely needed.

The bartender hadn't reached her yet when someone stepped up beside her. She only noticed because he stunk of smoke and stood far too close.

She looked up—and gasped.

Gordon.

She shot a look over her shoulder, but a group of people were now standing between her and the table, blocking her view of Colt. But even if they weren't, she wasn't sure she wanted him to see Gordon so close to her.

"You shouldn't be here," she said firmly.

"Really? Where should I be?"

"Away from Amber Ridge."

One side of his mouth lifted, but the smile was all wrong. "Indie, right?"

NYSSA KATHRYN

"How do you know my name?"

"It's a small town. Information is easy to come by."

"I've got to get back to Colt."

She took a step away from the bar, but Gordon moved quickly, blocking her path and towering over her. "Wait. We've barely had a chance to get to know each other."

CHAPTER 12

Clara frowned at him when Colt returned to the table. "Where's Indie?"

"Getting a drink."

"You look like you could use one yourself," Noah said.

He needed a hell of a lot more than one after holding Indie on the dance floor.

Clara touched his arm. "Are you okay?"

"Just fighting like hell to get my wife back."

"You've already made so much progress in such a short amount of time. Hopefully this dinner with your mom will be the final step in Indie trusting your relationship is safe for her."

He frowned. "How would a meal with my mother help?"

Clara's mouth opened and closed. "Well...um...you know... family's important."

He stepped closer to her. "Clara...has something happened between Indie and my mother that I don't know about?"

Her eyes widened. "I...uh—"

"Colt!"

He looked up to see Waldo weaving toward them, his eyes glazed and a wide smile on his face, a beer in his grip.

Jesus. "I think you've probably had enough, man."

"It's my birthday. It's my *job* to drink a lot today!" A frown cut into his brows. "Sober me doesn't care about other people's business, but drunk me is nosy. Who's the old dude at the bar, talking to your wife?"

Colt straightened, his body stiffening. "What are you talking about?"

"There's some old dude with a creepy scar on his chin—"

Colt shot into the crowd, not waiting to hear Waldo finish his sentence.

His father was here, at the bar...and he was with Indie. He spotted them just as Indie stepped away from the bar.

Immediately, his father stepped in front of her, almost causing her to collide with his chest.

Colt saw red.

Two more strides and he grabbed the asshole by the back of his shirt and swung him around, shoving him back against the bar.

"What the fuck are you doing here and why are you near my wife?" Colt yelled.

Gasps sounded around him, the shuffle of people moving away.

Gordon's smirk could only be described as evil. "Hey, son. I was just having a chat with your lady."

Colt's fists tightened. Every part of him wanted to hit the guy. Ram his fist so hard into Gordon's face that he went down and didn't get back up.

"Come on, Colt. It was just a conversation. I wanted to ask if you were here."

The fuck he was. "You're trying to tell me you were just going to ask about *me* and leave her alone?"

"I'm not *trying* to tell you. I *am* telling you. I wanna talk to you."

A hand touched his arm. "Colt, step back. He's not worth it."

Noah. His voice was calm but firm.

Colt got in his dad's face. "We have nothing to talk about. The only reason I'm not planting my fist into your face right now is because that would make me just like you—a damn coward who preys on people weaker than me."

There was a small narrowing of Gordon's eyes. "Colt—"

"Obviously, you're still as stupid as you were twenty-six years ago, because you didn't heed my warning." His fingers tightened around his father's shirt. "Leave now. There is no scenario where you come out unscathed if you stay."

"Step outside with me, and I'll tell you what'll make me leave."

Colt could have laughed. He wanted money. "You're not getting a fucking cent. Get out. Before I make you." Then he shoved his father's chest and stepped back. Without another glance his dad's way, he took Indie's hand and stomped through the crowd.

He wasn't sure how he'd expected Indie to react. But she matched him step for step.

When they reached his Audi, he helped her in before sliding behind the wheel. He felt Indie's gaze on him the entire drive home. She didn't ask if he was okay. She didn't ask a single question. Instead, she just set her hand on his thigh, and that helped him regain a fraction of the sanity he'd lost in that bar.

It also reiterated everything he already knew. That she knew him better than anyone else. And her touch healed him.

He set his palm on top of hers and immediately she turned her hand over, interlacing their fingers.

When they reached the house, he went straight to her side to help her out of the car before setting a hand on the small of her back and leading her inside.

She slipped off her shoes as he locked the bolt, and again, he could feel her gaze on him.

When he finally turned to her, he said the two words he should have said long ago. "I'm sorry."

"For what?"

"Anything my father said to you."

"He barely said anything. Just that we'd barely had a chance to get to know each other, when I tried to leave."

A vein in Colt's temple throbbed. He hated the thought of the asshole saying a single word to her.

Indie took that final step toward him and pressed her palm to his chest. "Are you okay?"

"No." He couldn't lie to her. He'd *never* been able to lie to her. "Let me stay the night. I'll sleep on the couch—hell, I'll sleep on the floor. But don't ask me to leave...please."

Her brows flickered. The silence that passed almost had him believing she was going to say no. That she was going to ask him to walk out of this house, leave her unguarded, and then he'd barely get a second of sleep.

"I'll make up the couch," she said quietly.

The knot in his stomach unraveled. *Thank fuck.*

Instead of walking away, she dropped her head on his chest. His arms immediately wrapped around her, fitting her flush against his body. He breathed her in, needing everything she had to give. Her calm. Her soft. *Her.*

Seeing his father looming over her tonight had scared him. It brought back every nightmare from his childhood of his father standing over his mother during a drug-induced rage. Only then, he'd been helpless to do anything.

Not anymore.

Indie lifted her head, her beautiful green eyes boring into him. "You don't have to be scared for me."

"I will *always* be scared at the prospect of not being able to protect you. Because the idea of losing you kills me."

Her eyes softened. "You're not going to lose me. And I don't need protection. I'm very good at the swift kick in the balls."

He bit back a laugh. "What *do* you need, then?"

"Right now?" Her gaze dipped to his lips, and something primal erupted deep inside him.

Slowly, she lifted to her toes. He didn't dare move, scared that a single twitch would break the moment.

She cupped his cheek, her skin warm and so infinitely feminine.

Then, finally, she kissed him. The touch of her lips against his was soft and certain and real. It was gentle, coaxing his lips apart before she slid inside his mouth, then he was tasting her. And she tasted exactly how he remembered. Sweet like strawberries and a hint of honey.

The world didn't slow or speed up—it stopped. She stopped his world.

He curved an arm around her waist and turned them, pressing her to the wall. Feeling all of her against him. The cushion of her breasts. The heat of her thigh as her leg wrapped around his waist.

She was like water he'd been deprived of for months. The air he needed to breathe.

He lifted her, and her legs immediately wrapped around him, holding him in place.

There were so many nights over the last year that he'd missed her. Craved her. And finally, he was here—*they* were here—and she was choosing him.

He moved his mouth down her throat, tasting her skin. When he found the spot on her neck that he knew made her shudder, he sucked, and her entire body trembled.

He wanted to keep going. To kiss and stroke and taste every inch of her. But not tonight. Not after his father had tainted the evening.

He lifted his mouth and touched his forehead to hers. "You're magic, Indie. You know that? You do something to me that nothing and no one else could ever do."

Her hands curved around his neck. "It's called love."

* * *

INDIE SCRUNCHED her eyes and rolled to her side. She couldn't sleep. How long had she been lying in bed, not tired at all? Not even a little bit. One hour? Two?

All she could think about was Colt on her couch in the other room. And that kiss...God, that kiss. It had been even better than the first one. Emotional and intimate and *healing*. It was crazy, but she'd felt that reconnection after a part of their marriage had broken a year ago.

When Colt had first moved to California, she'd lived with him, and there'd been times when he'd come home from a long mission and all he'd seemed to want was to kiss and hold her like he had tonight. That was how he'd quieted the storm inside him. And she'd always tried to give him all of her.

But now, lying here by herself felt wrong.

She rolled to her other side.

Even though the lights were off, the moon cast gentle light over the room.

Her eyes landed on her phone. And like she had so many other nights, she reached out and opened her photos. Not her most recent photos. Her albums...or one album in particular. The same album she'd opened a million times before. Every time she missed him, this was where she went. Every time she felt like she couldn't breathe without him, this was the album that gave her air.

Pictures of her and Colt. Some of them smiling. Some laughing. She stopped on one where she was looking up at him, and he was looking down at her. Neither of them were smiling. She couldn't even remember who'd taken the photo. But the love... God, you could almost feel it.

Tears she couldn't stop pressed at her eyes. They were so happy. But this was before it had gotten hard and her mental health had taken such a turn.

She blinked away the tears before flicking over to messages. Her fingers just started moving.

Indie: If you had a do-over, would you do that day differently?

It was late. He was probably asleep. And even if he wasn't, he probably didn't even know what day she was talking about.

Her phone vibrated with a response.

Colt: I've asked myself that question a million times...and the answer is always yes.

Indie: What would you change?

Colt: I would have called an ambulance for my mother, then called you right away. Whatever we did next would have been a joint decision. But I would have been with you for that call from the IVF clinic. I would have held you when they told you that our last embryo didn't take. And I could have pulled you up from the water when you felt like you were drowning.

Tears spilled down her cheeks.

If that had happened, if Colt had been there for her to lean on, cry on, maybe it would have hurt less. Maybe she wouldn't have felt like the future she'd built in her mind had shattered, leaving nothing but blank space.

Colt: I'm so sorry I wasn't there when you needed me. Next time, I swear to you, I will be.

Indie: I need you.

Three words.

And only a few seconds later, the door opened. The bed behind her dipped, and she was enveloped by Colt's strong chest and arms. More tears fell. Tears of grief for that night and for everything else. That they never got their baby. The stolen months of trying and failing. The dream of becoming pregnant postponed again and again.

"Indie, tell me what you're feeling," he whispered into her ear.

"Every cycle, I got my hopes up that it was going to be different because of something that we did or changed, and then it was the same outcome. And I started to wonder…what's wrong with me? Why is my body broken?"

His arm tightened around her. "There is *nothing* wrong with you. You aren't broken. You are *perfect*. And this journey isn't over for you."

She wasn't sure she believed that. But she wanted to.

She nuzzled back into him, and it was only the feel of him around her, the beating of his heart against her back, that finally allowed her to sleep.

CHAPTER 13

Indie traced the outside of Sylvia's house with her gaze. She was late. A good fifteen minutes late. Yet that didn't seem to add any motivation to get her butt out of the car and inside the house.

What would Sylvia be like tonight? The mother-in-law from the start of her relationship with Colt, who was kind and nurturing and had made Indie feel like she was gaining a mother as well as a husband?

Or the mother-in-law she'd turned into a few years later? The one who made Indie feel small and underserving.

Come on, Indie. Just walk in. The sooner the night starts, the sooner it will be over.

One deep breath, and she unclicked her seat belt before grabbing her apple crumble from the passenger seat.

She wasn't the best baker, but apple crumble had always been her thing. Although, she had no double Sylvia would find something to say about it, probably when Colt left the room.

Colt had wanted to drive her, but if she'd agreed to that, the man would have seen every one of her nerves. And yes, she absolutely should have told him about the snide comments from his mother, now that he was out of the military. He wasn't working a dangerous job anymore. They weren't trying to lower stress for fertility. She should have been honest with him by now.

There'd been a few times when he'd asked if there was something going on between her and his mother, and the words had been right there on the tip of her tongue. But they hadn't come out. Maybe because of everything going on with his father. Or maybe she'd always find an excuse not to tell him because she didn't want to be the reason for issues between him and his mother.

And there *would* be issues. Colt would lose his mind.

She reached the door and paused. Maybe things would be better tonight.

She almost snorted. Unlikely, but a girl could hope.

She lifted her hand to knock, but the door opened before her fist hit the wood. Colt smiled at her, and just looking at him completely disarmed her. He was big and beautiful and sexy. And yes, something as plain as jeans and a white T-shirt made him look ridiculously hot.

It wasn't fair.

Her lips curved into a smile. "Hey."

"Hey yourself. I was wondering when you were going to come in."

"You were watching?" Crap. How long had she sat in her car? Five minutes? Ten? Longer?

He stepped forward and slipped an arm around her waist, his lips hovering near hers. "Absolutely, I was watching. I would watch you all day, every day, if I could."

Heat bloomed low in her belly. He kissed her, and even though his lips only touched her cheek, a warm shiver chased down her spine.

The smile on her lips slipped when she stepped into the living room and spotted Sylvia in the kitchen.

The older woman looked up from the cucumber she was slicing. "Indie, you made it." She dried her hands on a towel and crossed the space between them. When she pulled her into a hug, Indie tensed. She couldn't help it. After years of expecting the worst from this woman, she couldn't relax around her.

When they separated, Indie forced the smile back to her lips. "Hi, Sylvia. Thank you for inviting me over."

"Of course. I've missed having you in my home."

Yeah, freaking right.

A man stepped into the kitchen from the back door. It took her a moment to recognize him as Ben. She'd met him a few times over the years. He was older, maybe in his sixties, and there was a hardness to him. Despite his age, he clearly worked out. His arm muscles were thick, and even through the jeans, Indie could see the definition in his legs.

Sylvia turned. "Ben, you remember my daughter-in-law, Indie. Indie, Ben will be joining us for dinner."

Ben stepped forward and shook her hand. "It's nice to see you again, Indie."

"You too." She turned back to Sylvia and held out the apple crumble. "I made a dessert."

"Wow, an apple crumble. How brave of you."

Indie frowned. "Brave?"

"Well, if I remember correctly, you don't really bake or cook. Remember that goulash you tried?" Sylvia chuckled and turned, setting the apple crumble onto the counter.

The goulash had been perfect. And Indie was pretty sure Sylvia hadn't even tried it. She'd put some on her plate but never touched it, only eating the potato bake *she'd* made.

Colt wrapped an arm around Indie's waist. "I love Indie's goulash."

There was a small tightening of Sylvia's eyes. It was so subtle, Indie almost missed it.

"I didn't know you were a goulash fan. Maybe I'll make you mine next week." Sylvia slapped her hands on her hips. "Now, I hope we're all hungry, because I've made *a lot* of food and Ben's grilled up some bison burgers outside that smell amazing."

The next twenty minutes were spent setting the table, finishing the food, and chatting. Sylvia did most of the talking, telling them about her book club and trips to the market. Something Indie had learned early on was that Sylvia liked to talk about Sylvia and Colt. And if the conversation ever switched over to Indie, Sylvia was great at switching it back.

When they finally sat at the table, Indie was just serving herself a burger when Sylvia glanced at her.

"Indie, I'm so sorry. I've been doing all the talking and haven't asked anything about *you*. How have you been?"

"Good. Still running my photography business. Not much has changed."

Sylvia's brows lifted. "Oh, you're still doing that?"

"Of course she is. It's her job, Mom," Colt cut in, brows flickering.

"I know, I was just clarifying." Sylvia forked up some potato salad. "I assume because you and Colt have been apart, you haven't done any more rounds of IVF?"

Colt opened his mouth to respond, but she squeezed his leg under the table before answering. "No more rounds. We might actually be done with IVF."

"Oh, that's good. It was so stressful for you both. I always wondered, if you really want a child, why don't you adopt?"

Her muscles tightened. She *hated* when people asked that. It was shocking how often that was the automatic question from most people. "Adoption is not a replacement for infertility, Sylvia."

"Well, of course not, but you tried the natural route. And sometimes nature has the final word, you know?"

The muscles in Colt's thighs bunched. "Mom."

"I'm not saying it to insult anyone. I just think there's a reason some people can't reproduce. To try to play God in this arena feels unethical and—"

"*Stop*."

Indie flinched at Colt's tone. Sylvia's eyes widened too. Even Ben's fork paused halfway to his mouth.

"How Indie and I extend our family is between her and me."

Indie's heart tapped at an eager rhythm, partly because of Sylvia's words and partly because of Colt. Because of the anger in his voice toward his mother. He'd never spoken to her like that before. At least, not in front of Indie.

Was this why Sylvia had become so unkind toward her? Because she thought Indie's use of IVF was unethical?

The shock on his mother's face shifted to annoyance, then a forced smile. "I'm sorry. You're right. It's between you two."

But the second Colt looked away from his mother, she glanced at Indie. And there was such coldness there. Accusation even. Because she blamed Indie for the way Colt had just spoken to her? Or was there more to it than that?

* * *

COLT WATCHED HIS MOTHER CLOSELY. He was noticing things tonight that he'd never seen or heard before. Small comments here and there. Little digs that could almost pass as innocent. About Indie's job, her cooking, her appearance, and what the fuck was that comment about IVF? His mother had *never* said anything like that to him, or even around him, before.

Had she said these things to Indie before? Is this what she'd been hinting at? Had this been an ongoing thing he wasn't aware of?

He glanced at Indie as she ate her dessert. The corners of her lips tipped up slightly, and to most, she would look happy.

She wasn't. Her lips were too thin for the smile to be real, and there were strain lines beside her eyes.

While his mother and Ben spoke, he squeezed her thigh and leaned over to place a small kiss on her cheek before whispering, "Are you okay?"

"Of course."

Too quick, and not even close to true. "I need you to tell me the truth."

"Let's just finish the meal. I'm really okay."

He stared into her eyes, searching. For what exactly, he wasn't sure. He only looked up when Ben's chair scraped back against the hardwood floor.

"I should go clean the grill. Colt, will you join me?"

And leave Indie alone with his mother when he had no fucking clue what was going on? That was the last thing he wanted to do.

But he needed to talk to Ben about his father. And maybe Ben had information for him.

He looked back at Indie. "Are you okay if I go outside for a few minutes?"

"Take all the time you need."

He still didn't want to go.

He leaned in and kissed her again, this time enjoying the softness of her lips against his before reluctantly lifting his head. As he rose, he glanced at his mother to see an emotion on her face that he couldn't place. Maybe concern. Maybe unease.

What the hell was going on? Whatever it was, he was sure as hell going to find out tonight.

He cleared the plates from the table and set them by the sink before following Ben outside.

"We need to make this quick," he said, the second they were outside.

Ben stopped at the grill. "Everything okay?"

"I'm not sure. Did you notice anything off in the way my mom interacted with Indie tonight?"

"Off how?"

Colt shook his head. "Don't worry about it. That's my job, not yours. Any update on Gordon?"

"I've checked everywhere. Every motel. The RV park. I contacted Airbnb owners. As far as I can tell, Gordon's not renting any accommodation in Amber Ridge."

"What does that mean? That's he's living in his car?"

"Maybe. Although he doesn't have a car registered in his name, which means he's either not driving, is using a fake ID, or is driving a stolen vehicle."

Jesus. "I'll let Jesse know. Maybe he can look out for stolen cars, or even get his deputies to check the streets for someone sleeping in a vehicle. I'll get him to check abandoned houses too."

"Good idea." Ben looked around before glancing back at Colt. "Sylvia didn't want me to tell you but...he was here the other night."

"*What?*"

"The silent alarm gave him away. Because you weren't home, I stayed the night. I took off after him but lost him around Fourth Street. He's also been calling your mom, but she hasn't answered any of his calls. He even left a message on her phone." Ben took out his cell and hit a few keys before playing a voice message on speaker.

"Sylvia. It's me, Gordon." Gordon's voice was gruff, and it made fury pulse between Colt's ears. "I need to see you so we can talk. I know I've made a lot of mistakes. I'm trying to do better. Let me make amends."

"Bullshit." The word was out of Colt's mouth before the message had ended. "He expects us to believe that?"

"He expects your mother to believe it."

"What did she say when she heard it?"

"Nothing. She went quiet and walked away."

He scrubbed a hand over his face. "The other times he's been back...has she ever considered letting him back into her life?"

"Not once."

"Good."

Ben watched him closely. "It's because of you, you know."

"What is?"

"The reason she would never take him back. She hates herself for allowing you to be around him for eight years. And she hates *him* too."

"She said that?"

"Not in those exact words."

Colt shook his head. "It's not her fault. All the blame lies on the bastard."

"It's not me you should be telling."

With a long exhale, he opened the back door.

That's when he heard his mother's words.

CHAPTER 14

*I*t was worse than she'd thought. Far worse than she ever remembered any meal with Colt's mother being. Usually, she saved her subtle digs for when Colt wasn't around. When he stepped out of the room or was too busy in conversation with someone else to hear. Tonight, the woman either didn't realize her insults weren't so subtle or she didn't care.

Indie cleared her throat as she used the tongs to move the meat from the plate to a container. "Dinner was lovely, Sylvia."

"I thought you didn't like it, since you barely touched what was on your plate."

Yeah, well, stomaching food was tough when someone was telling you that you're playing God for wanting a child. "I wasn't very hungry."

"Hm."

It was the most disapproving "hm" she'd ever received.

Maybe this had been a mistake. She couldn't make a relationship better if only one of them *wanted* it to be better.

"I'm sorry about Gordon." Her words were quiet but true. Despite her dislike for this woman, she *was* Colt's mother, and from what Colt had told her, she'd suffered protecting her son. "I'm glad you were able to separate from him."

Sylvia paused, plate in one hand, tap on. "Colt told you about what happened?"

"Bits and pieces."

The veins in Sylvia's neck visibly tightened. "So you're really getting back together with my son?"

Indie frowned at the question. At the surprise in her voice. Maybe even...disdain. "We're making progress. Is that a problem?"

"As a mother, it's my job to protect my son." Sylvia didn't look up as she rinsed the dishes in the sink. "I didn't do such a good job for the first eight years. I should have left Gordon earlier. I should have realized he wasn't going to change and put my son first."

"You kicked him out when you could."

"I could have done it sooner. But since then, I feel like I'm forever trying to make it up to him. All I can do is trust my gut with what I think is good or bad for him. The mom gut is strong and rarely wrong."

A sinking feeling began to churn in Indie's belly at where this conversation was going. She set the tongs on the counter and gave the woman her full attention. "What are you trying to say, Sylvia?"

Still, the other woman didn't look at her. "I know my son. I know what he needs. What he *deserves*. I know what will make him happy."

"And you don't think I'll make him happy?"

"You were so young when you started dating. I never thought it would last. Then you moved to California when he was stationed there, you got married, and I thought...maybe I was wrong. Maybe you *will* last, and you'll make him happy."

Indie's heart started to beat faster. Colt's mother had only been nice to her at the start because she'd assumed they'd break up?

Why did that hurt so much?

"Then you started trying for a baby." Sylvia shook her head. "I remember this one time when I visited you both. Colt was trying *so hard* to make you happy. He only had a few days of leave, and he was giving you everything you wanted. But you still weren't happy. You never smiled. You weren't coping."

"We were dealing with infertility. I was lonely. Colt was never home."

"Colt was going through the struggle to have a child too! And when he wasn't home with you, he was risking his life for his country. He needed *you* to be okay so that *he* could be okay. But instead of doing that, you left him alone in California to come back here."

"I needed to be with my family. Clara was sick, and I wasn't doing well out there."

"Did you ever consider that maybe *he* wasn't doing well, either? Did you ever think about trying to be stronger for him?"

"It wasn't about strength, Sylvia. I was in *pain*. I did IVF for years, basically alone. My body hurt. My heart hurt. I was drowning—"

"Then you should have learned how to swim!"

Pain...it cut through Indie's chest. Because those words spoke to every whisper of insecurity inside her.

A part of her always wondered if a stronger person *would* have been better for Colt. If maybe someone else would've been able to give him a baby. Or let go of the idea of carrying her own child. A stronger woman might not have run home.

Sylvia stepped closer. "I don't have a problem with *you*, Indie. I have a problem with the impact that you've had on my boy's life. You're not right for him. He needs someone who plants their feet when the storm starts, not someone who runs. He needs someone with *strength.* But you left him, forcing him to choose between the Marines and you. He left his home. His job. Why? Because you couldn't handle the fact that he was a soldier. You couldn't handle the journey to having a child. That's the definition of selfish!"

"Enough!"

Sylvia jumped at Colt's voice. Neither of them had heard him step inside.

Indie could barely move. So much of what his mother had said was true. Not everyone fell into a pit of depression after a few rounds of IVF. Some women had it so much worse than infertility with a husband who had significant work commitments.

Sylvia's eyes widened. "Colt, honey, I—"

"How *dare* you speak to my wife like that!" He took a couple steps toward his mother, but suddenly Ben was in front of him.

The older man pressed a hand to Colt's chest. "You should both leave. Come back and have this conversation another day, when you've cooled off."

Tears pressed at Indie's eyes, but she blinked them back.

True. It was all true. Sylvia's words weren't anything that hadn't whispered inside her when the world got quiet. Some days, they replayed over and over again.

Weak. Broken. Not for Colt.

More words were spoken around her, but they were unclear. A haze of voices and movement. She was too deep in her head. Until Colt slipped an arm around her waist and led her toward the door. But even then, her brain wouldn't stop. All she could think was that every word Sylvia had spoken had already been spoken in her own head.

* * *

COLT WASN'T ANGRY—HE was fucking furious. At his mother. Someone he'd rarely been mad at before. He could barely focus on the damn road in front of him.

Her words echoed in his head.

You're not right for him.

His fingers tightened around the wheel. What else had she said before he walked in? Was this the first time such awful words had come out of her mouth?

He'd always loved his mother. Since he was eight years old, it had just been the two of them. They'd both been protective of each other. But *this*? This hadn't come from a place of love. Love was supportive. It was kind. This was some cruel bullshit he couldn't begin to understand.

He shot a glance at Indie in his rearview mirror. When he'd stepped out of his mother's house, she'd been pale and quiet, and he'd had no idea what she was thinking. Had she bought into any of the shit his mother had spewed?

No. She had to know that she was more than he could ever deserve. She *had* to.

He'd wanted to ask—fuck, he had so many questions. He *would* ask. He wanted answers.

When he pulled into the driveway, he was out first, scanning the house, then the street.

Clear. Good. He didn't need another thing to handle tonight.

This time yesterday, he'd thought he only had one problem parent. Now he was fighting with both but in very different ways.

Indie stepped out of her car, and he placed a hand on the small of her back. Inside, she slipped off her shoes and went straight into the bedroom. He followed her, watching as she tugged her hair out of the elastic band, letting the fall of her long locks drape over her shoulders.

"How long?"

Her shoulders visibly tensed at his question. "How long what?"

"Don't do that, Cricket. Don't pretend you don't know what I'm talking about. How long has she been speaking to you like that?"

Indie swallowed before taking off an earring. "She's never been so direct. Usually, it's just backhanded remarks. Subtle digs here and there."

Just? There was no *just* about it. "What has she said?"

"It's often about my infertility. Referencing people we know who *could* get pregnant. Making a point to tell me that theirs was a natural conception. She also makes digs about my looks, comments about me looking tired."

Tears shone in Indie's eyes, and it fucking gutted him. "Why didn't you tell me?"

She turned to face him, those tears still there as she wrapped her arms around her waist, like she was trying to protect herself from something. "Because she wasn't *always* like that. And when she started, you and I already had our own problems...and your job was dangerous and important."

"*You're* important."

"And because she's your mother. She's your only family."

"Not my only family. You're my wife." He took another step forward. "I will *always* choose you."

A tear slipped down her cheek. "Maybe that's the wrong choice."

"What the hell are you talking about?" This time when he stepped forward, she stepped back. And everything in him rebelled against that distance between them.

"Everything she said was true. You were the one working the dangerous job. You were dealing with so much, yet *I* fell apart because I couldn't have a baby."

"Don't downplay what you went through, Indie. The injections. The hormones. Then the negative tests that put you right back where you started, again and again. It wasn't just your body that suffered from the process. It was so much deeper than that. I saw it. What I was going through was nothing compared to you."

"It killed me. But maybe I should have been stronger. I left you in California, and I still couldn't find peace here."

He lifted a hand to wipe her tears, but she took two more steps away, her back hitting the wall.

"Why do you keep pulling away from me?" It went against every part of him that just wanted to touch her. Draw her in close.

"It didn't work the first time."

The first time? This was *still* their first time. They'd never stopped and started again—it was one marriage. "Do you love me?"

"It's not that simple."

"Do you love me, Cricket?"

"You know I do."

He closed the space between them and cupped her cheek. "Then it *is* that simple. I love you too. I love you so much that I would give up everything I know for you, and none of it would feel like a sacrifice."

She leaned into his hand, her eyes closing, more tears falling down her cheeks.

He leaned in and kissed a tear. "You, Indie Reed, are my wife. You're my entire world. And you *are* strong. You're the strongest woman I know. And you're mine."

Her chest rose and fell. "But—"

"No buts. You are all I want. You're all I've ever wanted." Then he dropped his head and kissed her.

CHAPTER 15

$\mathcal{T}$he room quieted. The kind of quiet that silenced not only the world around her but those voices in her head. The ones telling her—*screaming at her*—that she wasn't enough. That she wasn't strong enough or brave enough. It all went away at the feel of his lips on hers.

He cupped her other cheek, his tongue slipping between her lips. He tasted sweet and deep and familiar.

When he suddenly lifted his head, she wanted to groan. To grab him and pull him back. Instead, she looked up at him. Traced the lines beside his black eyes. The curve of his hard jaw.

There was so much emotion in his expression. A mixture of need and desire and pain.

She swallowed hard, trying to calm her racing heart. "What are you thinking?"

"I need to know that you want this," he whispered, sounding almost scared, an emotion that was so out of place on a man so powerful. "I choose you, Cricket. In the small easy moments. And the big hard ones. I'll always choose you."

The big hard ones...there'd been so many.

"I choose you too. Tonight. Tomorrow. Forever."

His eyes darkened. And he dipped his head again and kissed her, his tongue slipping straight inside, curving, almost dancing with hers.

The peace and fire and desire...it filled every hollowed-out part of her.

He lifted her into his arms like she weighed nothing, but she still didn't feel close enough. She needed skin against skin. She needed him, all of him, right now.

Quickly, she reached for the hem of his T-shirt and pulled it up.

With one arm, he helped her, yanking it over his head. Then his lips covered hers again, and suddenly he was everywhere. He was all she could feel and his scent surrounded her.

He slipped the straps of her dress down, and cool air brushed the tips of her nipples. But only for a second, before he took one between his lips. Then he was sucking and she was gasping, grabbing the short locks of his hair.

Her head was back, her eyes closed. He swirled the bud in a circle with his tongue, and all she could do was try to breathe. Draw the air into her lungs even though it was difficult.

With desperate fingers, she reached for the bottom of her dress, Colt helping her.

Then all she wore were panties. And there was something so safe about wearing almost nothing in Colt's strong arms, held in place by his body.

He *was* her safety. He'd *always* been her safety.

He found her lips again, kissing her slowly, deeply, as he moved to the bed. The soft mattress dipped as he laid her down. His weight over her felt warm and familiar.

He lifted his head, his gaze searing into her own.

"It's been so long," she whispered.

"And yet, it feels like no time has passed at all."

It was so true. This strange in-between of feeling like both a lifetime and a blink.

He lowered his head and kissed her, so softly it was almost a graze. The next kiss touched her neck, then her chest. On his way down her body, he claimed her other breast, taking her nipple inside his mouth and rolling it with his tongue. Her back arched and air hissed between her teeth.

When he shifted again, light kisses brushed over her hip bone, his breath whispering over her skin as he moved.

She barely felt him slipping her panties down her legs, or the slight shift in his body so that he settled between her thighs.

When his tongue ran over her clit, she arched and cried out, the sound shattering the quiet. He tasted her again, and her entire body trembled.

She grabbed at the sheets, clenching them in her fists, trying to anchor herself. His arms slipped around her thighs, widening her legs. And when his mouth latched to her clit and sucked hard, she was on fire. Her body burned.

"Colt!" His name was something between a scream and a moan.

When his fingers touched her entrance, she tensed. Then he slid two inside.

It was both too much and not enough at the same time. She stood on the edge of that cliff again, both *wanting* him to push her over the edge but also needing to stay exactly where she was for as long as possible.

His fingers began to move inside her, slow, rhythmic thrusts while his kisses trailed up her hip bone, then her side.

She was panting. She couldn't get a single full breath in. When he took her mouth again, his tongue plunged straight inside, and she fell into the hole that was Colt. Losing herself in him as her hips thrust to meet his fingers.

Desperately, she reached down his body and unbuckled his jeans. Once the zipper was down, she slipped her hand inside his briefs and wrapped her fingers around his length.

His entire body stilled, and the cords of muscles that ran from his neck down his arms tensed and rippled.

She'd always loved that she could affect him as much as he affected her.

She slid her hand to the tip, running her palm over him, before shifting it back to the base.

"Indie." Her name was either a growl or a warning, she couldn't tell. It didn't matter—she didn't stop. She continued to move over his length, remembering what he liked. Wanting to bring him to the same spot on the edge of that cliff where he'd pushed her.

Suddenly, he gripped her wrist and lifted it above her head before kissing her again, the weight of his body pressing her into the mattress.

When he rose, she wanted to groan...or maybe she did, because his lips curved. He pushed down his jeans and briefs, and then her mouth went dry.

It didn't matter that she'd known this man, *loved* this man, since they were teenagers. It didn't matter that she knew his body better than she knew her own. She'd always feel that breathless, can-barely-think-or-move stillness at the sight of him.

He crawled over her and settled between her thighs. She felt him right there. It took her two tries to wet her dry throat, but even then it didn't really work.

He brushed a lock of hair from her cheek. "Do you want me to wear something?"

She could have laughed. They'd tried for a baby for so long, they hadn't worn a condom for nearly a decade. "No. I want to feel all of you inside me."

His eyes darkened. Slowly, he slid inside.

Her eyes shuttered as he filled her. Stretched her.

"God, I've missed you," he whispered, his lips grazing her cheek.

Tears burned in her eyes. "It's like a piece of me has been missing since you've been gone. And now I have it back."

He lowered his temple to hers. "We can both be whole again."

* * *

COLT DROPPED his head into the crook of Indie's neck.

Fuck, she was tight. He couldn't move. He could barely breathe. It was like he was fucking chained exactly where he was.

He'd missed her. God, he'd missed so much about her. Her scent. Her warmth. The breathy sighs she made when he was inside her.

She wrapped her leg around his waist, making him sink deeper. A guttural growl tore from his throat.

This feeling right here...this was what he'd almost lost forever. This euphoria. This peace. It was something only she could make him feel.

"Colt." Her breath whispered across his skin, her fingers dragging over his back. "Move."

Then, as if to illustrate her point, she tilted her hips back then forward.

Shit, she was going to kill him. He lifted his hips before thrusting back into her. The moan that escaped her throat shattered whatever control he had left.

He lifted his head and kissed her again, his hips moving in rhythmic thrusts. Every time he returned to her, he felt that *thing*. When air suddenly felt easier to breathe. When peace didn't feel foreign or out of reach.

He shifted his mouth to her neck and grazed his teeth across her skin before sucking, getting lost in the sweetness that was Indie.

This was his home. And he didn't want to be anywhere else.

He reached for her breast and cupped her. Finding the tight bud of her nipple and rolling it with his thumb.

130

Her head tilted back and she groaned. A deep groan, one he'd heard in his fucking dreams too many times.

He loved that sound. He loved everything about this woman.

He moved his hips harder. Faster. And she met him thrust for thrust. Her hips rising, her hold on his shoulders tightening.

When he needed more, he slipped his hand down her body and found the tight bundle of nerves between her thighs. The first stroke made her entire body jolt. He ran his thumb over her clit, fire burning in his veins at the scrunch of her eyes. The way she showed every degree of desire on her face.

"Colt…"

He found the sensitive spot behind her ear and sucked, before whispering, "I'm here, Cricket. Let me catch you."

Another roll of her clit, and she cried out, her back arched, her nails cutting into his shoulders as she broke.

He kept thrusting, his mouth never leaving her neck, sucking and tasting. Claiming. While his thumb still moved over her clit.

Every sound she made. Every whimper and moan made his world narrow to just her.

He tried to hold off, but then he looked at her and saw the complete abandonment of all inhibition. And he lost himself. He fell so fucking hard that he shattered into a million pieces.

The groan that flew from his throat was almost painful, and he dug his head into the crook of her neck, thrusting two more times before finally stilling.

The sounds of their heavy breaths were loud in the quiet, the stillness, in complete contrast to the chaos of moments ago.

When he lifted his head, it was to see Indie's eyes closed, the smallest hint of a smile on her lips. He took a moment to study her. To trace every perfect inch of her perfect face.

"God, you're beautiful."

Her eyes opened, the curve of her lips transforming into a full, glorious smile. "You're not so bad yourself." She lifted her hand and cupped his cheek. "I missed you looking at me like that."

"I've missed everything about you." He lowered his head and kissed her. A slow, gentle graze of a kiss.

He dropped to the bed beside her and immediately tugged her against him. She pressed into his side, and it was like no time had passed. Like twelve months of separation that had almost killed him just disappeared.

"Colt." The hesitation in her voice made some tension return to his shoulders.

"Yeah, Cricket?"

She pushed up and looked at him. There was sadness in her eyes. Maybe a bit of regret. "I'm sorry about your mom."

"Why are *you* sorry?"

"Because you guys are so close. And you went through a lot together."

"I *thought* we were close. But if she really loved me, then she'd love *all* of me—including the part that chooses you as my wife."

Indie swallowed. "I should have told you how she made me feel."

"I wish you had." He slipped a lock of hair behind her ear. "No more secrets."

"No more secrets." She wet her lips. "I love you."

"You have no idea." He lifted his head and kissed her.

She sighed, a sound of contentment.

But the second she laid her head back on his chest, Colt's smile disappeared, his mind going back to his mother. What she'd said to Indie earlier that evening.

It wasn't okay. Any of it. And it would *never* happen again. Tomorrow, he'd be making sure his mother knew that.

CHAPTER 16

*I*ndie rolled from her belly to her back.

Light...too much freaking light.

What was the time?

She cracked one eye open. Definitely later than she usually woke up. Had she gone to bed late last night?

She frowned, only for her pulse to stumble then race when it all came back to her. Colt's mother. The quiet drive home. Then everything that had happened after that.

Sex...with Colt. Good sex.

Ha. Sex with Colt was never *good*. It was breathless and dizzying and body-and-soul consuming.

She scrubbed her eyes. Coffee. She needed a giant mug of coffee.

But wait...where was Colt?

Both eyes popped open and she scanned the room. The open bathroom door. The empty walk-in closet.

He wasn't here. Well, not in the bedroom anyway. Had he left? Or was he somewhere else in the house?

She threw back the sheets and stood, the slight ache in her core another reminder of what they'd done last night.

Heat flushed her cheeks. She'd missed him. God, she'd missed him so much. It wasn't just the act of having sex that she'd missed. It was the intimacy. The closeness.

On her way to the door, she lifted his discarded shirt—which was now folded on a chair—and tugged it over her head.

She was about to start her search in the kitchen when she heard sounds in the hall bathroom. She changed direction and cracked the door open. Her throat dried instantly. Hell, it was like the Sahara Desert. All thanks to Colt.

He stood in front of the mirror, his very wet, very *muscled* back toward her.

Holy shit, he was hot with a towel slung low around his waist.

"That is exactly why I tried to sneak out, Cricket."

Her gaze flashed up to meet his eyes in the mirror. They were like dark pools of heat.

She swallowed. Nope, still dry. "You tried to sneak out on me?"

"Hell yes, I did. Because otherwise, I wouldn't make it out of the house at all."

Her lips curved into a small smile. "You think I have that kind of power over you?"

"We both know you do." He turned, and his dark gaze ran down her body. "You look great in my shirt."

"That's good, because you're not getting it back."

"Really?" He stepped forward and wrapped his arms around her waist. "What if I ask *really* nicely?"

"Depends...does the request come with any form of touching?"

A low growl rippled from his chest, and he lowered his head to kiss her. And even though they hadn't been able to keep their hands off each other last night, she suddenly felt starved of his kisses.

She leaned into him and ran her fingers over his chest, absorbing the dampness of his skin.

"Where are you sneaking off to?" she finally asked, when he lifted his head.

The humor left his face and a darkness took its place. Anger. "I'm going to talk to my mom."

"Oh." That was all she said. Because honestly, she didn't know *what* to say. Last night, Colt had reacted exactly how she'd known he would. Actually, no, it was worse, because Colt had heard the words for himself. "I hate that this is hurting you."

"It's not your fault. But I need to remind my mother that you're part of my life. A big part. And if she can't be kind to *you*, she doesn't get *me*."

Which sucked, because he shouldn't have to remind his mother of that. She knew they were married.

"Is there anything I can do?" she whispered.

"Yeah. Stay home with the doors locked. You don't have any shoots today, do you?"

She laughed, but there was no humor behind it. "No. That rumor sure worked and seems to have lost me most of my clients."

"The rumor you mentioned at the bar?"

"Yeah. Apparently, people around town have been gossiping about me. Something about money and my business. I don't know the details, but it sounded like I didn't come off quite so well, and that's possibly why people haven't been booking me."

A muscle in Colt's jaw clenched. "Do you think my mother started it?"

Oh God, she did not want to answer that question. But no secrets—they'd promised each other last night. "I'd be lying if I said it hadn't crossed my mind. But honestly, I don't know. I never thought she'd go so far as to ruin my livelihood."

But then, she'd never thought Sylvia would be so brazen as to say everything she'd said last night, with Colt so close by.

"I'll find out." His tone was heavy.

He went to step around her, but she grabbed his arm. "Colt,

135

wait… I don't want to be the reason you and your mom fall out with each other."

"You wouldn't be. You didn't ask for any of this. It's all her. And it's *her* choice what she does next."

"Will you come straight home after and tell me how it went?"

"I'll do you one better—I'll come home and take you car shopping."

She rolled her eyes. "I don't need you to buy me a car."

"I'm not. I'm forcing *you* to use *our* shared money to buy a safe vehicle."

"Same thing. Like I've said, I still have my money from the Subaru. I can buy my own car, thank you."

He growled and stepped closer. "My money *is* your money."

"But—"

"No. No buts. You're my wife. That makes everything that's mine, *yours*. Okay? And maybe while I'm gone, you can get those wedding rings out of storage."

Shit. "I'll look for them." It wasn't a lie. She *would* look. She just had no idea where they were.

"Good." He lowered his head and kissed her, and she slipped her hand behind his neck and deepened the kiss.

A low, guttural sound vibrated from his chest before he pushed her back against the wall, the warmth of his body in complete contrast with the cool tiles at her back.

He was just inching her top up when the ringing of a phone sounded from behind them. Colt's phone.

He growled. "It better be important."

She chuckled, missing him the second he stepped away from her.

Colt frowned before putting the cell to his ear. "Ben. Is everything okay?"

Whatever Ben said made Colt straighten. "I'm coming now."

Nerves punched Indie in the stomach as she waited for him to hang up. "What's wrong?"

"It's Mom. She's in the hospital."

* * *

COLT PULLED into the parking lot of the Amber Ridge Hospital. His mother being here wasn't a new thing. Suffering from asthma and chronic obstructive pulmonary disease meant she'd made frequent visits since he was a kid. She had better and worse days.

Was it worse today because of everything that had happened?

Or maybe it *wasn't* worse. Maybe this was a ruse to get him to come to her...just like it had been the night Indie had asked for a break a year ago.

He hadn't thought his mother could even do something like that. But after last night? He wasn't sure *what* the woman was capable of anymore.

He climbed out of his Audi and crossed the parking lot, heading toward the room number that Ben had texted him.

Everything his mother said last night played over in his head again and again. And it made him angrier each time. The reason it hurt so much was because he'd trusted her. From his father, he expected to be stabbed in the back. But not from his mom.

The one good thing to come out of last night? Indie. She'd finally let him in. She'd finally let him love her again.

He wasn't going to mess that up a second time. He was going to protect their marriage at all costs.

He turned the corner to see Ben standing halfway down the hall.

Colt stopped in front of him. "Hey. How is she?"

Ben shot a glance toward the closed door, then back to Colt. "Not too good. I woke up to her calling out for me. She was short of breath and had chest pains. I brought her straight in and she was put on oxygen. The doctor ran some tests and we're waiting for the results, but he said, based on her history, it could just be a flare-up."

"Thanks." He wrapped his fingers around the doorknob, but before he could step in, Ben grabbed his arm.

"Are you okay after last night?"

"No. But I'm her son. I need to at least see her."

Ben studied him for a moment. "She shouldn't have said what she said. But she loves you."

"Then she needs to accept Indie in my life."

Ben nodded slowly. "I agree. Good luck."

"Thanks."

He stepped into the room. His mother lay in the center of the bed, an oxygen mask on her face.

At the click of the door closing, her eyes popped open and went straight to him. She tugged down the oxygen mask. "Oh, Colt, honey. I'm so glad you're here."

Colt's brows drew together. She said it nonchalantly, like the previous night had never even happened. He shoved his hands into his pockets. "How do you feel?"

"Better. But it was so scary. I barely slept last night and woke up to the worst chest pain this morning. I couldn't breathe. Thank God Ben was there."

"I'm glad he's staying with you."

"Me too."

He stopped beside the bed. "The doctor said you're okay."

"At the moment. I'm scared to see what the tests show. But darling, I'm just so glad you're here." Sylvia reached for his hand, but he stepped back.

His mother frowned. "Colt—"

A knock at the door had them both looking up as a middle-aged male doctor stepped into the room. "Is now an okay time, Mrs. Reed?"

"Oh, yes, come in. Dr. Leeroy, this is my son, Colt."

The doctor dipped his head. "It's nice to meet you." He looked back at Sylvia. "I have good news. Your breathing has improved, and your oxygen levels are back to where they should be. I've also had a look at your test results—they also show everything's fine. It was just a flare-up."

His mother sighed loudly. "What a relief."

"I'd still recommend taking it easy over the next few days and keeping up with your medications. We'll schedule a follow-up appointment, just to make sure you're managing everything effectively, but I think you'll be okay to go home today."

"Thank you, Doctor."

The doctor dipped his head and stepped out.

His mother looked up at Colt and smiled. "Isn't that great news? And with you and Ben at the house, I'll be well looked after."

Did she really think he was just going to forget about everything from the previous night and move back in with her? "I'm not going back to your house, Mom."

Sylvia looked confused. "Because of last night? Colt, I didn't mean to hurt Indie's feelings."

"Hurt her feelings? You told her she wasn't right for me. You made her believe she wasn't strong enough to be my wife. You told her that IVF was unethical, and that God basically didn't want her to become pregnant!"

His mother opened and closed her mouth. "You're my son. I was trying to protect—"

"I'm an *adult*, Mom. It's not your job to protect me. Your only job is to love and support me. When you hurt Indie, you hurt *me*. Do you understand that?"

Her face paled.

He took a breath before asking his next question. "Did you start a rumor about Indie's photography business?"

The smallest widening of her eyes was all the confirmation he needed.

Fuck.

"You did." The reality hit him like a fucking freight train. How? How had he not seen any of this?

"I didn't start a rumor," she denied. "I simply...had some *conversations* with friends about her money situation."

"What *situation*?" Colt asked through gritted teeth.

Sylvia squirmed uncomfortably. "Just that one of the reasons she married you was for your money."

The *fuck*? That wasn't even slightly true. "What else?"

She swallowed. "I may have mentioned that when you stopped funding her lifestyle, she left you. And without your money, she probably had to resort to shortcuts in her work. Like AI edits and cheaper photography equipment. Just small talk!"

Jesus fucking Christ. "You *told* people that?"

"It's what I believed," she said stubbornly. "It's what I *still* believe. I don't think her motives around you are innocent, and as I mentioned last night—"

"Stop. Just stop. You tried to *ruin* her business, and you're *still* pushing the bullshit." Out. He needed to get the hell out and breathe. "I'm leaving."

Sylvia pushed up. "Wait—when will I see you again?"

"When you can be better. When you can fix what you've broken."

"Colt, please, I did this for you—"

"I never asked you to. *Indie* is my entire world. And I am *not* letting you hurt her anymore."

CHAPTER 17

*I*ndie put her camera bag into the back of the car before sliding behind the wheel.

The family photo shoot had gone overtime because the ten-year-old boy wouldn't smile for the first half hour. Just flat-out refused. It had taken a chocolate bar and a promise of extra TV time from the mom to get him to finally crack half a grin. Now it was almost dark, and Colt wouldn't be happy.

She cringed when her phone rang. That would be him.

"I know, I'm late," she said, before he could get a word in.

"Where are you?"

"I'm just leaving her house now."

"Do you want me to come out there?"

"No, I'll be home in fifteen minutes."

"Fine." The single word was almost growled. "But no stops."

"So you don't want me to pick up a pizza from Burt's?"

Colt chuckled. They both knew how inedible those pizzas were. Heck, they were barely pizzas. "Not tonight. Maybe next week."

"Or the week after, no rush."

"Drive safe, Cricket."

"Always do."

She hung up and started the engine, and to her absolute surprise, it actually started on the first try. Well, maybe her evening was about to turn around.

She'd ordered a new Subaru. Well, actually, Colt had, because he'd refused to let her put down the deposit, but it wasn't due to come in for another couple weeks. Colt had pushed for a new Volvo or BMW, claiming there were more safety features, while she'd been eyeing a secondhand Nissan.

The compromise had been a new Subaru.

She pulled onto the road and started heading home.

Since finding out Sylvia had started the rumors about her, Indie was even less inclined to spend Colt's money. And yes, she knew she shouldn't be letting Sylvia have that effect on her, but she did. Indie had never wanted Colt for his money. If anything, it only ever made her more hesitant about their relationship, because she knew she couldn't match the monetary value that he brought to the marriage.

After everything else, she shouldn't have been surprised the rumors were started by Sylvia. Still…it hurt. Maybe because it felt so malicious. And because she had no idea *why* Sylvia had done it, given Indie and Colt were already separated at the time. Just to hurt her? Or was there more to it than that?

Was she trying to drive Indie out of town by ensuring she couldn't work in Amber Ridge?

God, Indie had no idea.

And the pathetic part was, even after everything Sylvia had done, Indie still felt guilty that Colt wasn't speaking to his mother.

Sylvia called him every day. Some days he answered, some days he didn't. The rational part of Indie's brain knew it wasn't her fault. But there was also this other part that said if Colt had married someone else, maybe he wouldn't have had to choose between his wife and his mother. Maybe Sylvia would have accepted another woman.

A loud bang from her engine made Indie jump. Then she saw smoke. Thick clouds of smoke that blocked her vision of the road.

Shit.

She quickly pulled over to the side of the road and turned off the engine. Should she get out? She was still ten minutes from home, and there was nothing around her but forest.

The smoke grew thicker and her pulse sped up. Could the engine explode or something? Damn, now she was scared. Out. Definitely out.

She grabbed her keys, then her phone from the middle console and her camera bag from the passenger seat. She was stepping behind her car when lights appeared down the road. She expected the driver to slow beside her. Maybe roll down their window and ask if she was okay.

Instead, they passed her and parked just in front of her car.

She frowned, her stomach doing a little twist. Then she saw who it was.

Gordon Sharp. He climbed out of a beat-up old Toyota Camry.

No.

She quickly lifted her phone and tried to unlock it, but the tremble in her fingers caused her to hit the wrong number.

"Hey." He stopped in front of her and she took a big step back. His clothes were dirty, like he hadn't washed them in days, and the stench...God. Maybe it had been more than days. "Indie, right?"

Did she have a weapon in her car? There was a wrench—she could use that. But how would she get there in time? "What do you want, Gordon?"

"You look scared. You really don't need to be. I just want to chat."

"Really? Is that why we're doing this on the side of the road while it's dark and there's no one around?"

"Well, I went to see Colt yesterday at the park but he wasn't there, and some guy told me to fuck off. I've tried calling my son, and he won't answer. Not sure if he's listening to my phone messages, asking him to talk. So I found your address and got to your house just as you were leaving today. Thought I'd follow you."

She gasped. "You've been *following* me? Wait—did you do something to my car?"

"Like I said...we need to talk."

"You want to talk to Colt? I'll call him right now. But I should warn you, he won't be happy you're here."

"Exactly." Gordon stepped closer. "But the thing is, if I wanted to hurt you, I could have already. I don't want to hurt you...not right now, anyway. Consider this a little warning to my son. He can either hear me out and give me what I need. Or the next time I pay you a visit, I might not wanna just talk."

Fear kicked her in the belly. "You're threatening me?"

"I'm simply sending a message that I'd like to speak to my son, and if that doesn't happen, bad things will follow." One side of his mouth lifted, and he stepped back. "You have a good night, Indie. Hopefully your safe little town *stays* safe."

Her heart still drummed frantically as she watched his Toyota pull onto the street. And the second he was gone, she grabbed the trunk of her car to keep herself upright.

With shaking fingers, she lifted her cell and called Colt.

"Indie, where are you?"

"M-my car broke down."

He cursed. "I'll come to you. Are you safe?"

Noises sounded over the line. The rattle of keys. The click of a door opening.

She pressed a hand to her chest, trying to slow her racing heart. "Your dad was here. He did something to the engine."

"What?" Colt's voice was darker than she'd ever heard it before.

"Colt...I need you."

An engine roared over the line. "Send me a pin of where you are, Cricket. I'm coming now."

* * *

COLT PRESSED his foot to the floor, rage battering his insides. His father had done something to her damn car? He'd approached her alone?

If the man was here right now, he'd be breathing his last damn breath. But he wasn't, and in seconds, Colt was going to be with Indie. He needed to calm the hell down...for her.

"You still there, Cricket?" He kept his voice soft even though he wanted to fucking rage. She'd been on the line the entire drive because there was no way he was cutting contact with her.

"I'm still here."

There was a tremor in her voice, and he hated it.

He forced his Audi faster until, finally, her car came into view. The smoke coming from the hood was thick, but it was *her* that he focused on. The way she stood beside the Honda, arms wrapped around her waist in a protective gesture. Even in the approaching darkness he could see how pale she was. The fear in her eyes.

His fault. This was *his* damn fault. Noah had said his father stopped by the park, wanting to talk to him. Colt had ignored it. Just like he'd ignored every call and voice message the second he realized the number was his father's.

He pulled in right where Gordon had parked, and as soon as he reached her, he wrapped her in his arms.

She was shaking. He cursed and tugged his sweatshirt over his head before helping her into it. Then he cupped her cheeks. "Are you okay?"

"I'm fine."

Not true. Not even a little bit. "What did he say?"

"That he wants to talk to you. To tell you what he wants and if he doesn't get it, bad things will start happening in this town."

Air hissed between Colt's teeth. He was going to kill him. Murder the fucker in broad daylight. "Did he touch you?"

"No. But he did say that if he wanted to hurt me, he could have already."

The son of a bitch.

He lifted her camera bag. "Do you need anything else from the car?" He tried to keep his voice calm, even though calm was the last thing he felt.

"No."

"Let's go. I'll call a tow on the way home." He set a hand on the small of her back and led her toward his Audi. He set the camera in the back and had just opened the passenger door when he stepped on something that made a crackling sound.

He leaned down and picked it up. A wrapper.

"Big Sky Jerky," he read, almost under his breath.

"It must have fallen out of your dad's car. He parked in the same place as you."

The chill hit him so fucking hard, it sank right down to his bones.

It wasn't that homeless guy, Milo. It was his father. *He* was the person staying in the old cabin at the park.

Indie touched his arm. "Hey, are you okay?"

"I'm fine." A damn lie if ever he'd told one. "Let's get you home."

He waited for her to climb in before he closed her door and looked at the wrapper again. Then he crushed it in his fist.

He knew where his father was now. And tomorrow, the asshole would be getting exactly what he wanted...a visit from Colt.

CHAPTER 18

*J*ndie rolled from her back to her side, immediately reaching to the other side of the bed for Colt so she could feel his warmth and run her fingers over the hard ridges of his chest.

Her fingers touched cold sheets.

Her eyes flew open. The room was too light for it to be night, but not light enough for it to be late morning. It had to be early.

Quickly, she turned on the bedside lamp. Sure enough, the room was empty.

"Colt?"

Silence. There wasn't even the sound of movement from elsewhere in the house. Had he gone somewhere? When had he left?

She tapped the screen of her phone. Seven.

Quickly, she shoved off the sheets and climbed out of bed. After pulling on Colt's sweatshirt that was flung over a chair, she searched the house...every inch of it. The hall bathroom, the living room, the spare bedrooms. It was when she reached the kitchen that she saw the note.

Hey, Cricket, just ran out. Won't be long. House is locked. Please don't go out without me. C.

Out? Out where?

But she already knew the answer to that. He wouldn't have left her to work at the park this early, especially after what had happened last night.

He *would* go to find his father.

Had he figured out where Gordon was staying?

Dammit. This was bad. Really bad. On a normal day, she trusted Colt to do the right thing. But after last night, she wasn't sure what he was capable of.

She rushed back the bedroom and lifted her phone. Her finger hovered over Colt's number, but she hesitated—he might already be with his father. And even if he wasn't, would he listen to her?

She hit a different name.

Her brother answered on the second ring. "Indie, is everything okay?"

"I need you to find Colt."

"What do you mean, find him? Is he missing?" The rustle of movement sounded over the line.

"Last night, Colt's father made my car break down so he could talk to me."

"What the fuck? Are you okay?"

"I'm fine. But he told me that if Colt doesn't talk to him, he'll be back. He basically threatened me."

Noah cursed again. "And now Colt's gone to find him. Do you know where he is?"

"No."

"Did Gordon tell you where he was staying last night? Or did he give you any clues as to where he might be?"

"He didn't say anything about where he's been." She paused, frowning. "But Colt found a jerky wrapper, which we think fell out of his dad's car, and he went really quiet when he saw it."

"A jerky wrapper?"

"Yeah. One of those Big Sky ones."

"*Shit.* I know where he is. I'm going now."

"Noah…" There was a beat of silence. "Please make sure he doesn't do anything stupid."

"You can trust me to look after him, Indie."

"I know I can."

She hung up, but that pit in her belly didn't go away. It sat there, wide and hollow, making her want to *do* something. To go out there and help Noah find Colt. But that would be the opposite of help; she'd just be putting herself in danger. And she *did* trust her brother to look after him…if he got there in time.

A distraction. That's what she needed. She'd shower, then continue the search for her wedding ring. She'd already gone through every storage tote she owned, but it had to be there because that's where she'd put it. She just must've missed it.

In the bathroom, she stripped off her clothes and climbed into the shower. It took her less than thirty seconds to realize this was the worst idea. A shower was exactly where her mind took on a life of its own and a million worst-case scenarios ran through her head. Of what Colt might do to his father. Of the lengths he'd go to, just to make sure his father didn't hurt anyone he loved.

His dad clearly didn't shy away from a fight, and Colt wasn't a kid anymore. He was a former special operator. He was deadly. And he was also angry.

There was also the possibility that Gordon might be armed and hurt Colt.

Her heart rattled against her ribs.

No. He wouldn't do that. He wanted something from him. And he couldn't get it if Colt was hurt or dead.

Five minutes. That was all she lasted under the stream of water before she got out and grabbed a towel. Once she'd pulled on some yoga pants and a long-sleeved oat-colored top, she headed into the kitchen.

Coffee next. A strong coffee.

God, what she wouldn't do for one of Mrs. Gerald's chai spiced lattes, but that wasn't an option right now. She couldn't go out by herself, and it wasn't like the small town of Amber Ridge had DoorDash or Uber Eats.

Maybe when Colt got home, she could convince him to take her. And a piece of pie. Yeah, she definitely needed pie.

She'd just finished making coffee when she heard a knock on her door.

She frowned. It was still early and she wasn't expecting anyone.

Slowly, she crossed to the front door and looked through the peephole. The pit that formed in her stomach when she woke to find Colt gone widened.

Sylvia. The older woman held a tray with three coffees and a paper bag. Ben stood by the Mercedes that was parked on the street.

Oh, Jesus. This was not what she needed before coffee. She didn't feel emotionally equipped to deal with the woman's back-handed abuse. Or more recently, direct abuse.

But what was she supposed to do? Not answer?

With a deep breath, she pulled the door open.

Sylvia's brows lifted. "Indie. I thought Colt was staying here."

"He is. He's out right now."

"Out where?"

"That's a question you can ask *him*."

Annoyance pinched her brow. "I would, but he's refusing to take my calls. It's why I came over with coffee and breakfast."

"Well, I'm sorry he isn't home. He'll probably be home later. If you'll excuse me." She started to close the door.

"Wait! It's clearly important to my son that you and I get along." Sylvia swallowed, like the words left a sour taste in her mouth. "So, I think this is something we should work on."

Indie could have laughed. "Getting along isn't something you work on, Sylvia. You either do or you don't. And with the way you feel about me, and the things you've said about me, I don't see us *ever* getting along."

"So what? I'm just supposed to let my son cut me out of his life?"

"Again, that's between you and him—"

"Will you stop saying that!" Sylvia cut in. "I know you don't understand the bond between a mother and her child—"

"See, *that*—that right there is why you and I will never get along. Because you say these things aimed to hurt me without even *trying* to understand the pain that infertility has brought to my life." She stepped forward. "I *grieve* the child I've never held. I see them in my mind. Their little fingers wrapped around my thumb. Their chubby cheeks. Yet I've never held them, and I don't know if I ever will. It's a sense of loss and pain that you couldn't even begin to comprehend."

Tears stung her eyes, but she forced the words out because she needed Sylvia to hear this.

"And there's a sense of inadequacy that comes with infertility. Like my body is broken, and I don't know how to fix it. And every time you take a jab at me about how I'm not supposed to be a mother, or how I don't understand what it's like to be a mom, you push me deeper into the darkness that swallowed me a year ago—and you make every fear and inadequacy come alive again."

Sylvia's face paled.

"I was hurting," Indie said quietly. "I'm *still* hurting, but a year ago, I thought that pain would cut me in two. It's a kind of sadness that made me feel empty. I did everything I could to survive, including ending things with Colt so he was no longer forced to choose between us. And instead of checking in on me, your daughter-in-law, instead of asking if I was okay or what you could do to help while my world was crashing down around me, you demeaned me. Every time you saw me, you went out of your way to make me feel every bit as broken as I thought I was."

Sylvia didn't say anything, but the look on her face was one Indie had never seen. Something between shock and understanding…and perhaps a bit of shame. But maybe Indie was just seeing what she wanted to see.

She blinked away the tears. "So no, I won't be *trying to get along* with you. I will be working on my relationship with Colt and continuing to protect my mental health. Now, I need to go."

Once the door was closed, she leaned her forehead on the wood.

She wasn't sure if she was expecting to feel relief after finally telling Sylvia how she felt. She didn't. She just felt kind of hollow. Like she'd lost something she'd never even had—the mother-in-law she'd always wished for.

* * *

COLT CLIMBED out of his Audi, the cool morning air skimming across his skin. He barely felt it, the need to find his father consuming him.

Soon, Randy's crew would be here, this forest would be crawling with people, and Gordon would be gone.

So, he had a time limit.

He moved down the newly updated trails, his footsteps quick, fueled by adrenaline.

When the cabins came into view, a small light came from one of the windows.

Good. He was here.

The door to the cabin opened and Gordon stepped out, a backpack slung over his shoulder. He didn't look up as he turned back toward the cabin and pulled the door closed.

Colt took the steps up to the deck two at a time, and the second Gordon turned, he swung, nailing his father in the face.

Gordon grunted and dropped before rolling to his side and grabbing his face. "What the fuck?"

Colt didn't pause. He grabbed his dad and pulled him to his

feet. Then he shoved him hard against the cabin, the wood groaning under the impact. "I told you to *leave her alone*."

Blood dripped from a cut on his father's cheek. "Jesus Christ, you got a good hit. I taught you well."

"You didn't teach me shit. You *tried* to teach me how to be weak. You showed me you're a fucking coward. But you didn't teach me anything."

Amusement flitted across his father's face. "I taught you how to be *angry*...and I can see that anger in your eyes right now. You wanna kill me. But the little Boy Scout inside you is fighting it."

"You're right. I *am* fighting the urge to kill you. And I'll win, because unlike you, I have some damn self-control. Now tell me what you want so you can get the fuck out of town."

"You know what I want—the money I'm owed."

"What the fuck are you talking about? You're not owed a damn thing."

"Your mother hired Ben, and he forced me to sign divorce papers. I gave up everything—money, the house, all of it. I got scraps compared to what I should have walked away with."

Colt lowered his head. "You don't deserve shit, and my mother isn't giving you another cent of her money. There's nothing here for you—*leave*."

His father scoffed. "You think I'm scared of you? I'm not. I'm staying, and I'll make your life *hell*—your mother's life hell, and that pretty piece of ass's life hell—until I get what I'm owed."

Colt didn't think. He swung a second time, nailing his father in the face and once again sending him to the planks.

As he lunged toward him for more, strong arms pulled him back. "Colt, *no*."

He shoved at Noah. "Get the hell off me! I'm going to kill the bastard."

"No, you're not."

"He *threatened* Indie and my mother."

His father laughed. He wouldn't be laughing in a second when Colt tore his fucking head off.

Noah pulled him back and moved in front of him before pressing his hands to Colt's chest. "You kill him and you go to jail. That won't help Indie. She needs you here. You'd also become just as bad as him."

Colt's chest heaved, the anger tightening his fists.

"Colt, you're better than him," Noah pushed. "So *be* better."

He *was* better. "Fine."

Noah stepped to the side, but Colt knew his friend was ready to grab him again if needed.

Colt looked at his father on the porch. Gordon was back to grabbing his cheek and looked as pathetic as he was.

"You go near my wife or mother again, and I will kill you and hide the evidence. Do you understand?"

His father spat blood out of his mouth. "Get ready to murder me then, because I'm not going anywhere until I get my money."

Noah grabbed Colt's arm before he could step forward. "We're going." But before they did, Noah turned back to Gordon. "You need to leave, *now*. You step foot on this property again, you'll be arrested for trespassing. You understand me?"

Gordon just raised a brow, almost in challenge.

Colt could barely breathe through the tightness in his chest, the fucking fury, as Noah pushed him away.

They got all the way to the parking lot before Noah finally stopped and broke the silence. "Are you okay?"

"No. He got Indie alone last night."

"I know."

"He could have done *anything* to her."

"He didn't."

"What about next time? What about when he figures out he's not getting shit from my mother?"

"There won't be a next time."

"There might be."

Noah stepped closer, eliminating that small space between them. "Indie has you. She has me. She has Jesse and Becket. We all have her back. And your mom has Ben, who's shadowing her. No one is getting hurt. Do you understand?"

Colt scrubbed a hand over his face. "I hate this. I hate *him*."

"I know."

"I want to kill him. I *could* have killed him."

"But you won't."

"How do *you* know?"

"Because I know you. And you're a better man than he is." Noah gripped his shoulder. "Come on. Let's get you home. Indie's worried."

Colt nodded but spared one last glance at the mountains before he left. Gordon better leave Amber Ridge, and soon, or Colt was fully prepared to follow through on his threat.

CHAPTER 19

"*N*oah, that's too many chocolate chips!"

Noah grinned, looked Indie dead in the eyes, and added another handful. "I remember one very bossy eight-year-old telling me there was no such thing as too many chocolate chips."

"Well, that eight-year-old grew up and realized she couldn't survive off just sugar."

"Strange. I skipped that life lesson." He took a chocolate chip out of the bowl and tossed it into his mouth.

She chuckled before pulling the bowl across the butcher-block countertop to give it a mix. "This is now chocolate chips with a side of cookie dough."

"So I made it better."

She shook her head, but a hint of a smile played at her lips, because fighting with her brother could quite easily be the best part of her day. "Thank you again for having me over."

She really meant it. The last thing she felt like doing was being in her house alone. Colt had wanted to try the new gym in town. Apparently, a former UFC fighter ran the place. And of course, she'd said yes. He hadn't even needed to ask her. Not after the last week. He hadn't been himself. Hopefully hitting a bag would help.

And she wasn't going to say no to eating cookie dough at her brother's new place.

"You know you're welcome anytime, Indie. Even if you just need a break from Colt, my home is your home."

Her gaze flicked to her phone, the mention of his name making her itch to call him. Check in and make sure he was okay.

Noah bumped her shoulder. "Hey. What's going on in your head?"

"Just thinking about what a great place you have here."

Noah's brows arched. He didn't believe her. But even though it hadn't technically been true in terms of what she'd been thinking, the place *was* nice.

Noah had bought a Craftsman home that was built almost a hundred years ago. Not that you'd know it by looking at the place. It had been updated, and it was beautiful. Open-concept layout. A restored fireplace in the living room, which made it feel warm and cozy. And a ton of wood cabinetry and exposed shelving in the kitchen.

Noah put another chocolate chip in his mouth. "I was lucky Old Man Peters put it on the market right as I was looking."

"It was meant to be. Now you just need a woman to keep you company."

"I don't mind being alone. In fact, I'm kind of enjoying my newfound freedom after being in the military for so long."

"How are you doing with that? And be honest. I'll know if you're lying, because your eye does that twitching thing."

Something crossed Noah's face. An expression that came and went so quickly, she couldn't place it. "I have good days and bad days."

"But you felt ready to come home, right?"

"It's one thing to feel ready, another to actually follow through. Keeping busy helps."

She watched him closely. The smallest hint of a frown. The way he wasn't making eye contact.

There was something bothering him. Was he struggling with his transition into civilian life? Or was it something else?

She nibbled her bottom lip. "If you want to talk to someone, I have a great psychologist who helped me a lot. And I still have monthly appointments with them."

Noah cocked his head. "Thank you, Indie. But I don't need to talk to anyone. And even if I did, I'm too busy with the park. We should be up and running in the next month or so. Did Colt tell you we're going to have an opening night?"

Was he changing the subject on purpose?

She wanted to push. She didn't. He'd talk when he was ready. At least, she hoped he would. "He didn't, but there's been a lot going on. Is there anything I can do to help?"

"Just show up." He frowned. "As long as it's safe, that is."

Argh, she hated that Gordon was still hanging around. He hadn't done anything in the last week, but Ben had reported seeing him. "I just wish he'd leave or do something to get himself arrested."

Noah tensed. "If the latter happens, let's make sure no one gets hurt in the process."

Goose bumps crawled over her skin. She wasn't so much scared for herself—more scared of Colt and his reaction if she or his mother got hurt.

She scooped out a spoonful of batter and rolled it into a ball. "Have you hired anyone for the park?"

"Actually, I interviewed the first person today. The position was only supposed to work the front desk, but she's done IT courses and could create our website too."

"That would be handy. But if she was your receptionist *and* IT person, what would her job title be?"

"I'm thinking Administrative Assistant with Web and IT Responsibilities."

Indie chuckled. "I think only the first part is an actual job title. Did you like her?"

"Yeah, she's twenty-two and from Bozeman. She showed me some of the websites she's designed, and they're good."

Did her brother's voice get warmer when he spoke about her? She rolled another cookie, not looking at Noah when she asked, "Is she pretty?"

"I'm not answering that."

Her head shot up. "Why not?"

"Because if I hire her, I'd be her boss."

"And as her boss, you can't find her pretty?"

"No, I can't." He grabbed another chocolate chip.

It was probably true that a boss and a subordinate dating was a bad idea. But the sister in her liked the idea of her brother dating. Although, twenty-two *was* a bit young for her thirty-five-year-old brother.

Noah turned and started making coffee. "How are you and Colt doing?"

"Good. Really good, actually." She used a fork to press the cookie to the tray. "It feels different from a year ago. Which is good. I need different. Although, his mother hasn't changed one bit. I really thought maybe I'd gotten through to her the other day, but she hasn't tried to talk to me since. She calls Colt every day though."

"Does he answer?"

"Sometimes. But they almost always end up arguing and he hangs up. I don't understand her." She would've thought that if Colt really was as important to Sylvia as she claimed, the woman would at least try to change. But so far, she seemed fixated on the fact that Colt, as her son, should treat her well without any promises to do better.

"You know what's happening between them isn't your fault, right?" Noah said quietly.

"I know. I still feel awful for Colt. He and his mom have been through so much together. I wish she and I could've had a better relationship for his sake."

"You could. But that's up to her."

"I know you're right. It just kind of sucks."

He stepped closer. "You realize that it wouldn't have mattered *who* he brought home. No one would have been welcomed into her life."

She frowned. "What are you talking about?"

"She's spent the last twenty-six years leaning on Colt, relying on him for the support she didn't get from her husband. *Any* woman he brought home was going to pose a threat to her relationship with her son. That's why she was only kind to you until she realized you weren't going anywhere. It has nothing to do with you as a person."

She looked down at the remaining dough in the bowl. "She told me it was because I wasn't strong enough for Colt. That I'm weak because I couldn't handle being the wife of a Marine while also managing the stress of IVF...and I made him sacrifice his career for me."

"That's bullshit, and we both know it. She says that to justify the way she treats you. Deep down, she knows she's wrong—and calling it 'being a protective mother' is just *another* way of justifying all her wrongdoings."

"When did you become so wise?"

"Genetics. It skipped you."

She chuckled and threw a chocolate chip at his head. He caught it with his lightning reflexes and tossed it into his mouth.

When the cookies were in the oven, Indie took her coffee and cell to the couch and Noah sat beside her. Still, she itched to call Colt.

"He's okay," Noah said quietly.

She looked up at her brother. "How do you know?"

"Because I just need to hit the shit out of a heavy bag too sometimes. He'll come back feeling better."

She sighed. "I hope you're right. Distract me. Tell me something that will blow my mind."

An odd expression crossed his face.

She straightened. "What?"

"What do you mean, what?"

"You had that same look on your face when I was sixteen and you told me you broke the new necklace Colt gave me for my birthday."

"Damn, you have a good memory."

"Only for things like that."

There was a small pause. "I've been trying to get in contact with Bonnie."

For a moment, shock made the air feel stuck in her throat. "But she disconnected her old phone."

"Jesse has a friend who's good at finding information. They tracked down her new number."

Her chest rose in a silent gasp. Noah had their sister's number. He'd called her. Or at least, she assumed he had. "Did you talk to her?"

It had been years since either of them had spoken to Bonnie. And even though Indie was still mad as hell at her for leaving, she also missed her.

"She answered. Probably because she didn't know it was me."

She'd actually answered. Noah had heard their sister's voice! "And when she realized it *was* you?"

The muscles in his jaw clicked. "She made some excuse about why she had to go and hung up. But I'm not giving up. I'll give it a week or so and call again. I'm making sure our sister knows that she's welcome back home anytime."

Indie's brows dipped. She wasn't sure how she was supposed to feel about that. She and Bonnie had such a complicated relationship. While Indie had been the responsible one, Bonnie was the wild sister. Never listening to authority figures. Sneaking out in the middle of the night. Underage drinking.

But then Bonnie's high school boyfriend died, and a few short months after that, their parents. Then in true Bonnie fashion, she'd left town, not caring about anyone she left behind.

What would happen if she came home?

CHAPTER 20

*C*olt hit the bag hard with his gloved fist, then watched it swing back, the chain creaking as it moved.

He hit it again, harder this time, ignoring the ache in his arms. The exhaustion that pulled at his limbs. He'd lost track of how long he'd been here. Far longer than he should have.

An entire week had passed since his run-in with his father, and he still felt that searing rage. The pulse of frustration and hate. It flooded every quiet corner of his body.

Gordon had contributed nothing good to his life. And now, the asshole felt like he was *owed* something? The scumbag was owed *nothing*.

He needed to leave. And because he wouldn't, Colt had to look over his shoulder every time he left the house. He had to shadow Indie when she went on shoots just to make sure she was safe.

She'd told him it wasn't a big deal, but that was a lie. There were already stupid rumors affecting her business—thanks to his mother—and now she also had to tackle the fact that she couldn't give her clients privacy during their shoots.

When would it end? Gordon wasn't getting a cent of fucking money from him *or* his mother, so if he was smart, he'd already be gone. But his father had never been a smart man.

Colt knew full well that if he gave the son of a bitch money, he'd just be back again, asking for more. Nothing would change.

Two more punches followed by a kick to the bag.

From his peripheral vision, he saw someone approaching. The man was tall and broad, with dark hair and intelligent eyes.

Without even knowing the guy, Colt knew he was dangerous. After years as a Marine, it was something he'd picked up. Sometimes it was as simple as watching how a person moved.

The man stopped beside Colt, arms crossed. "Hey. Colt, right?"

He lowered his fists and turned, regulating his heavy breaths as he took the guy in. The laser-blue eyes. The short brown hair. The small scar on his left brow.

Definitely dangerous. It radiated off him. "How'd you know my name?"

"Looked at your paperwork. I'm Zane Merrick, the owner."

"The UFC fighter." This place had only opened a few months ago. And yeah, word traveled fast in this town.

"Former UFC," Zane corrected. "And you're military."

"You hear that around town?"

"No, I can see it in your combat stance. It's defensive. Hands up, chin tucked. You hit with purpose. Plus, you keep scanning the gym, giving away your situational awareness. Bet you've already identified every exit and entry point and categorized every person in here."

True. But that was also because there was a threat in the form of his father in this town. "How do you know all that?"

"I did a stint in the military before I got in the ring. Army Ranger."

Colt snorted. "That's not a *stint*. That's an elite group of soldiers trained for direct action missions."

Zane nodded slowly. "It is."

"Would have taken a lot of work for you to get there, only to leave."

"I could say the same for you."

True again. "Why come to Amber Ridge?"

"Why not?"

The guy was keeping his cards close to his chest, but then, so was Colt.

"You're going at that bag pretty hard. Everything okay?"

"Not really." Not even close to okay.

Zane shot a glance over his shoulder before looking back to Colt. "If you ever want a real workout though, let me know. We have floor space for striking and grappling. We also have a ring."

The ring was hard to miss. It was an octagon-style ring that centered the room and was a real focal point. "Thanks. I'll keep that in mind."

"You do that."

When Zane walked away, Colt turned back to the bag and started punching again. Memories of his father's fists flashed in his mind. The anger in his eyes when he was high.

Colt could almost feel the fear that had paralyzed him for so much of his early childhood. Fear of his father's fists. And on that last night, fear of the men who'd entered his house.

"I'm going to kill you, boy!"

Colt sprinted through the living room and into the library, his heart beating so hard it felt like it might punch right out of his chest.

He didn't try to silence the loud thuds of his feet against floorboards. Speed was more important than silence. His mother wasn't here to protect him and his father had sent the nanny home. It was just the two of them.

But he was glad his mother wasn't here. She always got hurt when she was, and Colt hated his dad for that.

He slammed the library door closed behind him and ran straight to one of the floor-to-ceiling bookshelves. In the bottom corner, he removed the false panel before slipping into the small hole. He just fit.

His mother had hidden him here so many times. Then, when he'd gotten bigger, he'd hidden himself. Another year and he'd probably be too big.

Quickly, he pulled the panel closed behind him, then lifted the butcher knife. He couldn't remember when he'd first hidden it here. He'd never had to use it, but he'd made a promise to himself that the next time he heard his father hurting his mom, he would.

His father wasn't even supposed to be home. It was supposed to be just him and Anita, his nanny. But then he'd stumbled through the door, and Colt had seen his red eyes. Glassy eyes. Unfocused.

Whenever Colt saw him like that, he knew to run. Because whatever came next wasn't good.

The library door crashed open, making Colt flinch. He closed his eyes and worked hard to control his breathing, his fingers wrapped so tightly around the knife that his knuckles ached.

"I know you're in here, boy. I just need the details of the accounts. I know your mother shares them with you."

He was eight. Why would his mother give him that sort of information?

But then, his father rarely made sense when he got into these rages.

Colt hit the bag harder, the memory making him want to go back and kill the man who'd terrorized the child version of himself.

Colt shut his eyes, every part of him wanting to run out there and pay his father back for all the times he'd hurt his mom. Kick the asshole's ass. But he was too small. He was no match for his dad. One day, though...one day, he'd teach the asshole a lesson.

Then he heard something...it almost sounded like the distant click of the front door closing. Colt's eyes flew open.

Was it Mom? No. Please. She wasn't due home for another hour.

His stomach twisted, one hand going to the false back of the book-shelf while the other still gripped the knife.

He wasn't going to touch her this time. Colt would make sure of it.

"What are you—"

His father's voice was cut off by a grunt and a mechanical click. "Gordon Sharp, you owe us money."

Who was that? The voice was deep and unfamiliar. And not really angry...but definitely dangerous.

It made Colt want to shrink back. Disappear into the wall.

"I'm—I'm getting it for you." His father sounded short of breath.

"You see, you said that a month ago, but we still haven't received anything. I'm losing faith in you, my friend."

"No! I'll have it to you, I promise. I just need the missus to tell me where the money is."

A deep laugh sounded, but it was a strange sound. Kind of like when a bully found someone to pick on. "I'm starting to think she cut you off. Which means we might have a problem. And do you know what we do with problems?"

"No, please—"

A pained shout came from his father. Colt slammed his empty hand over his ear and pressed the other to his shoulder, scrunching his eyes. He wasn't sure how long he stayed like that. It could have been minutes. It could have been hours. He started counting in his head. Long, slow counting that took his mind off whatever was going on in the library.

Suddenly, the panel opened.

Colt wrenched his hands from his ears and grabbed the knife—only to freeze at the sight of his mother.

Her eyes were wide and fearful. "Colt...baby! You're okay."

"Mom?"

She reached in and tugged him out, immediately pulling him against her chest. "Baby, I'm so sorry! I didn't know he was coming home early. I saw him on the camera. Are you okay?"

He nodded. He wasn't sure if it was a lie. Maybe. He wasn't hurt. But he didn't feel okay either.

"I was so worried." She pulled back again and studied his body. "Your father isn't here. And I'm going to make sure he doesn't come

home ever again. I'm calling someone for help. His name's Ben. He's going to protect us."

Colt nodded. He wanted to believe her. But he'd heard that promise before. And at just eight years old, he understood the threat that was his father. Knew the man wouldn't leave so easily.

And even if he did, he wouldn't stay away.

CHAPTER 21

"*H*ey! They're mine."

Colt took his gaze off the new lock he was installing on the cabin door to see Indie pulling her bag of M&M's out of Noah's hand.

"Really?" Noah asked in disbelief, making a grab for it, only for Indie to yank it farther out of his reach. "You're not going to share?"

She scoffed. "You just ate half the bag. I've shared. The rest are mine."

Colt chuckled. Indie had been editing photos on her laptop all day, while he and Noah worked on the cabins and Randy's crew had come and gone. The two of them had spent fifty percent of that time arguing and the other fifty percent joking like they were best friends.

It was a complicated relationship.

"Does she treat you like this?" Noah yelled over his shoulder.

"He doesn't steal my M&M's," Indie answered before Colt could get a word in.

"I once made the mistake of taking a chocolate egg from her Easter basket," Colt said, as he held the faceplate against the wood before driving in a new screw. "She yelled at me that it wasn't mine to take, that the chocolate had already been emotionally allocated."

"Hey, that was mid-IVF; it was a tough time. I may have cried."

Noah frowned. "What does 'emotionally allocated' mean?"

"It means it had been emotionally reserved for a future time when I might need comfort," Indie answered.

"I had to buy new chocolate."

"But Easter had passed," Indie added sadly. "So it was just normal chocolate."

Noah looked back at Indie. "Would you like me to buy you more M&M's?"

"That would be great. Thanks."

Colt just shook his head while Noah chuckled before looking at his watch. "I need to go."

"Hot date?" Indie asked.

"Nah, I promised Holden I'd help him move a few big things from his work shed."

"Need any help?" Colt asked.

"I think we'll be all right, but I'll message if that changes."

"You got it."

Once Noah left, Colt turned back to the door. "Five more minutes and I'll be done."

"No rush."

He tightened some screws. "You're happy he's home." It was an observation, not a question.

"I'm happy you're both home." There was a small pause. "Has he mentioned Bonnie to you?"

Colt stopped. Bonnie was Indie's sister. And even though she told people they didn't get along, the story was a lot more complicated than that. They'd never gotten along.

Bonnie had always been a rebel. Then came the night of Bonnie's high school graduation party. It had been a house party hosted by someone in her class. Bonnie had fought with her boyfriend and left him at the party. He'd driven home drunk, crashed his car, and died. It hadn't been Bonnie's fault, but his family blamed her. Then a few short months later, *her* parents had died in a car crash. It was too much for Indie's sister, and she had left town.

"Has he reached her?" Colt asked, trying to keep his voice neutral.

"Yeah, but she won't talk to him. Not a surprise. She's avoided us for this long—why would she start talking to us now?"

And there it was. The hurt. The pain she tried to hide. He lowered his tools and looked at her. "Are you okay?"

"Not really. When I think of Bonnie, I defer to anger because it's easier than feeling the hurt and the loss and the worry. God, I've been *so* worried about her for so long. But she doesn't care. She's never cared about anyone but herself. She needed to leave town, so she did. Who cares about anyone still here who loved her and also lost people?"

Colt crossed the space between them and sat beside her on the picnic table bench. "She'll come home."

"You don't know that. It's been thirteen years, and she hasn't so much as made contact."

"I *do* know that because my gut tells me she'll come home. And my gut's rarely wrong."

She leaned into his side, and he wrapped an arm around her. "What did your gut tell you about us?"

"That you're my wife. That you'll always be my wife."

She looked up at him. "Lately I've been thinking…maybe we should start exploring other options."

Colt frowned. "Options?"

"Adoption or fostering. I want to be a mother."

His arm tightened around her. "That sounds good, Cricket."

Her eyes softened. "I love you."

"I love you. And I would do anything for you." He meant that...*anything*.

She leaned forward and kissed him, her lips soft against his. And he drank her in. Slipping his tongue between her lips and tasting her.

Never again. Never again would he be away from her. Separated in any way.

He lifted her to his lap and her thighs immediately hugged his hips, the soft moans from her throat shifting into the air, toying with him.

He was just slipping his hands beneath her top when the ringing of his cell interrupted.

Goddammit.

He growled and pulled it out of his pocket to see it was his mother.

"Maybe you should talk to her," Indie said quietly. "You've ignored her last few calls."

He watched it for another moment before shaking his head. "It's getting late. I'll call her tomorrow."

The ringing stopped, and he quickly sent a text telling her he'd call in the morning, before shoving his cell into his pocket. It vibrated with a voice message. It could wait. "Let's get out of here."

They packed up and started the hike home. Colt scanned the trees the entire walk, his hand hovering over his concealed holster. If he was on his own, he'd probably welcome an attack. Because if his father did that, Colt would have cause to attack back.

Twenty minutes later, they were back home. He stepped into the kitchen and lifted his cell to listen to the voice message just as Indie's phone rang.

She frowned. "It's Jesse."

As she turned to answer it, his mother's voice message began. "Colt...help!"

He straightened, every muscle in his body locking at the fear in her voice. At her breathlessness. Was she running? There was the sound of wind over the line.

"It's Gordon! He...he shot Ben and he's going to—" Suddenly, his mother's scream pierced the line. Then his father's angry growl. A thud cut through the line—and it went dead.

Indie turned back to him, face white. "Colt, your mother and Ben have been rushed to the hospital. It's not good."

* * *

INDIE COULDN'T STOP her foot from tapping against the linoleum tiles of the hospital floor. It was a nervous gesture. But she didn't want to be nervous right now. She wanted to be strong for Colt. She wanted to be whatever he needed.

Sylvia's chest rose and fell in slow succession. The deep bruising on her cheek was dark, and God, there were so many tubes attached to her.

She was asleep. She'd been asleep since they'd stepped into the room.

Indie's heart broke for the woman. It didn't matter that Sylvia had never treated her well. No one deserved this.

Colt's boots thudded against the floor as he paced the room. He wasn't okay, and the need to make this better for him, to fix this, ran so deep it consumed her. But there was nothing she could do. She felt helpless.

The door opened, and she stood as a middle-aged man in a white lab coat stepped in, folder in hand. "Good evening. It's good to see you again, Mr. Reed. I'm sorry it's under such unhappy circumstances."

"Dr. Leeroy. This is my wife, Indie."

The doctor dipped his head in her direction. "It's nice to meet you, Indie."

"You too."

"How is she?" Colt asked.

"Your mother sustained quite serious injuries. Two cracked ribs. A broken finger and a fractured elbow. But it's the injuries to the head that we're most concerned about. She has a significant concussion, so we'd like to keep her here for a few days for monitoring."

Colt's muscles visibly tensed. Indie stepped behind him and touched his back, trying to offer just a little bit of comfort.

"But she'll be okay?" Colt asked.

"We'll keep monitoring, but after a lot of rest, I believe she will. She's heavily sedated tonight so won't wake until morning."

Colt nodded, but the action was sharp and short. She could feel his anger. It rippled off him in waves.

"Thank you, Doctor," Indie said softly.

She waited until the man closed the door behind him to step in front of Colt and touch his chest. "What can I do?"

"You're already doing it by being here."

It wasn't enough. But then, nothing felt like enough. She wanted to take away his pain. To make this mess better, but she couldn't.

A knock sounded at the door, and this time her cousin Jesse stepped in. He wore his sheriff uniform, and his usual easygoing smile was nowhere to be seen.

"How's she doing?" Jesse asked somberly.

Colt shook his head. "Not too good. Head injury is the worst. I need to know what happened."

"Until one of them wakes up, I won't have the details. But from what I can piece together, your mother and Ben were leaving the community center. She left bridge early and the people inside heard a gunshot. They called us, and one of the elderly members of the group had a gun. But by the time he got out there, he saw your father running away. Your mother was unconscious between the community center and the parking lot, and Ben was bleeding out by your mother's car."

"My father shot Ben, my mom tried to run, and he caught her and beat her."

"That's what it looks like," Jesse confirmed quietly. "And he took your mother's purse."

Nausea punched Indie in the belly. Gordon was so desperate for money that he'd shoot a man and beat a woman, only to take her purse?

"As soon as she wakes, we'll get her to cancel her bank cards," Jesse added. "We've also stationed someone outside her house in case he's stupid enough to try and access it with the keys that were in her purse."

"Is Ben okay?" Colt asked through gritted teeth.

"He's in surgery."

"Where is he?" Colt growled, and both Jesse and Indie knew he was talking about Gordon.

Frustration brimmed on Jesse's face. "We're looking for him."

"I need to find him."

Jesse stepped closer. "No. *You* don't. You need to let me do my job."

"And what? Wait for the asshole to attack again? Fuck that." He took a step toward the door, but this time Indie rushed to step in front of him.

"Colt. Stop." She reached up and cupped his cheek. "Jesse will find him. Please, trust him. Right now, your mother needs you. *I* need you."

The veins in his arms popped, but finally he turned back toward Jesse and scrubbed a hand over his face. "Fine."

"Go home. There's nothing more you can do here," Jesse said. "Get some rest. I'll put my deputies on the door."

When Colt didn't move, Indie took his hand and slipped her fingers through his. "Come on."

The drive home was quiet. Colt barely said a word, and she didn't know *what* to say. There weren't any words for situations like this. She just had to sit with him in this hard moment and be the support he needed.

Her mind flicked back to his mother in the hospital bed. The injuries she'd sustained.

Her ex-husband had done that. Someone she'd once trusted and loved. Someone she'd had a child with.

That was why she didn't trust Indie.

It made sense now. She'd trusted someone with her son before, and he'd hurt both of them. Now she'd always be afraid of history repeating itself. Noah was right. It wouldn't have mattered who Colt had chosen.

When they reached the house, Indie stepped into the kitchen. "I'll heat up the Chinese for dinner."

Colt scrubbed a hand over his face. "I'm not really hungry. I might take a shower." He lowered his head and pressed a kiss to her temple before leaving the room.

She hated this. All of it. They needed to find Gordon, and soon, and when they did, that asshole needed to be locked up so he couldn't hurt Colt or Sylvia anymore.

She took the takeout containers from the fridge. She'd just set them onto the counter when her phone buzzed with a call.

Clara.

Indie pressed the phone to her ear. "Hey."

"Indie, I heard about Colt's mother. Is she okay? Is Colt?"

Indie leaned her hip against the counter and closed her eyes. "No. Neither of them are okay. Syliva's going to be in the hospital for a few days, and I'm worried about Colt. He's barely talking to me, and I don't know whether to give him space or not."

"Oh, Indie. I'm sorry. You know, when Becket's upset, he says he needs space, when really, I think he just doesn't know how to ask for help."

Her gaze shifted to the closed bedroom door. "Should I go to him?"

"Do you *want* to go to him?"

"Yes." It was a full-body yes. Every part of her wanted to be close to him right now.

"Then go."

She nibbled her bottom lip. Clara was right. "Thanks, Clara. I'll call tomorrow."

She hung up and walked to the bedroom.

CHAPTER 22

olt gripped the edge of the bathroom counter.

He could barely breathe.

His fault. This was *his* fucking fault. His mother had called him for help. And yeah, on a deeper level, he knew he'd never have made it in time. But she'd been scared, *suffering* at the hands of that piece of shit father of his, and she'd called *him* for help. But he hadn't answered.

And Ben…the man who'd been more of a father than his own dad ever had, had been shot and was in surgery.

He tore off his clothes and stepped into the shower, making the water hot. So hot it burned his skin.

He'd said he wanted to kill his father so many times but never really meant it. Now though? If the man was in this very room with him, he wouldn't be able to stop himself. And he'd do it slowly. Make him hurt. Suffer the same way everyone around him suffered.

He pressed his palms to the wall of the shower and tried to breathe. To draw oxygen into his lungs even though the air was too thick.

The bathroom started to fill with steam. There was too

much anger inside him, and he didn't have anywhere to put it. It was trying to claw its way out of him. Hurting him. Choking him.

The door opened with a click, followed by the soft thud of footsteps.

Colt didn't move. He couldn't even look at her. If he couldn't protect his own mother, how would he protect his wife? He felt undeserving of her.

There was a creak of the glass shower door opening, then warm, familiar arms slipped around his middle and a cheek pressed to his back.

He just stood there, frozen. Still barely breathing. Still angry. Still wrecked.

"It's not your fault," she whispered, her words running over his skin, like cool water on the hot rage burning through him.

He lowered the temperature of the water and turned. Indie's brows were tugged together, her naked skin wet from the water that had slipped from his body to hers. And her eyes, those beautiful, soulful greens, seared into him.

She reached up and cupped his cheeks. "It's *not* your fault." She said the words slowly...firmly. Like she knew they were the only words capable of pulling him back from the edge.

"I didn't answer her call." Guilt. It coated each word.

"It wouldn't have changed anything if you had."

He swallowed hard. "I hate him."

"Me too. But *only* him because what he did is *all* on him. Do you understand? *You* are good. And you protect...you don't hurt."

"I didn't protect either of them tonight."

"Because you couldn't. And he knew that."

Colt latched onto those words like they were the only things keeping his head above water.

She leaned in and kissed his chest, her lips touching right over his heart. It was a heart that beat for Indie. It belonged to her.

She kissed him again, but this time over a small scar that sat close to his left shoulder, one he'd had since he was eight. One his father had put there.

And yeah, it took all the fucking pain away.

She looked up at him. "I love you, Colt Reed. You are the best man I know. And you're everything your father isn't."

He closed his eyes and gripped her hips, letting that kiss heal the broken parts of him. Letting her remind him of who he was, because she was the only one with the power to do so.

She pressed another kiss to his chest, but it wasn't enough. He cupped the back of her head, tilted her chin up, and kissed her. He slipped his tongue inside and let her taste, her softness, everything she was, lift him out of the dark place where his father put him.

She kissed him back, meeting him exactly where he was.

He lifted her and turned, pressing her back to the tiled wall, her entire front meeting his.

Fuck, he loved her. He loved everything about her with an intensity that should probably scare him. It didn't.

He reached down and held the soft mound of her breast in his palm, her moans weaving inside him, finding the hollow parts and filling them.

When he found her nipple, he swiped it back and forth with his thumb before rolling it in a circle.

She groaned.

So…fucking…beautiful. And his. This woman was his.

His mouth shifted to her cheek, then her neck. When he found that spot behind her ear that made her squirm, he lowered his hand to the V between her thighs and stroked her clit. Her entire body convulsed. He did it again, loving how damn sensitive she was. Absorbing every sound. Every tightening of her fingers against his shoulders. Memorizing her.

He shifted his thumb to her clit and slipped two fingers inside her. Her gasp was fucking magic. Piercing his chest, making his cock turn to stone.

He moved his fingers in and out in a rhythmic motion, his thumb gliding over her clit, sending her wild in his arms.

"Colt…" She reached down and grabbed his wrist. "Now."

Then she gripped the back of his head and tugged his mouth back to hers, but this kiss was fast and desperate. It was fire and need and desire.

He positioned himself at her entrance and slowly slid inside.

Fuck, she was tight. And she fit around him so fucking perfectly.

She tilted her head back and sighed before opening her green eyes and looking at him.

"Loving you is one thing I never got wrong," he whispered.

"You fought for us. You held us together, even when I felt like I was coming apart."

"I will *always* fight for us." He found her lips again and kissed her. Then he began to move. Long, deep thrusts that felt like coming home every time he returned to her. It was the peace and ecstasy that so many spent their entire lives chasing. And he had it in the palm of his hands.

* * *

EVERY INCH of Indie's body was on fire. Her fingers dug into his shoulders like if she didn't hold on she'd fall or break or something equally devastating. And maybe she would. Maybe Colt was and had always been her only anchor.

She barely felt the stream of water on her shoulders or the steam in the air. All she felt was Colt. He was everywhere. His body surrounded her, and his heat had slipped beneath the surface of her skin.

His thrusts grew faster. Harder. So deep and powerful it felt like she was going to break. The kind of shattering her body had only ever done for Colt.

She tucked her head into the nook of his neck and tried to breathe. To drag one breath in after the next.

When he found her nipple and began to play with the tight bud, she gasped. He rolled it and tugged, knowing exactly what to do to drive her crazy. To make her pulse speed up and her heart beat so hard it almost hurt.

She opened her mouth on his shoulder, not sure if she was kissing or biting him. Or maybe she was just stifling the screams.

When his hand returned to her core, her entire body tensed. He rolled his thumb over her clit and her body pulsed. He did it again, this time firmer.

She lifted her head and kissed him again, letting his tongue sweep inside her mouth. Letting him taste her. *Claim* her.

When his mouth moved from hers, she wanted to groan. But then he nibbled at the lobe of her ear before whispering, "I love you so fucking much, Cricket."

And that was it. Those deep, hushed words that whispered against her ear pushed her over the edge. She cried out, the sound a strangled scream as the orgasm hit her hard, making her entire body convulse.

Colt kept pumping, prolonging the throbbing in her core. Making her writhe and arch in his arms until finally, he growled. His teeth gently latched onto her neck as he shattered along with her.

Then he was just holding her, neither of them able to suck in a single full breath.

When she finally had the strength to lift her head, she cupped his cheek and looked at him. Her husband. Her entire world. "Are you okay?"

"I'm not sure. But you make me want to be."

At least he was honest.

This time she pressed a gentle kiss to his forehead, letting her lips linger before whispering, "They'll be okay."

"This time."

"There won't be a next time."

"We don't know that."

She swiped a trail of water from his brow. "There's you. And Noah. And Becket. And Holden. And Jesse and his deputies. An entire army of people who'll help to bring him in. You're not alone."

He leaned his forehead to hers and closed his eyes. "And there's you, keeping me sane."

"And I'm not going anywhere."

CHAPTER 23

*C*olt couldn't sleep. What had he gotten, two hours? Three? Whatever it was, it probably wasn't enough, but he wasn't going to get any more. Not tonight.

He watched the moonlight flicker over the road outside, telling himself he was here and not in bed because he didn't want to wake Indie. But that wasn't true. He needed to watch the house. Wait. Because his father *would* make an appearance, it was just a question of when.

He closed his eyes, and the night he'd met Ben flashed back in his mind.

Colt fisted his hands so hard that his knuckles ached. He was angry. Angry at his no-good father for making him run and hide again tonight. And that he'd brought those men onto their doorstep.

His mother could have been home. What then? What would they have done to her?

He and his mother deserved better. He was only eight, but he knew that much.

Colt looked out his bedroom window into the dark night. He should be sleeping, but he couldn't. What if his dad came back? Or worse, what if those men he owed money to came back?

Actually, he wasn't sure if that was worse. Would he prefer the devil he knew or someone new to terrorize his mother?

A door opened somewhere downstairs. It was so quiet the noise almost didn't reach him. But he'd become so attuned to any sound in this house over the years that he still heard it.

He shot up and pulled the knife from beneath his pillow. His mother had tried to take it from him, but he'd snuck it up here when she wasn't watching.

Then he ran—quick, silent steps out of his room and down the large hall. He'd just reached the top of the stairs when he saw a man beside his mother by the front door. Not his father. This guy was broader. And his eyes were clear rather than glazed over like his dad's.

Was he one of the assholes who wanted money?

He sprinted down the stairs, brandishing the knife. "Who are you?"

"Colt!" his mother gasped. "Honey, give me the knife."

"No! I want to know who he is." As a kid, he didn't have the height or the breadth to be much of a threat, but what he lacked in size, he made up for in anger.

The guy wasn't fazed. He stepped forward and crouched. "Hi, Colt. I'm Ben."

"What are you doing here?"

"Your mother called me. I'm going to stay with you for a little while. Make sure your dad and anyone else who wants to hurt you doesn't come back."

Colt's frown deepened. "You're here to protect my mom?"

"I'm here to protect both of you." There was kindness in his eyes but also a hardness. He reminded Colt of some guys who'd visited his school once. They'd worn uniforms and talked about their jobs in the Army.

"Do you know how to protect us?" Colt asked quietly.

"I was a Marine. Do you know what that is?"

Colt shook his head.

"It's someone who's trained to keep people safe. We're trained to be strong and brave."

Strong and brave...two things that, even at eight, Colt knew he wanted to be. He tried to be.

Ben held out his hand. "Give me the knife, son. You don't need that anymore."

For a second, Colt didn't move. He studied the stranger in front of him. He didn't want to trust a new person. But they needed help.

"I believe you." Just three words, then Colt handed over the knife.

Arms wrapped around Colt's middle, pulling him out of his memory and tensing his muscles. Then her familiar scent hit him. "Indie."

"Of course. Are you okay?"

Shit. He hadn't heard her coming. What if she'd been someone else? He needed to be more damn alert. "Yeah. I was just in my head."

"Want to talk about it?"

He covered her hands on his stomach with his own. "I was thinking about Ben. About the night I met him."

"Will you tell me?"

"He told me he was a Marine, and that he was trained to be strong and brave. He was everything I wanted to be."

"You were only eight."

"Yeah."

She stepped in front of him, studying him. "And you did it. You became a Marine."

"Yeah. But now he's in the hospital because—"

"Of your father," Indie interrupted. "He's there because of *Gordon*. And that's on him, no one else."

"I know you're right. It still hurts."

Indie's eyes flickered between his. "I'd like to come with you today to visit your mom. Is that okay?"

"Of course. I don't want you out of my sight."

"Good. I don't want you out of my sight either. Someone needs to protect you too, you know."

A smile played at his lips. "Are you going to protect me, Cricket?"

"With my life."

Fuck, he loved her.

But then the smile slipped from her lips. "What are you going to do when your mom gets better?"

That was something else he needed to think about. "I love her. I love her so damn much, and I want her to be okay. But I don't know how to have her in my life when she won't treat you the way you deserve to be treated. I'm not giving you up. You're my wife. You'll *always* be my priority."

She cupped his cheek. "Maybe you just tell her that. Put your boundaries in place and let her choose what she wants to do with them."

"You make it sound so simple."

"I'm pretty smart."

"I've never met anyone smarter or kinder than you, Indie Reed." He tugged her closer and kissed her cheek, then her jaw.

"Mm. You forgot pretty."

"You're not pretty. You're fucking gorgeous." He nuzzled her neck.

She chuckled. "Colt, I—"

Suddenly she stopped and gasped, before putting a hand to her belly.

His head shot up and his arms tightened around her. "What's wrong?"

"I think…" She stopped, hand still on her stomach. Then she ran out of the room.

What the hell? He followed her into the bathroom to see her drop and throw up in the toilet.

He cursed and dropped behind her, pulling back her hair and rubbing her back. Was she sick? Had she caught a virus or eaten something bad?

When she finally sat back, he studied her pale skin. "Are you okay?"

"Yeah, I kind of woke up feeling a bit nauseous but forgot about it when I saw you. Then…I don't know, it just hit me full force."

"We should see a doctor."

She shook her head. "No. I'll eat something and see if that makes me feel better."

"Indie—"

"Colt, I'm okay. Really."

He didn't like it. And if the nausea remained, he would be pushing for a visit to the doctor.

* * *

INDIE REMAINED close to Colt as they walked through the hospital waiting room, her hand in his.

Sylvia would be awake. What kind of mood would she be in? Would she be annoyed that Indie was there? Or might she finally start coming around?

They turned a corner and a man walking toward them made her frown. Why, exactly, she wasn't sure. Because of the tattoos down his arm? Because of his size?

He passed them, and she shook her head. She was just freaked out about Gordon. She shouldn't be judging a man because of a couple of tattoos.

They rounded another corner, and halfway down the hall, a deputy was stationed outside of Sylvia's room. Colt's fingers tightened around hers.

They stopped beside the guy. "I'm Colt, the son," he said, and showed his driver's license.

The deputy dipped his head. "Wade. Sheriff told me about you. Go in when you're ready. She's awake."

"Thanks." Colt turned to Indie. "Are you sure you want to come in with me?"

"Yes. I'd like to know she's okay. I also want to support you." She glanced at the seats in the hall. "But if you'd prefer I didn't—"

"No. I want you with me. And she needs to see us together."

Relief sent air rushing from her chest. A part of her had been scared he'd want her to wait outside. And she'd understand. Sylvia had just gone through something really traumatic—maybe he didn't want to risk upsetting her. But she was glad he wanted her with him, and hoped Sylvia would be okay with it.

"I'll be right by your side, then."

"Are you feeling okay?" he asked.

"So much better since eating something. I don't know what was going on." It must have been a low blood sugar thing. Either that or sleep- or stress-induced. Heck, it could be a whole list of things.

Colt studied her. "You let me know if you're not feeling well and we'll go straight home."

She nodded.

He lowered his head and kissed her forehead before pushing inside. Just like the previous night, nausea swelled in Indie's belly at the sight of bruises on Sylvia's face and the tubes attached to her body.

Sylvia's eyes popped right open, and the start of a smile curved her lips. "Colt, honey." Then she looked at Indie, and the smile slipped. Only a fraction, but she saw it. "Indie."

Guess things weren't any different.

Indie offered a small smile. "Hi, Sylvia."

Colt stepped forward and touched his mother's hand. "How are you feeling?"

"I woke up in so much pain this morning, but the lovely nurses gave me some more medication and now I barely feel anything."

"Good. And last night was quiet?"

"Your father didn't make an appearance."

"Thank God." Colt lowered into the seat beside the bed. "What happened last night, Mom?"

Real fear flickered in Sylvia's eyes, and even though so much had happened between them, Indie's heart hurt for the woman.

"Ben and I walked out of the community center. I wanted to leave early because I was tired. We'd just reached the car when Ben heard something. He shouted at me to get down. I heard a gun." Tears glistened in Sylvia's eyes. "He was shot. I wanted to help him, but your father stepped out from behind a car. I ran back toward the building to get help. That's when I was calling you. But he caught me before I could get inside."

Colt's muscles visibly bunched, and Sylvia took a moment to compose herself before she continued.

"He wanted money," she continued. "A lot. I said no. Said he wasn't getting a single cent from me ever again—and he just lost it. He was angrier than I'd ever seen him."

Colt's jaw pulsed, and Indie set a palm on his back, a gentle reminder that she was here.

"Did he say what the money was for?" Colt asked through gritted teeth.

"No. But we both know it's probably for drugs. That man could have all the money in the world and it wouldn't be enough to support his addiction."

Colt leaned forward. "I'm going to get him, Mom."

The fear in Sylvia's eyes intensified. "No! I told you, you need to stay away from him."

"Mom—"

"*No.*" She shook her head and forced herself to sit straighter. "I don't want you anywhere near him. Nothing good will come from that. Do you understand me?"

When Colt didn't respond, his mother leaned toward him. "It's not your job to protect me, baby. I'm your mother. *I* protect *you.*"

This time, tears blurred Indie's vision. This was why she didn't want Colt to lose his mother from his life. Because Sylvia loved him. She loved him so much. She just didn't always direct that love the right way.

The ringing of Colt's phone cut through the room. He pulled it out of his pocket and pressed it to his ear. "Jesse, you got anything?" He straightened. "Yeah, I'm already at the hospital with Mom. I can be there in a couple of minutes." He hung up.

"What is it?" Sylvia asked.

"Ben's awake. I'm going to go talk to him."

"I want to see him." Sylvia tried to climb out of bed, but Colt gently touched a hand to her shoulder.

"No. You need to get stronger first. I'll let you know what he says."

She huffed but lay back against her pillows.

Colt reached for Indie's hand, but she touched his chest. "Actually, I might wait here with your mom, if that's okay?"

His brows flickered. "Are you sure?"

"Yes. I'll keep her company."

He still didn't look convinced, but he nodded and flicked one last glance his mother's way before leaving the room.

When it was just the two of them, the older woman shook her head. "You didn't need to stay, Indie. I'm quite okay by myself."

"So nothing's changed? I was so hoping something would."

"I don't know what you're talking about. You already said everything you needed to when I came to your house the other day. And Colt confirmed it for me. There's nothing new you can say that I don't already know."

She swallowed before stepping forward. "I see why you're the way you are now."

Sylvia swung her gaze back to her, surprise in her eyes. That clearly hadn't been what Sylvia expected her to say.

"You can't forgive yourself for not leaving Gordon sooner. You blame yourself for allowing someone you trusted to hurt your son. So now it's easier to trust *no one*. But he never blamed you, Sylvia. So for him, there was nothing to forgive."

Tears appeared in Sylvia's eyes, her frown deep.

"I can't give him up," Indie pushed. "I tried that, and it didn't work...for either of us. I don't want him to lose *you*, either. But if you make him choose, he'll choose me."

Sylvia's chest rose on a sharp inhale, pain in her eyes.

"I don't say that to boast or to rub my importance in his life in your face. I say it as the simple fact it is. He'll choose me, and he'll lose *you*. And I don't want him to lose you, because you're his mother. His family. And he loves you. So don't make him choose."

A tear rolled down Sylvia's cheek. "I don't know how to trust you enough not to hurt him."

"That's fair. I left him once. But I did so because my head was underwater and I had to choose between pulling myself out and waiting for the storm to pass or drowning us both. I saved us by giving us a break. I healed myself so we could find our way back to each other."

"Are you healed now?"

"Mostly. I don't think anyone's ever completely healed of what hurts us, but I love myself enough to love him too. And I will never leave him again. I'll love him until the day I die. You can trust me with him. That's a promise I make to you. So, by choosing me, you'd choose him too."

The silence that followed felt long and drawn out. There was sadness in Sylvia's face. And some regret. Maybe also some confusion.

Finally, she said softly. "I appreciate you talking to me, dear. I'm going to think about what you've said."

It wasn't a promise that things would improve. But Indie had done what she could. The rest was up to Sylvia.

CHAPTER 24

*I*ndie crouched low beside the bay window and adjusted the zoom on her camera, the soft morning light through the sheer curtains casting a golden glow over the newborn baby. He lay on a white cushion and was wrapped in a white muslin blanket.

One leg had escaped, and Indie was struggling not to stare at those chubby toes. At his chunky thigh that resembled a soft marshmallow.

Then he tipped his head back and yawned. It made her chest ache.

She ignored the ache, forcing herself to focus on the job. She changed the shot to his face, capturing the creases of his shut eyes. The soft O shape of his lips.

Gorgeous. Baby Samuel was so gorgeous that when she looked at him, her heart both hurt and yearned.

"I so love his yawns." Martha, the mother, sighed.

"Well, being wrapped in a straitjacket makes him tired," her husband, Grant, said and chuckled.

Indie forced a smile to her lips. "Some babies love it, others hate it."

"Do you have kids?" Martha asked.

Indie tensed before forcing her muscles to ease as she snapped more photos of Samuel from above. "Not yet."

Yet...the word hung in the air, heavy and stagnant. She'd always believed she would. But now? Now she wasn't so sure. Yes, she'd said she might be ready to explore other options, but every time she started looking into it, her heart hurt. A physical pain at the prospect of letting go of the idea of carrying her own baby. Of never feeling those kicks or experiencing that swollen belly.

This was why she preferred not to do newborn shoots anymore. There was so much baby talk, and it always brought up questions about her own family structure...if she had *plans* for kids. And while dancing around those painful questions, she had to sit in this newborn bubble that had nothing to do with her.

"That man who walked you to the door is your husband, right?"

Grant nudged his wife's shoulder. "Martha, don't be nosy."

Indie shook her head. "No, it's okay. Yes, Colt's my husband. We're going somewhere right after the shoot, so he's just waiting for me."

Two weeks had passed since Sylvia's attack, and Colt was still trailing her to every appointment. He escorted her to the door of each house. Followed her into the mountains when it was an outside shoot. And when he worked, she went with him to the park and edited.

It probably wouldn't be so bad if she hadn't felt so nauseous and tired lately. The stress and lack of sleep was really kicking her butt.

"Grant, do you want to kneel at Samuel's feet and put your hand on his waist?" Indie said softly. "And Martha, can you kneel at his head and touch his hands?"

The two got into the frame, and Indie stood above them to snap some images. When she took the side-view shots, she saw the look on Martha's face. The love. The devotion. It made Indie want to cry.

Crap, did she actually have tears in her eyes?

She quickly blinked them away as she snapped more photos. "That's beautiful, guys."

Good. That was good. She hadn't sounded as emotional as she felt at all.

"Do you want to pick him up, Martha? And then, Grant, you could cuddle in nice and close."

Martha lifted him, and Samuel did the newborn scrunch. Indie snapped the photo.

"He's so perfect," Martha whispered.

Grant got close beside her. "He really is."

Indie bit the inside of her mouth in an attempt to keep her composure. She clicked a few more photos.

Done. "That's it, guys."

Martha looked at her. "You got everything?"

"I did. They're beautiful. You have a gorgeous family."

The new mother beamed. "Thank you so much."

"You're welcome. I'll edit them and email through the gallery when they're done."

Martha handed her son to Grant. "I cannot wait!"

"I'll pack up and get back to Colt."

The other woman nibbled her bottom lip for a moment. "Sorry to be nosy. You said you were married but...I heard you were divorced."

"*Martha*," Grant hissed.

"What?"

Indie shouldn't be surprised. She'd probably heard Sylvia's rumors about marrying for money.

Indie packed up her camera. "We *were* separated, but we're back together now."

"Oh, that's great! I didn't think you could possibly be divorced, based on the way he looked at you."

The way he'd looked at her?

Martha's smile softened. "It was that dreamy, you're-all-I-see kind of devotion. I imagine it's how Grant and I have been looking at Samuel all morning."

"I'll have to take more notice next time." Once everything was in the bags, she rose—then immediately swayed and had to grab onto the wall to steady herself.

Martha gasped. "Indie! Are you okay?"

"Um, yeah, I'm sorry. I don't know what just happened."

"Here, let me get you some water." Martha ran down the hall.

"Are you sure you're all right?" Grant asked, concern in his eyes.

Indie nodded. "Absolutely. I probably just stood too fast. I'll wait for Martha by the front door. It was lovely to meet you."

She'd just reached the door when Martha returned with a bottle of water. "Here you go."

"Thank you."

"Are you sure I can't get you something else? Coffee maybe?"

Indie's belly rolled. "That's okay. For some reason, I've been really off coffee the last couple weeks." The kind of "off" that had her gagging at the very smell of it. Which *sucked* because chai spiced lattes had always been a highlight of her day, and she couldn't enjoy them lately.

"That's funny, I was off coffee my entire pregnancy. Grant actually had to stop drinking it around me because just the smell would make me gag." Martha bumped her hip. "Maybe you're pregnant. Any other symptoms?"

Indie's brows lowered. Nausea. Fatigue. Dizziness. Turned off certain foods.

They were all pregnancy symptoms.

But no. She couldn't be pregnant. They'd tried for years.

Infertile. It was a label that had been stamped all over her medical files.

But what if she wasn't?

The question hit her so hard, for a moment, she couldn't breathe.

No. She could not get her hopes up, only for them to come crashing down.

She tried for a smile but was sure it came out all wrong. "I should get going. I'll have the photos back to you within the next two weeks."

"Thank you, Indie. I'm so excited to see them."

She stepped outside, but her pulse was still racing.

She *did* have the symptoms. And hell, now that she thought about it, her period was late. But then, she'd never been too regular, so she hadn't put any thought into it.

She slid into the car and opened her mouth, not sure what she was going to say to Colt. Then a voice sounded over the car's Bluetooth.

"How about next week?"

Randy?

"No, that's too soon," Noah said, his voice also coming through the speaker. "I don't want to risk the safety inspector doing the final walk-through too early."

"It's not too early," Randy pushed.

Colt leaned over to her and whispered, "Sorry, we're almost done. Ready to go to your aunt Pam's?"

She nodded stiffly, even though it was the last place she wanted to go.

Colt frowned. "Everything okay?"

"Of course. Newborn sessions are just a bit emotionally draining."

Concern flickered through his eyes before he leaned closer and kissed her forehead. When he pulled onto the road, her gaze went to the window, but she wasn't really seeing anything.

She wasn't pregnant. There was no way. And wondering if she was would just end in pain and disappointment.

* * *

Randy and Noah were still talking, but Colt was barely listening. Something was wrong with Indie. She said she was fine, but she was pale. The frown on her face was too deep and had been there since she'd climbed into the car.

Was it just because of the newborn shoot, or was it more than that?

He pulled up in front of her aunt Pam's house, half a dozen cars already there. "I need to go. Randy, I'll continue this conversation later. Noah, I'll see you when you get here."

He didn't wait for their responses, just hung up, but Indie was already out of the car and walking toward the house.

He cursed and rushed to catch up with her. "Hey, what's wrong?"

"Nothing."

Not true. Fuck, she was barely looking at him.

They stopped at the front door and he grabbed her arm. "Cricket, I can tell something's not right. Tell me what. No secrets, remember?"

Something akin to fear flashed in her eyes.

Shit. It was bad. He stepped closer. "Is it my father? Did you see him somewhere?"

No, that wasn't possible. Even though Colt had been on a work call, his eyes had been on the house and the street the entire time.

"I told you," she said quietly. "This isn't the best time to talk about it. And I haven't been feeling great. Can we discuss it later?"

He touched her forehead. She didn't feel hot. But she hadn't been herself these last couple weeks. Nauseous. Tired. He'd put it down to stress.

"Indie—"

The door opened, and Becket stood on the other side, beer in his hand.

Dammit.

"Sorry, I was coming out to grab something from the car." Becket frowned. "Everything okay?"

Indie gave a jerky nod. "Of course." She slipped past Becket into the house.

The urge to tug her back was strong. Hell, Colt had to fist his hands to forcibly stop himself.

Becket looked back at him. "What's going on?"

"I don't know." But he sure as hell was going to find out.

He squeezed Becket's shoulder before stepping inside. Everyone was out back, drinks in hand, smiling and laughing, but his gaze went straight to Indie. She was standing with Clara and her aunt. She was smiling, but it was strained.

What the hell was going on?

Colt grabbed a beer from the cooler and joined Jesse and Holden. The guys were best friends and had served on the same Ghost Ops team. Now, Holden dated Clara.

Holden smiled at him. "Hey. How're you doing?"

"All right." He'd been better. A hell of a lot better. He looked at Jesse. "Have you found Gordon?"

"Maybe. Five minutes ago, I got a call about a lead. They're checking it out right now."

"What lead?"

"There's an abandoned house out on Clifford Avenue. One of the neighbors has reported seeing someone there the last few days."

Colt cursed. "What the hell are we still doing *here*?" He turned, but Jesse grabbed his arm and tugged him close.

"My guys are probably already there. Let them do their job."

"What if he gets away?"

Almost on cue, Jesse's cell rang. He stepped away to answer

the call, but Colt didn't take his eyes off him. He saw frustration flicker over Jesse's face. Then anger.

Something had gone wrong. They hadn't caught him.

Shit.

Jesse stepped back, keeping his voice low. "Gordon had a gun. He started shooting as they approached the house."

"Anyone get hurt?" Holden asked.

"One of my deputies, Luke. Wade, one of the new guys, had to choose between helping Luke or chasing down Gordon. He helped Luke."

Colt swallowed the acid in his throat. "Gordon got away."

Jesse's gaze went back to Colt. "Yeah. I have to go. Wade's new to the department. I need to be with him for the debrief. I'll keep you updated."

A part of Colt wanted to go with Jesse. Hear exactly what his deputies had to say firsthand. But then his gaze caught on Indie across the yard. She was watching him, and she was still too damn pale.

She needed him.

Noah joined him, a frown on his face. "Hey. I saw Jesse leaving in a rush. What's going on?"

"Gordon shot a deputy."

Shock widened Noah's eyes. "Shit!"

Yeah, shit.

Becket approached, and the guys updated him on what was going on. Everyone needed to know the details. The more eyes looking for Gordon, the better.

As they spoke, Colt watched Indie. Sky approached the women with a tray of prawns from the grill. That last bit of color drained from Indie's face. Suddenly, she spun and jogged across the yard to the house.

Colt went after her, crashing inside and following her all the way to the bathroom. She dropped to her knees in front of the toilet and vomited.

He cursed as he knelt behind her, pulling her hair out of the way and rubbing gentle circles on her lower back.

That was it. He needed answers. Whether those answers were from her or a doctor, he didn't care. But he needed them *now*.

When she eased back, he helped her up and watched as she flushed the toilet and rinsed her mouth in the sink.

"What's going on, Cricket?" he asked softly, gripping her hips from behind.

She took some deep breaths before lifting her head and looking at him in the mirror. "I don't want to say it in case I'm wrong. God, I'm scared to even *think* about the possibility because hope can be so dangerous." Her words sped up, each rushing into the next. "I got my hopes up every time, and every time they turned out to be wrong it hurt more and more. But I've been sick and tired and dizzy, and Martha said she hated coffee too and—"

"Indie." He tightened his fingers on her hips, and she stopped. "Breathe."

Her chest rose and fell.

"Just tell me what's happening. Let me be in this with you."

She swallowed, her gaze meeting his in the mirror, before those quiet words left her lips. "I think I might be pregnant."

CHAPTER 25

S hock. Uncertainty. Concern. It all played over Colt's face. And yeah, she felt it too.

"You think that because you've been sick?" he asked, voice quieter than a second ago.

"And tired. And off coffee. Then this morning, I got dizzy—"

"You got dizzy? Why didn't you tell me?"

"I'm fine. Martha got me some water. I just stood up too fast."

He took her hand and pulled her toward the door. "Let's go."

"Where?"

"To the doctor."

"No." She ground to a stop.

He turned back to her. "*Yes*. We need to know one way or another. We need to talk to a doctor and—"

"I'm scared." Two words. They were said quietly, but God, they sounded loud in the small bathroom.

"Scared of what?"

"That the doctor will tell me that I'm not pregnant and this is all in my head. But I'm also equally scared that he'll tell me I *am* pregnant. Then I'll start believing we'll get our baby, only for something to happen and suddenly we lose the baby—and I get really sad and angry at the world again." Panic exploded inside her at the thought. She couldn't even imagine getting that positive test, only to lose them. But the truth was, a loss in the first trimester was common. Too common.

"Hey." Colt stepped closer and cupped her cheeks. "You're not alone. I'm with you every step of the way."

"I know. And I know that should probably be enough, but I'm still scared."

His thumb caressed her cheek. "Why don't we make a doctor's appointment for tomorrow? It will give us a few hours to wrap our heads around all of this."

Tomorrow. Would it feel any less scary then?

She nodded, because what else could she do? They *did* need to know one way or the other.

Suddenly, she needed to feel his arms around her. She needed his closeness and his breath at her ear and the calm of his heartbeat against hers.

She leaned into his chest, and the second his arms wrapped around her, the fear quieted. Not all the way, but enough to make her heart stop thumping so loudly.

"I'll step out front and call the doctor now," he said quietly, after they parted.

"Okay." And she'd go back to the yard and pretend everything didn't suddenly feel different.

The next couple of hours were a blur of smiles and nods and trying to focus on conversations that she was barely following. She forced herself to eat something, even though her stomach rebelled. She wasn't sure if that was nausea or nerves.

Clara kept watching her. But then, of course she did—they were best friends. They knew each other too well to hide anything.

Noah did the same.

They were just cleaning up when her brother touched her arm. His voice low, he asked, "What's wrong?"

"Nothing."

"Don't lie to me. I can see something's going on."

She cocked her head. "You're one to talk. You've been quiet all afternoon." Despite the distraction, she'd noticed.

His brows lowered. "Bonnie called."

Indie gasped, momentarily pulled out of her own haze. "When?"

"Last night."

"What did she say?"

"Not much. She just seemed to want to ask questions. About me and Amber Ridge. About you."

Bonnie had asked about her? "Did you find out anything about *her*? Where she's living? What she's doing?"

"She said she's working at a women's shelter as a programs coordinator."

Indie pulled back. She'd never pictured her sister working a job like that. But then, she didn't know who her sister was at all anymore. "It sounds like she's doing okay. And it's good that she called you."

He bumped her hip. "*You* could call her."

She shook her head quickly. "No. She never liked me."

"She liked you, Indie."

She scoffed. "All we did was argue."

"You're different people."

Yeah, and that was probably part of what had driven Bonnie away. Indie had always wondered, if they were closer, would Bonnie have stayed? Would they have leaned on each other while going through the grief of losing their parents?

Noah squeezed her shoulder. "This is good, Indie. This is progress."

She nodded. It was true.

Colt joined them, immediately wrapping an arm around Indie's waist. "Ready to go?" His voice was gentle. Cautious even.

He'd kept an eye on her all afternoon. And when he wasn't

watching her, he was touching her. An arm around her waist. A hand on the small of her back.

She leaned into him. "Yeah, I'm ready."

They went around and said goodbye to everyone, and by the time she slid into the passenger seat, she was exhausted. She leaned her head back and closed her eyes.

"You okay, Cricket?"

"Just tired."

He squeezed her thigh, then turned on the car. When they got home, Colt put his hand on the door, but she touched his arm before he could get out.

"I should have asked," she said softly. "Are *you* okay?"

"I'm right where you are, Cricket. Nervous to test, and just as nervous not to."

She studied his dark chocolate eyes. "I'm sorry."

"For what?"

"I've made so much of this infertility about *me*. I was struggling so much that I never really checked in on you. But you wanted a child just as much as I did."

He leaned toward her. "I did want a child. I *still* do. But more than that, I want you to be happy."

"I don't deserve you."

"I think it's the other way around."

It wasn't.

She turned and climbed out of the car. Inside, he closed and locked the door before heading into the kitchen. "Hungry?"

"After all that food at Aunt Pam's? Definitely not."

He chuckled. "I'll make us some hot drinks."

"I'm just going to change." She slipped off her shoes and headed into the bedroom. She was about to take off her jeans when she stopped at the light breeze on her neck. Frowning, she turned.

The window was open. But there was no way her or Colt would have left it like that.

That meant—

A figure suddenly moved in the mirror behind her. She opened her mouth and screamed, but the sound was cut off by Gordon's arm wrapping around her throat and the knife he pressed to her skin.

Colt crashed into the room, fear then pure rage cutting across his face.

* * *

PREGNANT. Indie might be pregnant. It still didn't feel real.

The doctor could tell them she wasn't. And fuck, it would hurt.

But he could also tell them she *was*.

He closed his eyes, allowing himself for just a second to consider the possibility that she was pregnant. That their child was growing in her belly after years of trying and failing.

He'd wanted kids for so long. After growing up as an only child, he'd always wanted lots of kids. He'd dreamed of a loud home full of family.

But more than that...he wanted to be a dad. And he'd sure as hell do a better job than his own father.

He'd just opened the fridge when the scream cut through the air.

Indie.

He took off, sprinting through the house, his feet pounding against the floorboards before he crashed into the bedroom. And what he saw made his blood run cold.

Gordon Sharp stood behind Indie, one arm wrapped around her throat while the other held a knife inches from her cheek.

Indie's eyes locked with Colt's. The fear almost gutted him. But there was also something else in her expression—anger.

"What the hell are you doing, Gordon?" Colt growled.

His father raised a brow. "I'm holding a knife to your wife's throat. You don't think you can muster up a 'Dad' for me?"

"What I *think* is if you harm a fucking hair on her head, I will *gut* you."

His father laughed, but the sound was almost manic. "You're not too bright, are you, kid? *I'm* holding the knife. So I make the rules."

"What do you want?" Each word was forced out through gritted teeth.

"You know what I want…the money I'm owed."

The asshole wasn't owed a fucking thing. But now wasn't the time to remind him of that. "And what? You think I just keep a pile of cash sitting around?"

"If you want your wife to come out of this in one piece, I think you'll figure out how to get it to me."

Fury pulsed through Colt's veins.

"I have cash," Indie said, voice quiet, almost breathless. "It's in my safe in the walk-in closet."

"How much?" Gordon growled.

"Thousands. I sold a car, and they paid me in cash. I never put the money in the bank. It could tide you over until Colt and Sylvia get you the rest."

Colt frowned. Was that true?

"If you're lying to me—"

"I'm not," Indie interrupted.

"I'll get it for you," Colt said, taking a step toward the closet.

"*No.*"

Colt stopped, his hands fisting at the way the knife in Gordon's hand inched closer to Indie's skin.

"You think I'm stupid?" Gordon gasped. "She and I will go. And if there's a gun in there, I'm slicing her neck open."

Every part of Colt screamed to cross that small distance between them and ram the knife into his father's throat. But it was too close to Indie's neck. He wouldn't make it in time.

Instead, he angled his body to the side and got his phone from his pocket. He stepped forward, half of his body hidden by the dresser, using it to shield what he was doing. Only looking down in the small milliseconds that Gordon took his eyes off him.

He hit Jesse's name but silenced his end and put the call on speaker. Jesse would hear everything, while Gordon would hear nothing. The station wasn't far. He could only pray they didn't take long.

As Gordon stepped into the walk-in closet, Colt inched forward and set the phone face down on the dresser. One step forward, then the next. He wanted to be as close as possible in case he needed to act.

They stopped just inside the closet and Indie pushed clothes aside. Gordon had loosened his hold on her throat, but that knife was still close to her face. He couldn't see the safe from where he stood, but the soft beeps of her typing in her passcode were loud in the otherwise quiet room.

What's your plan, Cricket?

He had to hope, pray, that she wouldn't give Gordon any reason to hurt her. But hell, Gordon probably didn't need a reason.

Blood roared between Colt's ears as he prepared to lunge forward.

The click of the safe door opening sounded. Gordon's eyes widened—and he took the arm away from her throat to reach inside. When he pulled his hand back, he held a wad of cash.

She was telling the truth.

Gordon was still holding the cash when Indie thrust her hand inside and pulled out a pistol.

"What are you—"

Gordon's words were cut off when she fired at his foot. He cried out, shoving her hard against the doorframe.

Colt had already lunged, wrapping an arm around his father's middle and sending them both to the floor in the bedroom.

Gordon growled, swinging to dig the knife into Colt's side, but Colt was faster, gripping the man's wrist and smashing his hand to the floor so hard that Gordon cried out.

Colt squeezed, and Gordon dropped the knife. He tried to lift a knee, but Colt immobilized his body with his own before throwing his other elbow into his father's cheek.

The hit was so hard that Gordon's head dropped, eyes closing, body unmoving.

Colt turned back to Indie—and fear immediately seized his chest. She lay on her side in the doorway, blood coating her head.

No...

He grabbed the knife in case Gordon woke and tossed it deep into the closet before dropping beside her. "Cricket, can you hear me?"

Nothing.

He rolled her to her side and touched her pulse. It was strong. Good.

Sirens wailed outside, but he ignored them.

"Come on, Cricket, I need you to wake up."

The front door opened on a bang. Then footsteps.

When Jesse stepped in, Colt's gaze flew to him. "We need an ambulance!"

CHAPTER 26

a strong, rhythmic beeping pulsed between Indie's ears.

She squeezed her eyes shut. Where was she? And what was that sterile smell?

A deep ache in her head made her want to groan. But it wasn't just the ache that bothered her. Her head felt heavy and foggy, and even with her eyes closed, the world was spinning.

Then she became aware of something else. A warmth wrapped around her hand. Fingers. Familiar fingers.

Colt.

She forced her eyes open, needing to see him. To understand what was going on.

His dark hair was the first thing to enter her vision. His head was down, so she couldn't see his eyes, but the tension in his shoulders was obvious.

"What happened?"

His head shot up, eyes flaring. "Cricket! You're awake."

"Yeah." She turned to take in the room. "I'm in the hospital."

"Do you remember anything?"

She frowned. "We got home from Aunt Pam's. I went into the

bedroom. And..." She gasped, her eyes flashing back to Colt. "Gordon!"

The frustration on his face shifted to something darker. Something that made him look irrefutably dangerous. "He grabbed you. Put a knife to your throat."

"I shot him in the foot."

Just the smallest hint of a smile twitched at his lips. "Yeah, you did good."

"What happened next?"

"I disabled him. He's here, in the hospital. You're safe."

Gordon was in the hospital. They had him. "So he won't be able to come after us again?"

"After shooting a deputy and Ben, attacking Mom, and then everything that happened tonight, he won't be out for a while."

Relief hit her so hard that tears filled her eyes. "Thank God."

Colt stroked the back of her hand. "I'm sorry."

"Why are you sorry?"

"It's because of me that he attacked you. Because you're my wife."

"No. It's because of *him* that he attacked me. You didn't ask for any of this."

"But if you weren't married to me—"

"I am. And there is nowhere else in the world I'd rather be than by your side."

For a second, his gaze bore into hers, and even though she tried, she couldn't figure out what he was thinking. Then he lifted her hand and kissed the back of it. "I love you."

"It can't be as much as I love you."

He chuckled, like it was a joke.

A knock sounded at the door, and a woman wearing a white lab coat, who had wisps of gray in her hair, stepped into the room.

She smiled warmly. "Hi. Is this an okay time?"

"Of course," Indie nodded.

The woman stopped at the end of the bed. "I'm Doctor Frankie. I've already met your husband, but it's nice to officially meet you, Mrs. Reed."

"You too."

The doctor pushed her glasses up her nose. "Do you remember how you got here?"

"Bits and pieces. I know I was shoved against a doorframe."

"That's correct. You had a concussion, which caused you to lose consciousness, and that's why we've been monitoring you. We've done a CT scan, and there's no sign of internal bleeding or serious trauma, which is great news."

Indie nodded, but that little movement caused a flicker of pain in her head. She cringed.

Colt noticed and his fingers tightened around her hand.

"You're probably feeling a bit groggy," the doctor continued. "Maybe nauseous with a headache. That's all normal after a head injury."

"Okay."

"And the baby's fine."

Air stalled in Indie's lungs, those four words hanging in the air, suspended, like they weren't meant for her.

For a moment there was silence. A heavy silence that no one seemed to want to break.

It was Colt who asked the question. "She's pregnant?"

"Yes." The doctor frowned slightly and shook her head. "I'm sorry, I thought you knew."

Indie forced herself to breathe before asking, "Are you sure?"

"Very. Your beta HCG levels are strong. At least six weeks."

Tears gathered in Indie's eyes. "I'm pregnant." The words almost felt too big and heavy for her to hold. She turned to look at Colt. "We're having a baby."

Colt's face was a mixture of relief and happiness and shock all merged together. "We're having a baby," he repeated quietly, his eyes locked on hers.

The doctor continued to talk. Indie caught some words, like *rest* and *monitoring* and *symptoms*. But most of it was a blur.

After years of trying. Years of invasive procedures, blood draws, hormone crashes, and hope that grew, only to shatter, she finally heard the words she'd longed to hear.

When the doctor left the room, Colt looked down at her, and there was so much love in his eyes. He was the father of her child. The love of her life. And they were having a baby together.

Gently, he set a hand over her stomach before lowering his head and kissing her belly. The small action made more tears gather. This was all she'd wanted for so long.

When he lifted his head, he looked at her again. "What are you feeling?"

"Happy. God…happiness barely touches the surface of what I feel. But I'm also scared. So much can happen during a pregnancy. I don't think I'll feel safe until I'm holding our baby in my arms."

He cupped her cheek. "We'll handle anything that's thrown our way together."

"Thank you."

He leaned forward, his lips hovering over hers. "You don't need to thank me for loving you."

Then he closed the last bit of distance between them and kissed her. At the feel of his lips against her, some of that fear dissipated, and the familiar safety Colt invoked returned.

* * *

COLT HELD Indie as she slept, the TV a quiet drone in the background. They were on the couch and had gotten home from the hospital less than an hour ago. Noah had fixed the lock for the window in the bedroom, but he was still on high alert.

She hadn't said it, but she'd been hesitant to go into the bedroom. He'd suggested a movie, knowing full well she wouldn't last very long. Hell, it had been almost midnight when they'd gotten home. She'd held out for the first five minutes before falling asleep on him.

He brushed a lock of hair from her cheek, a tightness clutching at his lungs when he surveyed the wound on her temple. At the memory of her unconscious on the floor and the panic that had spread through his limbs like wildfire.

And all while she was pregnant.

The sudden urge to get up and go to the hospital, find his father, and make sure he never hurt Indie again was strong.

He wouldn't. Indie needed him with her. But the fucker *would* go to jail, and if he ever got out, Colt would personally make sure he went right back in.

He grabbed the remote and turned off the show. He wasn't even sure what they'd put on. Some romantic comedy on Netflix. Indie had sent a questioning glance his way when he'd chosen it, but she loved that sort of stuff. Besides, it hadn't mattered what they watched, he'd just wanted to hold her. Place a hand on her belly and imagine it swelling with their baby.

Gently, he slipped his arms behind her back and knees and lifted her into his chest.

Her soft hum made him want to hold her closer. Tighter. But then, Indie had always had a way of making every primal, protective instinct in him come to life.

In the bedroom, he laid her beneath the sheets. Her eyes fluttered open, and a small smile stretched her lips before she whispered, "Hey."

"Hey, Cricket." He lowered to the side of the bed. "How are you feeling?"

"Like I hit a doorframe with my head."

A small growl vibrated from his chest. "I'm sorry."

"Don't do that. This wasn't on you." She swallowed. "Today was crappy. Tomorrow will be better."

"I hope so."

"I know so."

He lowered his head and kissed her temple. "Sleep. I'm just going to make sure everything's locked up."

Her eyes fluttered closed. "Don't take long."

"Nothing can keep me away from you for long." He meant that. He loved her too much to lose her.

He waited for her breathing to even out before stepping out of the room and texting Jesse.

Colt: You've got eyes on Gordon, right?

Jesse: I do. He just got out of surgery for his foot. He'll probably be in for another couple of days, maybe longer.

Colt's jaw clenched. He wanted the man locked up, and he wanted him locked up today.

Jesse: As I mentioned at the hospital, he has a deputy stationed at his door and is cuffed to the bed. He's not going anywhere.

So why did Colt have a pit in his gut?

Because today he'd seen Indie with a knife pressed to her skin, and it was something he'd take a long time recovering from.

Colt: Thanks.

He'd just finished locking up the house when his cell rang, his mother's name on the screen. For a second, he considered not answering. But it was late. Really damn late. If she was calling, it had to be important.

"Hey, Mom."

"Colt, Ben just woke me up to tell me they have Gordon, but you were attacked?"

He'd called Ben just so he was aware of what had happened. "Indie was attacked. But she's okay. We both are."

"Thank God! I was so worried."

"He has a deputy on him now, and the second he's out of the hospital, he'll be locked up."

"What a relief." Emotion clogged his mother's voice.

"How are you doing?"

"I'm okay. Bruising's almost gone and the broken ribs and other injuries hurt less every day."

"That's good. Ben said he was doing well when I called."

His mother scoffed. "He's acting like nothing happened. I caught him trying to lift a dresser yesterday. Honestly, if I don't chain that man to a bed, he doesn't rest. It's like he forgets he was shot."

A small smile tugged at Colt's mouth. "Sounds like Ben."

"Can I come visit tomorrow? I'd love to see you."

"You mean us."

There was a small pause. "Yes. Well, of course."

He shook his head. She *still* didn't get it. And at this stage, if she didn't get it, she never would. "Mom, it will *always* be us. It's been *us* since we started dating in high school."

"I know. I—"

"No. I don't think you do know. I appreciate you checking in, but as I've said before, I need minimal contact right now."

"Colt—"

"Indie will need to rest tomorrow anyway. I'll try to stop by in the next week or so. I'm glad Gordon's in the hands of the police so we can all be safe now."

Then he hung up and leaned his head back, the frustration tugging at every part of him. He loved his mother. What they'd gone through together at the hands of his father had created a bond he'd thought was unbreakable. And his mother had given him the best life after Gordon was gone.

It was probably why this hurt so much. Because he'd expected more from her.

When the lights were off, he moved back to the bedroom to see Indie curled into a ball on her side of the bed.

Damn, she was beautiful. Every time he looked at her, he was reminded that she held his heart in the palm of her hand.

He stripped down to his briefs and climbed into the other

side. Then he slipped an arm around her waist and tucked her close.

She sighed and nestled closer.

This. Her. It was everything he'd craved the last year. It was all he needed. All he'd ever needed. And he would do whatever it took to protect her, body and soul.

CHAPTER 27

"We had our first fight this morning."

Indie's lips curved as she lifted her peppermint tea, coffee still not sitting well in her belly. She didn't love the tea, but it was supposed to be good for nausea. "You and Holden had a fight? About what?"

"We went out to that new Italian place for dinner. I was dressed very casual—leggings, my hair was in a claw clip, and I had no makeup on. Basically invisible."

Indie scoffed. "You're never invisible, Clara." The opposite. Her cousin was gorgeous.

"No, I looked terrible. And this waiter comes over and asks how we're doing. He smiles, hands us menus. That's it. That's all he does."

"Sounds very standard."

Clara threw her hands up. "Exactly! Well, the second the waiter leaves, Holden says he was flirting with me."

"What gave him that idea?"

"He said the guy's gaze lingered and he had a *tone*."

"What kind of tone?"

Clara lifted a shoulder. "I don't know, a flirty one that I somehow missed. Anyway, he spends the entire dinner eyeing this guy like he's about to wage a war against him. I get annoyed, tell him he's overreacting. Then when I go to the bathroom, the waiter hands me his number."

Indie almost choked on her tea. "*What?* Holden's a million feet tall and all muscle. What was he thinking?"

"I know! And I was so mad because *he* was right and I was wrong. I didn't talk to him for a full hour."

Indie laughed. It wasn't the worst thing to fight about. "I'm sorry. Kind of cute that he was so overprotective though."

"Yeah. And we did have *really* good makeup sex later that night."

"Sounds like you should fight more often."

"You know, I was thinking the same thing." Clara sipped her sweet tea. "Tell me about you. How's your head?"

Indie swallowed. "My head's good." It had been a week since the attack. She'd rested a lot during that time and was finally feeling ready to be out and about, especially now that she didn't have to worry about Gordon. "Actually, there's something I've been meaning to tell you. I didn't earlier because there was so much going on with Gordon and my concussion, and there were often other people around when I saw you."

Clara set her glass onto the table, a frown between her brows. "What?"

"I'm pregnant."

Her mouth dropped. "No."

"Yes."

"Yes?"

"Mm-hmm."

Suddenly, Clara screamed before jumping out of the booth, rounding the table, and throwing her arms around Indie. "I'm so happy for you!"

"Thank you."

"I can't believe you let me go on about that waiter and makeup sex when you were sitting on this information!"

Indie chuckled. "Hey, I liked that story."

When Clara pulled back, she had tears in her eyes. "You're really pregnant?"

"Really, really. But it's early. I'm still in my first trimester."

"But there's a baby growing in there."

Clara's tears made wetness fill Indie's eyes. "I don't know how."

"Because Colt's home. Because you love each other. Because things are right in the world."

"Now that Gordon's been arrested, it kind of feels that way."

"How else are you feeling?"

"A mix of happy and shocked and sick and scared."

Clara frowned. "Why scared?"

"Because there's a reason women aren't supposed to tell people in their first trimester. The chance of miscarriage—"

"No. Don't say that. Don't even *think* it. You are safe. Your *baby* is safe."

"You can't promise me that."

"I shouldn't, but I am anyway. Because my gut tells me I'm right."

Indie's lips curved. "I wish I had your faith."

"You will." Clara slipped some hair behind Indie's ear. "I'm going to be the best auntie for this little baby."

"You really are. You're amazing."

"Only because I have an amazing cousin who also happens to be my best friend. Now, when can I stick needles into you?"

Indie laughed, and they spent the next half hour talking about all things baby. Colt's reaction. Her symptoms. Where she planned to put the nursery.

When it was time to go, they both headed outside, where

Clara pulled her into another big bear hug. "I am *so* happy for you. You're going to make the best mother. You deserve this pregnancy."

"Pregnancy?"

Indie gasped—and turned to see Sylvia behind them, purse in her hands. "Sylvia, I didn't see you."

Sylvia stepped closer. "Indie? Are you pregnant?"

Crap. She'd wanted Colt to tell his mother when he was ready. Too late. "I am."

Sylvia's gaze lowered to Indie's stomach before rising again, her expression shocked. "Congratulations, dear."

Indie dipped her head. "Thank you."

Sylvia offered a small smile before stepping around her into The Tea House.

Clara cringed. "I'm so sorry."

Indie shook her head. "It's not your fault. I didn't see her either."

They said goodbye and Indie headed down the street. She'd parked at the print shop because she'd picked up some photos she'd printed for a client before meeting Clara. They were gorgeous; she always loved seeing her photos in print. With the rise of the digital age, prints had become less and less common. But there was something so special about seeing the photos framed or in a book.

As she stepped into the parking lot, she texted Colt.

Indie: I have to tell you something.

His response was immediate.

Colt: Are you okay?

Indie: Yes, but your mom overheard me talking to Clara. She knows about the pregnancy. I'm sorry.

Colt: Why are you sorry?

Indie: Because you should have been able to tell her.

Indie unlocked her car door and climbed in. There'd been a

delay on her new car, so she still had another week to go. Colt wasn't happy.

She was actually a bit sad to say goodbye to this one. Since its trip to the mechanic, it had been a lot more reliable.

Colt: How'd she take it?

Indie was about to respond when a figure flashed in her rearview mirror from the back seat. All she saw was dark hair and eyes. She didn't have time to scream before something wrapped around her neck and pulled tight. So tight she couldn't breathe.

Panic clawed at her throat, her hands going to the rope and trying to rip it away, but she couldn't get her fingers beneath it.

A mouth suddenly touched her ear, humid breath against her skin. Then a man's unfamiliar voice. "Where is he?"

He eased the rope off just a fraction so she could speak. "Who?"

The rope tightened again. "Don't fuck with me, woman. I *will* hurt you. Where's Sharp?"

Sharp... *Gordon.*

"Hos...pital," she choked out. "Room two-five-eight."

The rope tightened again, and suddenly she couldn't breathe at all. Not a single breath. Pain cut through her chest, the panic making her heartbeat roar between her ears.

His breath was hot against her ear as he growled, "That asshole owes me money. And if I don't get it from *him*, you better believe I'll be back to take it from his family."

Terror clawed at her insides.

Air. She needed air! It felt like her chest was going to explode. Like the rope around her neck was going to cut her in two and suffocate her at the same time.

Then suddenly, the rope disappeared.

She dropped forward, sucking in huge gulps of air, her hands going to her aching throat. Tears burned her eyes, and even though she could breathe, it still felt like she was choking.

She stumbled out of her car, her chest heaving, fear alive in her bones.

Someone stepped toward her. Another man. He was big, but everything else about him was a blur. She was about to scream when he spoke.

"Hey, are you okay?"

She collapsed into his arms, and he caught her.

* * *

"How the hell did you guys get this done so quickly?" Colt asked as he looked at the finished office. There was fresh paint. New carpet. A big window, which gave a view of the mountains. They just needed the reception desk and some more furniture for the attached office and they'd be done.

But it wasn't just the office that was finished—the entire park would be ready to open in the next month.

He hadn't been here nearly as much as he'd wanted to be, but he'd tried to make up for that in the last week since his dad had been arrested.

"I've got a great group of guys," Randy said, crossing his arms.

Noah's gaze ran over the mountains outside. "I can't believe we're doing it."

"You'd *better* be doing it after all that work." Randy chuckled. "We're still waiting on your signage, but most things are ready to go. The zip line. The mountain bike trails. The cabins. You still organizing a food truck?"

"I haven't advertised yet, but I will," Noah answered.

"What about staff?"

"We've spent the last few weeks interviewing," Colt said. Not that there'd been too many candidates. In the small town of Amber Ridge, there were only so many people looking for work.

"We've got enough to get us started," Noah confirmed.

"Am I still meeting the new receptionist today?" Colt asked.

Noah looked at his watch. "She's due any minute. I'm going over the website she's started building with her."

At that exact moment, a short blonde stepped in. She looked young, but that was expected. How old had Noah said she was? Twenty-two?

A smile widened on Noah's face. "Addison, hey."

"Hi, Noah. And please, call me Addie."

"Addie, meet Randy, the man responsible for the magic of this park coming together so quickly. And my partner, Colt."

She shook his and Randy's hands. "It's nice to meet you both."

"You too." Colt frowned. "Are you new in town?"

"I am, but I'm from Bozeman. A good excuse to try living in a new area and meeting some new people without going too far. Plus, I love this outdoorsy kind of stuff."

Colt took in her makeup, the perfectly curled hair, and the fake long nails. Didn't exactly scream *outdoorsy*, but maybe he was wrong. "Well, it's good to have you on the team."

"Thanks. It's good to be here." She nibbled her lip and glanced behind her out the door. There was something about the way she did it, a hesitation that made Colt frown. Was she feeling uneasy?

Noah cleared his throat. "Would you like to go into the office? There are some drawers we can use as a makeshift desk."

She chuckled. "Sure."

Noah turned to Colt. "Want to join us?"

"I'm just going to take a walk around first."

"Got it."

The second the two of them disappeared into the office, Randy whistled quietly. "Watch those two. I see a little some-thing-something in their future."

Colt frowned. "What are you talking about?"

"You didn't see it?" Randy shook his head. "Guess I've been watching too many of those rom-coms with the missus. I'm going to check on my guys."

Colt's gaze flashed back to the office door. No. It couldn't be right. She was too young for Noah.

He stepped outside and his phone dinged with a text message.

Indie: I have to tell you something.

Shit. What was wrong?

Colt: Are you okay?

Indie: Yes, but your mom overheard me talking to Clara. She knows about the pregnancy. I'm sorry.

Colt: Why are you sorry?

Indie: Because you should have been able to tell her.

No. Not him—*them.* He'd planned for both of them to tell her together.

Colt: How'd she take it?

He waited a second for her response as he walked down the path. When it didn't come through, he stopped.

Colt: You still there?

Nothing. Not even the dots to say she was responding. She might have gotten distracted with something or someone, but after the few weeks they'd had, he doubted she'd leave him hanging.

The sudden need to hear her voice drowned out every other concern.

He called her cell. It rang. No one answered. What the hell was going on?

He opened the Find My Friend app on his phone to see she was in the parking lot behind the print shop.

He was moving before he could stop himself, heading straight to his car. He didn't care that he was probably overreacting. He didn't care that his father was under watch at the hospital. He *needed* to see her. He needed to know that she was okay.

He sped into town, breaking every damn speed limit he passed. When he finally got there, what he saw made blood roar between his ears.

Indie was sitting on the steps at the back of a shop. She was leaning forward, and her back was heaving, like she was breathing fast.

A man was kneeling in front of her, his hands on her shoulders.

It wasn't until Colt was parked and out of his car that he realized he knew the guy. He'd met him.

The new gym owner—Zane.

"What the fuck are you doing touching her?" Colt shouted, as he closed the distance between them.

The man looked up, standing, but it was Indie who made Colt's blood run cold. Her cheeks were tear-stained, her neck red like fire.

The fuck?

He grabbed Zane by the shirt and shoved him into the building. "What the fuck did you do?"

"Colt, stop!" Indie shouted, jumping to her feet.

"Did he hurt you?" Colt growled, his hand already fisted and cocked, ready to hit the asshole.

Zane didn't react. Not a single fucking muscle. "I saw her climbing out of her car like this. I came to help."

Colt froze. "What?"

"It's true," Indie rasped. "He called the sheriff's office and was waiting with me. I was going to call you once I caught my breath."

Colt's hands dropped and he turned to her. "What happened?"

A sheriff's car raced into the parking lot, closely followed by another car carrying two deputies.

Jesse ran out and stopped beside Indie. "Hey, what's going on?"

Her eyes filled with tears.

Fuck. Colt wrapped his arms around her, just holding her. Then, softly, he urged her back down to the steps. Both he and Jesse knelt beside her.

"What happened?" Colt asked again, trying to keep his voice gentle when it was the last thing he felt.

"I climbed into my car, where I was texting you, and suddenly a rope was around my neck. It was a man. He wanted to know where Gordon was. I told him, and he told *me* that if he doesn't get the money he's owed, he'll be back to get it from Gordon's family."

That familiar rage crawled up Colt's throat, begging to break free.

Indie had been hurt again. Threatened. She could have been *killed*.

"Did you get a look at the guy?" Jesse asked gently.

Indie shook her head, more tears in her eyes. "All I saw was dark hair and dark eyes. Then he put the rope around my neck and I just panicked. I'm sorry."

"Hey. You have nothing to be sorry about." Colt cupped her cheek, and when one tear fell, he swiped it with his thumb. "You got out of it and you're alive. That's all you had to do."

"I'm pretty sure I saw the guy get onto a Harley-Davidson Road Glide," Zane said. "He was parked in the side alley."

Colt rose. "You saw him, but you didn't grab him?"

"I saw a guy running and jumping onto a bike. Thought he looked suspicious. Came into the parking lot, saw she wasn't doing too good. Decided the guy was probably gone, and thought it was best to stay with her and make sure she was okay."

It made sense. And the anger wasn't really aimed at Zane. It was all on himself.

Jesse asked, "You get a license plate or description?"

"Guy was six two, brown hair, athletic build. License plate A-B-Q two-two-four."

One of Jesse's deputies wrote it down while Jesse nodded. "Appreciate it."

Colt lowered in front of Indie again. "We're going to the hospital."

She touched a hand over her belly, eyes widening. "Do you think—"

"I think we shouldn't worry, but it's best just to get checked out."

She nodded quickly before leaning into him, and he just spent another moment holding her.

CHAPTER 28

$\mathcal{C}$olt climbed out of his Audi. The hospital was the last place he wanted to be. He should be home with Indie, making sure she was resting. But after what happened yesterday, he needed to talk to his father. He had words he needed the man to hear. Questions he needed answers to. Whether he'd get those answers though, he wasn't sure.

The bruises on Indie's neck were on constant replay in his mind. She'd told him she wasn't in pain. But there was no way she wasn't hurting. And he saw that in small moments when she thought he wasn't watching. In subtle flickers of unease. In the way she cringed when she touched her neck.

He stepped inside and strode down the hall.

Everything about the previous day felt like a nightmare he couldn't escape. Hell, everything involving his father from the last month and a half felt like a nightmare.

It was time for it to end...all of it.

He rounded a corner to see Jesse and one of his deputies standing outside a room. Jesse wore a grim expression, but then, Colt had expected it. Jesse didn't want him here, but Colt had pushed. Thank fuck Jesse had agreed.

"You sure you want to do this?" Jesse asked, the second Colt stopped in front of him.

"No. I need to."

Jesse's brows drew together. "Can I trust you to be in there by yourself?"

"He's cuffed to the bed. There's not much he can do."

"I'm not worried about him."

"As much as I want to make him hurt for the things he's done, I won't." But only because he couldn't afford to be arrested when Indie needed him.

Jesse stared him down. "Okay. Go. But, Colt…be careful. He's going to try to get a reaction out of you."

Colt knew that. He was expecting it.

He pushed through the door to see his father on a bed in the center of the room, his right hand cuffed to the frame, his foot raised and bandaged.

Gordon's brow lifted, almost looking amused. "You finally decided to come see your old man?"

"Who do you owe and how much do you owe them?"

His father sighed. "Not even a hello?"

"Answer the question, Gordon."

"I take it they paid you a visit."

Colt stepped forward, not feeling anything but revulsion for this man. "You know what I don't understand? How did my mother ever see anything redeemable in you? How did she ever look at you and think, yes, this guy is someone I want to spend time with? Make a family with. *Love*. Because when I look at you, I see nothing but scum."

"Your mother saw who I *wanted* her to see. A good guy. Husband material. *Father* material. She had money. I didn't." He lifted a shoulder. "It's as simple as that."

Simple? Nothing about that sounded simple. Manipulative. Underhanded. Psychotic. *Those* words fit better. "So you openly admit to using her."

"I admit that when I met your mother, I saw what she could do for me. I saw all the ways she could support my addiction. I saw everything I could get out of her. I also saw how much she wanted a man in her life. She was easy prey."

"Yet you couldn't manage to keep her."

"The bitch cut me off. Do you know what they did to me the day those assholes came to our house, wanting that money from me? They cut off my right fucking toe!"

Was Colt supposed to feel sorry for him? "You got into bed with criminals. What did you expect?"

"I *expected* your mother to support her fucking husband! To give me the money I needed to get them off my back. Instead, she kicked me out. Hired that asshole protection of hers, who forced me to sign divorce papers. It was *her* fault, all of it!"

He was delusional.

His phone vibrated with a text. He pulled it out and scanned the screen.

Jesse: I know who attacked Indie.

He shoved his cell back into his pocket before looking back at Gordon. "Actually, it was *your* fault. Everything you've ever done in your life has gotten you exactly where you are. You deserve everything that's happened to you."

That anger returned to his father's face. It was unfiltered and unhinged. "You say shit like that to me, yet you expect me to offer information?"

"You were never going to tell me anything."

"So why are you here?"

"To tell you in person that I will do everything in my power to make sure you spend the rest of your useless life rotting in prison. And if you ever *do* get out and try to hurt anyone I love again, you'll either be sent straight back behind bars or straight into the ground."

His father tried to pull at his restraints, anger reddening his cheeks. "You have no idea what I'm capable of!"

"I do—and it's very little. Because you're *nothing*. You've *always* been nothing." Colt turned.

"Get back here, kid!"

Colt ignored him and stepped into the hall.

Jesse frowned. "Everything okay?"

"Same shit, different day. What did you find?"

Jesse shot his gaze to the door, then back to Colt. "We ran the plates of the Harley-Davidson. The owner is a Roman Korr. He's been in the system before. He works for a guy named Chester Vane, who runs an unofficial lending operation."

"Do you have his location?"

"It's going to take a bit of time, but my team's working on it."

Colt's jaw clenched, frustration throbbing at his temple. "Is my father going to be in here much longer?"

"There was a complication with the surgery. He needs to go back under. The doctor said another week or so."

Jesus Christ. He just needed this to be over.

* * *

"HOW ARE YOU FEELING?"

Indie rolled Noah's question around her head as she watched him move in her kitchen from where she sat on the couch. "About the pregnancy or the guy who attacked me in my car?"

A darkness slipped over Noah's face. It looked eerily similar to the one Colt had worn since yesterday.

He filled a saucepan with milk. "Both."

"Well, in regards to the pregnancy, I throw up every morning. I've realized that hunger is not my friend, so I've actually started keeping dry crackers on me wherever I go. And don't even get me started on the exhaustion. But at the same time, the symptoms are almost comforting, like my body's reminding me it's making a baby and doing what needs to be done."

"That's great. After everything you've done to get here, you deserve it." A frown formed between his brows as he added cocoa powder to the pan. "And the other stuff?"

"I've been trying not to think about it." Although, she was not always successful. This morning, she'd made Colt check the back seat of the car three times before she felt safe enough to get in. *Three.* That fear probably wouldn't go away for a while.

"You know you're safe with Colt, right?"

Was the fear as thick in her voice as it felt in her chest? "I know. I'm mostly scared something will happen to me and hurt the baby."

Even thinking about the possibility made a shudder crawl down her spine.

"Nothing is going to hurt you or the baby." The ringing of Noah's cell cut through the room. "Hang on, it's Addie." Instead of putting the cell to his ear, he hit speaker while he continued to prepare the hot cocoa. "Addison, everything okay?"

"Addie," the voice on the phone corrected.

Indie frowned at the instant smile on Noah's face. Did he call her that, knowing she preferred Addie? Just to get a reaction out of her?

"Addie. What's happening?"

"I'm just finalizing details for the opening party and someone named Burt called. He offered to donate some pizza—"

"No!"

Indie chuckled under her breath.

Addie was quiet for a second. "Really? He seemed really nice. He won't charge you. Said something about how proud he was of you and Colt."

"Addison—"

"Addie."

"Here's my pro tip, now that you're living in Amber Ridge. Don't eat Burt's pizza. *Ever.* Don't even smell it. It's not like any of the pizza in Bozeman. In fact, I would go so far as to say it's the worst pizza in Montana. Maybe America."

"It can't be—"

"It is."

Oh, it definitely was.

"Um. Okay. I'll let him know we don't need any."

"But say it nicely. In fact, don't worry about it. I'll call him tomorrow. I like Burt."

"You like Burt, but not his pizza?"

"Yeah, he's great."

"Uh…okay. I'll leave it with you, then."

"Good. Everything else okay?"

"Yeah. It's been easy. You've left some great notes."

"I *have* been told that I'm the master of note leaving. Call if you need anything else."

"I will."

Noah hung up, another ghost of a smile on his face as he lifted two mugs and carried them into the living room.

"Who told you you're the master of note leaving?" Indie asked, unable to wipe the smile from her own face.

"Plenty of people."

Yet he couldn't name a single one of them. She took the steaming cup of cocoa from his outstretched hand. "I'm sure that's what it is."

He lowered beside her. "What *what* is? And why are you smiling like that?"

"You like her."

He scoffed. "She's younger than me."

"You like her."

"She works for me."

"You *like* her."

He shook his head. "Can we talk about something else?"

He liked her. She didn't need his confirmation to know she was right.

She lifted her mug and sipped the warm liquid. It was good. Really good. But that shouldn't surprise her. Her brother was good at everything. Had been his entire life. Someone should really hurry and wife the guy up.

"Okay," she finally answered, the smile falling from her mouth as she said her next words. "I don't believe you're doing as well with the fact that you're not a Marine anymore as you want people to think."

There was a small tightening of his eyes. "I'll *always* be a Marine, Indie. Once a Marine, always a Marine."

"Okay, I'll rephrase. I don't think you're doing as well being home as you want me to believe."

"Indie—"

"And if you don't want to talk about it, that's okay. But I need you to know that I'm here if you ever do want to talk."

He scrubbed a hand over his face, and she noticed the scar peeking out from beneath the short sleeve of his shirt, on his biceps. It was long and red, like it was still kind of new.

"What's that?" She leaned forward to touch it, but Noah shot off the couch. "Noah—"

"It's nothing."

"It's not *nothing*. It's a scar!"

"People get scars in the military, Indie. It happens." There was a thread of something in his voice. Annoyance, maybe? It wasn't like him at all.

"That looked like a knife wound," she said quietly.

"I'm going to do a perimeter check."

Before she could say anything more, he was out the front door.

What the hell was that? Why was he acting so strange at the mention of a scar?

She had questions, and it was so unlike Noah to not tell her things.

The questions were still flickering through her mind when his phone rang from the table. She glanced at the screen...and her muscles immediately locked.

Bonnie.

She hadn't spoken to her sister in years. Thirteen, in fact. It had been thirteen years.

Slowly, she reached for the phone and pressed it to her ear. "Bonnie?"

Silence. It filled the line. Then, "Indie?"

Bonnie's voice...it made immediate tears gather in her eyes and a million emotions rise in her chest. Some good. Most sad.

She swallowed the lump in her throat. "How are you?"

"I'm okay. What are you doing answering Noah's phone?"

"He, um, stepped outside. I saw your name on the screen and..." And what? Wanted to talk to her? Ask her where she was and why she hadn't come home in thirteen years?

"Congratulations," Bonnie said.

Indie frowned. "What?"

"Noah told me you're pregnant."

He had? "When?"

"Last night."

"Oh. You talk regularly?"

"Lately, yes."

How often was regularly? Weekly?

"I've called most days in the last week," Bonnie explained.

Hurt kicked at her ribs, but she wasn't sure why. Noah had told her they were talking, but not daily.

"I should go."

"Bonnie, wait—"

But her sister had already hung up.

The door opened, and Noah stepped in.

"All clear," he said, as he locked the bolt. When he stepped into the room, he looked down at the phone in her hand. "Everything okay?"

"Bonnie called."

"Really? And you spoke to her?"

"I did. She mentioned you've been talking daily."

He ran a hand through his hair. "Indie...I wanted to tell you."

"Tell me what? That you've been talking to our sister so often? That's between you two."

"She asked me not to say anything."

More hurt. But maybe it shouldn't. Of *course* she didn't want Indie to get involved.

Noah crossed the room and sat beside her. "I'm sorry. But I was scared that if I didn't agree, she'd cut contact."

She swallowed hard. "Is she okay?"

"She seems happy. And safe."

Indie nodded. "Good. That's good."

Noah's brows flickered before he touched her knee. "Hey. Are *you* okay?"

"Yeah. I just haven't heard her voice in a long time, and I had so many questions, but she couldn't wait to get off the phone with me."

"I'm sure that's not true."

"It was."

He squeezed her knee. "I'm going to get her home."

"How?" The word was barely a whisper.

"I'm not sure yet. But I will. Trust me."

She did. She trusted her brother with her life. It was her sister she was worried about.

CHAPTER 29

"We don't have to go."

Indie capped the blush stick and turned to look at Colt in the doorway. He stood, hands in his pockets, eyes intense as he watched her. "Of course we have to go. You, Noah, Randy, and his team have worked so hard to get the park ready. We're not missing the opening party."

"We've also worked hard to keep you safe." He took a step toward her that almost felt predatory, his gaze lowering to her neck. The bruises were barely visible under the thick concealer.

"I'm sorry Jesse hasn't found the guy yet." Technically *guys*, plural…if you counted both the man who'd attacked her in the car and the guy he worked for.

She swallowed hard, trying not to let Colt see the fear. He had enough to deal with.

He closed that last bit of space between them to stand behind her, then he curved his arms around her waist. "I want this to be over. I want you to be safe and for us to not have to look over our shoulders every second of every day." His palm flattened on her belly. "I want us to be able to focus on our family."

She set a hand over his. "We will."

"I hate him for this."

Colt didn't need to explain that "him" was his father. She knew. She turned and cupped his cheek. "I'm sorry."

"You don't need to be sorry about anything. You are the best thing in my life, Indie. You're the reward for the all the shit I've had to live through." A small smile stretched his mouth. "You and Peanut."

"Peanut? I thought the baby was Dumpling?" At least, that's what he'd called them at their scan earlier that week. The one where they'd gotten to hear their baby's heartbeat, and she'd cried so many tears she thought she'd never stop.

He lifted a shoulder. "I'm liking Peanut more. She's pretty small."

Indie's heart thumped. "She?"

"I'm feeling girl."

"Really?"

"Yeah. With green eyes. Beautiful long waves in her hair."

If hearts could explode, that was exactly what hers would be doing. "I was kind of hoping for a boy with dark eyes."

He lowered his head, his mouth hovering over hers. "That can be our second."

Second...she could barely believe they were pregnant with a first. Two felt out of reach right now. But before she could overthink anything, he kissed her. And she sank into him. This man made her want to believe in the unbelievable. He made her want things that, a week ago, she'd been too scared to want.

His tongue ran across the seam of her lips. She opened and he slid inside, tangling his tongue with hers.

A deep, primal growl slipped from his chest before he turned them and pressed her to the wall. "We're staying home."

His hand had just inched beneath her shirt when she gave his chest a big shove. "We absolutely are not. This is important. Plus, I want to meet Addie."

"Addie?"

She slipped past him, grabbed her phone, and popped it into her purse. "Yeah, your new receptionist slash IT woman slash whatever else she does."

"Why do you want to meet *her*?"

"Because I'm ninety percent sure my brother has a thing for her." She moved to the door. "Actually, ninety-five percent sure. So, pretty certain."

"You're the second person to say that. What am I missing?"

"You're not missing anything. You just don't have my sisterly intuition."

He shook his head, but there was a hint of a smile on his face.

The second they stepped outside though, that smile dropped. He tugged her closer and his gaze scanned the street, like he was searching for danger. She didn't miss the way his hand hovered over his concealed holster.

The drive to the park was quick, with Indie filling the quiet by talking about the photos she was editing. She'd become really good at trying to distract Colt lately. And even though he engaged with the conversation, she knew his mind was always partly on their surroundings. On making sure they were safe.

The great thing for her was that business had picked up over the last few weeks. She'd booked more shoots in the last month than she had in the entire last year. Maybe the rumors were finally dying down.

When Colt reached across and held her hand, she ran her finger over his gold wedding ring. "So...I have to tell you something."

Colt shot her a look, concern in his eyes. "What is it?"

"I've lost my wedding ring."

"You lost it?"

She cringed. "I put it away somewhere safe and...I don't know where it is! I've searched every box in the spare room so many times. I even checked the outside shed. I don't know what happened, I—"

"Hey. It's okay. It's just a ring."

"No. It was your *grandmother's* ring. It's been in your family for generations."

He pulled into a parking spot at the park and turned to her. "It's just a piece of jewelry. Besides, if you put it away, then it has to be somewhere. I'll help you look again."

"You're not mad?"

"At you? Not possible."

She scoffed. Because it definitely was possible. But at least he didn't seem upset. "Thank you."

He lifted her hand and kissed it, causing a shiver to roll down her spine.

Then she turned and looked at the entrance sign to the park. "Wow. It brings back so many memories."

"I know. I feel fourteen years old every time I come here."

"Back when you were hopelessly in love with me but didn't know it yet?"

"Oh, I knew it."

They'd gone to the same school since they were kids but didn't start dating until high school.

"But, if I remember correctly," Colt said slowly, "it was *you* who asked *me* to go to the tenth-grade dance with you."

"The only first move I ever had to make."

He leaned forward. "I've been chasing you ever since." He kissed her.

It was only a knock on the glass that had them separating. Noah stood outside, a grin on his face.

Indie climbed from Colt's Audi and hugged her brother. "Congratulations."

"Thanks, Inds. And thanks for the photos you took for the advertising. They're great."

She lifted a shoulder. "I barely had to edit them, the place looks so good."

Colt walked around the car and shook Noah's hand. "Hey."

"Ready?"

"To open the place we've slaved over for the last two months? Absolutely."

Colt set a hand on the middle of her back, and they headed down the path. As they moved, her brother and husband continued their conversation, but she didn't miss their covert scans of the forest. And God, it just made her so damn mad. That a day that should be a celebration for both of them was tainted by Colt's father's actions.

When they reached the cabins, Indie couldn't stop the smile from spreading across her face. Everything looked perfect. The freshly oiled wood. The lit firepit surrounded by the cabins.

There was also music and a good crowd. A big food table and balloons.

But then Indie's gaze caught on something else. Or more accurately, *someone* else. The pretty blonde by the food table. The one Noah was walking straight toward.

That had to be Addie.

Indie watched the way Noah's eyes softened when he spoke to her. The almost nervous fiddling of Addie's hands.

"Don't," Colt whispered.

She looked up at him innocently. "Don't what?"

He gave her a pointed look. She, of course, ignored it and walked over to her brother, dragging Colt behind her.

Noah stepped back. "Addison, this is my sister, Indie. She's also Colt's wife. Indie, this is Addison, our new right hand."

The other woman extended said hand. "Hi, Indie. I go by Addie."

"It's nice to meet you, Addie. I hear you're new in town."

"I am. Although, I only come from Bozeman, so not far."

"Bozeman is beautiful."

Addie's brows rose. "You've been?"

"Of course. Their pizza makes ours taste like cardboard.

Although, that's not hard. And I love the mac and cheese from Montana Ale Works."

Addie sighed. "Oh, I miss their mac and cheese. It was a weekly order for me."

A mac and cheese fan. She distinctly remembered that had been one of Noah's favorite foods growing up. If that wasn't a sign of a good match, she didn't know what was.

* * *

It was crazy that in the middle of everything they were going through, Colt could be smiling. But it was hard not to. The park was filled with everyone he loved. Indie. All of his closest friends. Randy's entire team. They could have easily fit more, but smaller was smarter right now.

If it were up to him, he would have canceled altogether. But Indie was right—with him, Noah, Jesse, Becket, and Holden all in the same spot, this should be the safest place in Amber Ridge.

"How are you doing?" Becket asked as he came to stand beside Colt.

He lifted a shoulder, the cold bottle of beer in his hand still full. "I'll be better when there isn't anyone out there gunning for my family members." His gaze landed on Indie. She was standing with Sky, Aspen, Clara, and her aunt Pam. There was also a dog that followed Sky everywhere. It wasn't exactly the cutest dog he'd ever seen, but it seemed to adore Sky and Becket.

"This town is a magnet for trouble," Becket said under his breath, as he lifted his own beer to his lips.

Colt shot a look at his friend. He and Sky had also found themselves in danger not long ago. Apparently, it was bad, and they'd both barely gotten out of it with their lives. "Are you and Sky doing okay?"

"Better than okay. I love that woman."

Colt nodded toward the dog by Sky's feet. "I see you got a dog."

Becket chuckled. "We did. And you know, I'm not hating it."

"Really? I thought dogs weren't your thing."

"They're not. But Bella is." Becket turned to him. "Hey, I don't think I've congratulated you in person, brother. Congratulations, you're going to be a dad!"

"Thanks. It feels surreal. We spent so long trying and being told we couldn't make a baby, and now, suddenly, Indie's pregnant."

"Maybe that wasn't the right time, but this is."

He could have laughed. This was the *worst* time. Indie had been threatened. Their lives were still in danger. Which made protecting her even more important.

Becket gripped his shoulder. "You know we're all looking out for her, right? She's family."

"I know. I just hate that we have to. She should be safe to walk the street on her own."

"I've felt that frustration, brother. I know it well."

Someone walking through the trees had Colt straightening. Then he realized who it was.

Burt. Not only Burt but also his nephew Pete, who worked as his delivery driver. And they were holding pizza boxes. A lot of them.

Jesus Christ.

"You ordered pizza from Burt?" Becket laughed.

"No." He wove through the crowd, but Addie got there first.

"Um, hi. Who are you?"

"I'm Burt." He smiled at her, his voice loud and larger than life. He still wore his red apron from the shop.

She shook her head. "No. I'm sorry. I explained you didn't need to bring pizza."

"Didn't need to? This is for Colt and Noah. They're family. I *had* to."

"But—"

Noah touched Addie's arm. "No, it's okay."

"My boys!" Burt shouted. "You reopened the park! I would hug you but…pizza."

Colt chuckled. "It was nice of you to do this."

"Of course. Like I said, I had to." He looked back at his nephew. "Come on, Pete."

Pete wore his usual bored expression as he followed his uncle to the food table.

Addie turned to them. "I swear I told him not to come."

"I believe you." Noah sighed. "It's fine."

"Burt means well," Colt agreed.

"Although, now he'll stay, and we'll actually have to eat it," Noah said with a frown. "That could be a problem."

"I can sneak slices away while he's not watching," Addie said. "Stash them somewhere."

Noah grinned. "I knew you'd be a good fit here."

"I'm sure I can wrangle some more people to help you," Colt added.

Addie checked her watch. "It's almost time for you guys to speak. Are you ready?"

"Speak?" Colt asked. Who the hell said anything about speaking?

"Just a quick thank you," Noah said like it was nothing.

Of *course* Noah knew about this. So why the hell hadn't he said anything?

Addie moved over to the music and turned it down before lifting a microphone. "Hi, everyone. If I could have your attention?"

The crowd quieted.

"I'm Addie. I take care of the admin side of things here. And I'd like to call up Noah Hayes and Colt Reed, the new owners of the park and the men responsible for the reopening!"

The crowd roared and cheered, and Colt was pretty sure he heard Becket hooting. He followed Noah toward Addie.

Noah spoke first. Because of course he did. He'd probably rehearsed an entire speech. He covered all the main points, thanking Randy's team, mentioning everyone who'd contributed to the opening.

As Noah spoke, Colt found Indie in the crowd again. She was watching him, a soft smile on her face. And he felt the same thing he always felt when he looked at her. Love. But not the kind that just lived in the heart. It took over every part of him. His bones. His blood. It was all he felt sometimes.

When Noah handed the microphone to Colt, there wasn't much more to add. "I think Noah covered most of what needed to be said, but he's always been the more organized of the two of us." The crowd chuckled. "I will add that there's one person who has helped me get here...my wife."

He watched as her smile widened.

"Indie, you're my best friend. And I've made some pretty crappy decisions in my life, but coming home to you was the best one by far. Well, second to loving you."

There was an audible sigh from the crowd.

"This park may be under my and Noah's names, but it has your fingerprints all over it," Colt finished. "I love you, Cricket."

The crowd clapped, and tears gathered in Indie's eyes.

Then someone from his peripheral vision caught his attention. His brows flickered at the sight of his mother, Ben by her side. She wasn't supposed to be here.

He gave himself a mental shake as he returned his attention to the crowd. "Have a good evening, everyone. And eat—there's so much food!"

He handed the microphone back to Addie. She turned the music back on, and the crowd returned to their conversations while Colt wove through the group, his gaze never leaving Indie. She met him halfway.

"That was beautiful," she whispered.

"*You're* beautiful." He gripped her hip. "I know I've brought a lot of baggage to our marriage with my parents—"

She touched a finger to his lips. "I love you, and nothing your parents do or say has anything to do with that. I love *you.*"

"I never had a good example of a father, and he never showed me how a good husband was supposed to act. But I will spend my life trying to do better than him."

Sadness flickered through her eyes. "You are nothing like that man. You're the best husband, and you'll be an amazing father. I know that because I know *you.*"

She said it with so much certainty. Like it was a guarantee.

He lowered his head and kissed her, letting her soft lips smooth the jagged edges of his nerves.

When he lifted his head, frustration slipped into his tone. "My mother's here."

"I saw her. You should talk to her."

"I never get out of that talk feeling good."

"Maybe tonight will be different."

Maybe. Maybe not. "Come with me."

"I would but...this is your night. I don't want to make this about her and me. I'll wait here with the girls."

He kissed her temple before heading toward his mother. She held a glass of champagne and was looking over her shoulder.

"Looking for Ben?" he asked.

His mother turned back to him. "No, someone just bumped into me. Didn't even apologize. Gosh, some people are rude." She shook her head. "Anyway, Ben's just talking to someone. You know how much he loves to chat."

Colt nodded slowly. "I didn't know you were coming."

"Margaret at the grocery store mentioned it." Hurt tinged her voice that he hadn't told her. But had she expected him to invite her? As far as he was aware, nothing had changed.

"Are you staying safe?" he asked.

"Thanks to Ben. Are you and Indie?"

"We are."

"And…the baby?"

"Baby's good. We heard the heartbeat yesterday. It was strong."

His mother's eyes widened. "Wow. That's…I mean, it must have been very special, especially after all you two have been through."

"It was."

She nodded quickly. "Well, I'm sure you have lots of people to talk to. I'll go find Ben. I just wanted to come and support you. I love you, dear. And I'm proud of you."

"I love you too, Mom. And thanks."

She touched his arm before walking away.

Was it possible she was finally coming around? She'd asked about Indie. Asked about the baby and acknowledged how hard it was to get here.

Time would tell.

He was just heading back to Indie when a flash of movement in the trees caught his attention.

He stopped, his gaze narrowing.

Then he saw it again. A man. Just a blur because he was running away.

Fuck.

Colt took off, sprinting toward the forest. A voice shouted his name. Either Becket or Jesse, he wasn't sure. He didn't stop or slow.

He sprinted around trees and leapt over roots. Wind whipped across his skin and his heart pounded in his chest. He ignored all of it.

He could just see the guy ahead. The distance between them was shortening.

Then the sound of a motorcycle roared.

There was a road ahead.

No.

He pushed his body to move faster, needing to catch this guy. Needing this to end.

But he hadn't yet reached the road when he saw the asshole jump behind someone on the back of a bike and the two people rode away.

He'd lost him. *Shit!*

Jesse stopped beside him and was already pulling his cell from his pocket and calling the station.

Colt cursed again, his hands on his head. He wanted to fucking hit something.

When Jesse hung up, he looked at Colt. "What the hell was he doing here?"

"I don't know." He had no fucking clue. Watching?

But his gut told him it was more than that.

CHAPTER 30

*I*ndie glanced at Colt. His fingers were wrapped so tightly around the wheel that his knuckles were white. Everything about him was hard and angry and almost felt unreachable.

The second he'd returned to the party, he'd swept her away.

Why tonight? Why did those jerks have to ruin it for him?

"How are you doing?" she asked quietly, her voice sounding loud in the quiet car.

The muscles in his forearms flexed. "I don't like that I don't know what he was doing there."

"Maybe he was waiting for a chance to grab someone but was scared off by you and Jesse?"

Colt shook his head. "I think there was more to it."

She touched his thigh, feeling the muscles in his leg ripple beneath her palm.

When they reached the house, Colt got out first, Glock in hand as he circled the car. He helped her out, but his gaze didn't stop moving, continually scanning the street.

They stepped inside, and Colt checked every inch of the house before he let her out of his sight.

When everything was clear, she slipped off her shoes, watching as he holstered his weapon. "I'm sorry we had to leave your party."

"Noah's more the party guy anyway."

She sighed. It was true.

Over the next hour, they heated up some food and got comfortable on the couch. They were on the second episode of *Yellowstone* when Colt's cell rang. He pulled it out to show Ben's name flashing on the screen.

Nerves fluttered in her belly. Was something wrong? He'd only be calling at this time if something was wrong, right? Was it Sylvia?

Colt put the cell to his ear. "Ben, is everything okay?"

There was a pause. Then Colt's jaw tightened.

"We're coming now." He hung up and turned to her. "Mom's in the hospital again. They were driving home when she lost consciousness. Ben's not sure what happened, but she was grabbing her chest before she passed out. It might be her heart."

Air got stuck in Indie's throat. Oh God, that wasn't good.

She turned off the TV and rushed to throw her shoes on.

Neither of them spoke on the drive to the hospital, but Indie didn't move her hand from Colt's thigh. He drove faster than he should have and tension radiated off him.

Was it a heart attack? Something else?

They pulled into the hospital parking lot, and it didn't take them long to find Sylvia's room. Indie's pulse picked up speed at the sight of her so still in the bed, with so many tubes attached to her.

Ben rose from the chair beside her bed.

"Do they know what's wrong?" Colt asked.

"Doctor said she had a severe drop in blood pressure and something called bradycardia, which is a slow heart rate."

Colt's fingers tightened around Indie's. "What was the cause?"

"They're not sure yet. They're running some tests."

Colt's gaze ran over his mother. "Is she going to be okay?"

"She's stable right now."

That wasn't a guarantee.

Indie ran her thumb over the back of Colt's hand, wanting to soothe him. Needing to do something, *anything*, to make this just a bit better. In reality, she knew there was nothing she could do. They just had to wait.

He squeezed her hand before moving to his mother's bedside and touching her arm.

"I think someone did this to her."

Colt swung toward Ben at his quiet statement. "Why?"

"We left shortly after you. Sylvia was acting strange. Stumbling. She seemed confused. But she'd barely drunk anything. We were driving home when she grabbed her chest and passed out. I drove straight here."

He was right, that didn't sound like natural causes.

Colt's phone rang, and he looked at the screen before putting it to his ear. "Jesse."

There was a short pause.

"I'm here at the hospital too. So is Ben. Room twenty-four."

"Jesse's here?" Indie asked, once Colt hung up.

"Yeah. He has something to tell me."

There was something about the way Colt said it...like whatever Jesse had to say, it wasn't good.

Jesus. They did *not* need more bad news right now.

A couple of minutes later, the door opened and Jesse stuck his head in. "Hi. You guys got a sec?"

Colt glanced down at his mother.

"I'll stay with her," Indie said, stepping beside Sylvia's bed. "You guys go."

He lowered his head and kissed her temple. "We'll be right by the door."

When they left the room, Indie touched Sylvia's hand. "It's just you and me, Sylvia," she said softly, studying the woman's face.

"And I'd really like you to wake up because Colt needs his mother. I love him so much, and I am so grateful to you for raising him to be the person he is. I need to show you how grateful I am. And I truly believe that if you spend some time getting to know me, you might just decide that I'm not so bad. Heck, you might even start to like me."

Her lips twitched at the thought. But it was all true.

Sighing, she turned to see the window curtain was open. Instinctively, she moved toward it. It would be dark soon, and privacy was definitely needed right now.

She'd just reached the window when something made noise in the bathroom beside her. It was faint. Like a small shuffle.

She frowned. What was that?

She stepped into the bathroom, glanced at the mirror—and the second she did, Gordon stepped out from behind the door. She didn't have time to scream before he slammed her head against the wall and her world went black.

* * *

"What is it?" Colt asked, as he stepped into the hall.

"One of my deputies spotted Roman and Chester in the parking lot about half an hour ago."

Ben's eyes narrowed.

"Roman was here? Why?" So they'd gone straight from the party to the hospital?

"I don't know. I just got here, and I'm going to go check on your father now, but I wanted to tell you both first."

Colt opened his mouth to say that he wanted to go too, but a man in a white lab coat stepped up to them, clipboard in hand. It was the same doctor he'd met previously.

"Doctor Leeroy," Colt said, before the man could speak.

The doctor dipped his head. "Mr. Reed."

"Do you know what happened to her?"

"We found propranolol in her blood."

"What's that?" Ben asked.

"It's a prescription blood pressure and heart medication, although not a prescription that Sylvia should have. It didn't mix well with her medication and is the reason her heart rate dropped so low and she passed out."

"He drugged her," Jesse said quietly. "Roman."

"That's why he was at the party," Colt growled.

Jesse's phone rang. "Is everything okay?" There was a small pause, then Jesse's eyes flashed up at Colt. "Wade, the deputy I put on your father's door, is gone. And so is Gordon."

Colt's world narrowed. He turned and crashed into his mother's room.

But Indie wasn't there—and the window was open.

No.

He sprinted to the window and jumped straight out, but he saw nothing. Everything was still and quiet around him.

Jesse jumped out after him. "There's blood in the bathroom."

Gone. Indie was gone. And without needing any confirmation, he *knew* his father had her.

CHAPTER 31

*I*ndie groaned. Jesus Christ, her head ached. It felt like someone had taken a hammer to her skull.

She scrunched her eyes before opening them.

Darkness. It surrounded her. Then she noticed other things. The dull rumble of an engine. The gentle vibration beneath her.

She was in a car. The trunk of a car...that was why it was so dark.

How did she get here? *Think, Indie, think!*

They were at the hospital for Sylvia. Colt and Ben stepped out, then...

She gasped.

Gordon. He'd been hiding behind the bathroom door.

Dammit, why had she gone in there? Why hadn't she run out to Colt the second she'd heard something? *Stupid.*

She lifted her hands and pushed on the roof of the trunk. Of course it didn't move. But she still pushed again and again, her movements becoming quick and desperate, until her fists were basically pounding at the metal.

It was only when her hands began to ache that she dropped

her arms and swallowed a sob. She was stuck. Stuck until Gordon decided otherwise.

Panic clawed at her chest. She wasn't a claustrophobic person, but right now, the small space combined with the darkness and the knowledge that she couldn't get out made her want to crawl out of her own skin.

Breathe, Indie. Just breathe.

She closed her eyes, put a hand on her belly, and sucked in one full breath of air.

"It's okay, Peanut. We're going to be okay." Her whispered words sounded loud in the silence. But they were also comforting. A reminder that she was strong, and she *could* figure her way out of this. She had to, for her baby.

What she needed was a weapon.

Blindly, she reached around the trunk. Her fingers ran over cables, clothing...when she touched what felt like a flashlight, she grabbed it, feeling for the switch.

The second it turned on, light blinded her, causing pain to shoot into her skull and her eyes to snap closed. They remained closed for a few seconds before she slowly cracked them open.

Finally, her eyes adjusted. She turned her head. So much stuff, but none of it looked useful.

Hang on...

She reached out and grabbed a spray cannister. It was about the size of a water bottle. She turned it around.

Bear deterrent.

Yes! This could work. If she sprayed it into Gordon's eyes, she might give herself time to get away. Plus, Gordon had just had major foot surgery. He wouldn't be fast. There was a chance she could outrun him.

Hope began to bubble in her chest. But so did another emotion—fear.

Not fear for herself, but fear for the baby. What if she fought him and didn't win? That could put the baby at risk. But then, *not* running could be just as much of a risk.

No. She had to fight.

She just had to trust that she was going to be okay. And the baby was going to be okay.

The dull rumble of the engine stopped. Her breathing hitched, pulse taking off.

This was it. She turned the flashlight off and pointed the cannister up, finger on the lever.

Deep breaths. One...two...three...

The trunk opened and she sprayed the repellent.

Gordon cried out and grabbed his eyes. He keeled over and she forced herself up—until a wave of dizziness had her arms caving and her body falling back into the trunk.

No! She had to get up! Go. *Run.*

She pushed up again, this time locking her elbows. She stumbled out of the car, repellent still in hand, catching herself on a tree before she hit the ground.

Trees. They surrounded her.

She hadn't run far when a strong body crashed into her from behind, sending her to the dirt. She rolled to her back and lifted the repellent, but Gordon slapped it out of her hand before she could press the lever.

Then he pointed a gun right at her stomach.

"Move and I shoot," he growled, his eyes red and swollen.

Her skin went cold. "What do you want with me?"

He laughed, but the sound was manic. "I wanna see what you're worth to my son and ex-wife."

He yanked her up and pressed the gun into her back. "*Walk.*"

She didn't want to. But she also didn't want to get shot. So she walked. "How did you even escape?"

"How do you think? Chester and Roman."

"The men you owe money to?"

"The men I worked for."

She frowned. "You worked for them?"

"Yeah. Until Chester found out I stole from him. The only way to get out of that alive was to tell him about the gold mine my ex and my son were sitting on. So here I am. But they weren't happy when I got arrested."

She glanced over her shoulder. He wasn't just limping from his foot injury—there was blood seeping through his shirt. "Did they do that?"

"Yes." Gordon scowled before shoving the gun between her shoulders again to keep her moving. "Assholes fucking *branded* me. A warning to get them the money."

She frowned. "Did they tell you which room Sylvia was in?"

"Yeah. Smart bastard. Chester probably paid off some nurse. It's how he operates. I was supposed to grab Sylvia. But you were easier to grab. So this worked out better because I have no doubt my boy will pay good money for you."

Anger flared within her. That this man had a son who was good and decent, yet he had a father who only saw what he could get out of him.

"So what now?" Indie asked through gritted teeth.

He shoved the gun into her again. "We keep walking. Although, I should shoot you just for shooting me."

"It kept you out of prison a little longer," she retorted, suddenly remembering that he'd been cuffed to the bed. "What happened to the deputy on your door?"

"Fuck if I know. I don't ask questions."

"No, you just kidnap people."

"If Sylvia and Colt get me the money I need, you'll be free to go."

Would she? In every kidnapping story she'd ever read, the victim was never released once the bad guy got what he wanted. Something Colt would be aware of.

When a small old, falling-down structure came into view, she frowned. "What is that?"

"An old toolshed. It was part of the adventure park. When Colt kicked me out, I came here. They haven't touched it."

That meant they were close to the adventure park. Was anyone still around from the party? Would they hear if she screamed?

"We're too far," Gordon said, reading her mind. "And I'd shoot you and run before anyone got here. You're not leaving unless I get what I want."

"And how much is it that you want?"

He opened the rotting wooden door. Reluctantly, she stepped inside to see old tools, but also a makeshift bed with a thin sheet and a jacket rolled up as a pillow. Two cell phones sat on the counter.

"How much do I want?" Gordon repeated as he stepped in after her and pulled the door closed. "Everything they have."

* * *

COLT COULD BARELY THINK. Indie was gone. Someone had taken her from his mother's hospital room while he'd been right there by the door. It was a nightmare he couldn't wake up from.

And the blood...Jesus Christ. They'd hurt her.

He wanted to kill the asshole. But how the hell had his father escaped? Then how had he known which room his mother was in?

While Jesse had taken him to the sheriff's station, Ben remained with his mother as well as two deputies.

Noah paced beside him. They'd called Indie's brother the second they'd arrived at the station.

Colt forced himself to suck in air even though every breath hurt. A physical ache that competed with the mental and emotional pain.

"Got it," Jesse said from his seat behind his desk as he turned his computer screen.

Colt and Noah stepped forward to see the footage of the hospital hallway. Wade stood by Gordon's door. At first, everything looked normal. Then the deputy glanced at his phone before walking down the hall.

Just walked away.

The *fuck*?

Colt's eyes narrowed when two men passed Wade. Even from the back, Colt knew exactly who they were.

"Roman and Chester," Jesse said under his breath.

Colt leaned forward. "Stop. Can you go back slowly?"

Jesse pressed a few keys.

Colt saw it again. "Your deputy gave them a key."

"The key to Gordon's handcuffs," Noah said quietly.

A vein in Colt's temple throbbed. He watched as Chester stepped into the room while Roman took guard outside. Jesse sped up the video, and a few minutes later, Chester stepped out and the two men left. It was a few more minutes before Gordon came out. His face was pale, and he was holding his stomach.

"How the fuck did no one stop him?" Noah growled.

Not just because Gordon was a prisoner, but because he looked three seconds from passing out.

"The hospital sent this one too," Jesse said, clicking out of that clip and into a different one. The next clip showed Gordon walking straight into his mother's room, and mere seconds later, his mother was wheeled in.

"He knew she was going to be placed in that room," Jesse said quietly.

"How?" Colt wanted to fucking roar the question.

"They paid someone off," Noah said, the fury in his voice matching Colt's.

Jesse's cell dinged with a message, and he lifted it. "They just arrived with Wade."

"He's here?" Colt asked.

"Yes, but—"

Colt didn't listen to whatever Jesse said next. He stormed out of the office just as Wade was entering the building, a deputy on either side of him.

Colt went to grab him, but Jesse and Noah each took an arm.

"Don't," Jesse warned.

"She's gone!" Colt shouted at the pathetic excuse for a deputy. "Indie's fucking gone and it's your fault!"

"I don't know what you're—"

"Don't lie," Jesse cut in. "We have you on video handing them the key to the cuffs."

The guy's face paled. "He threatened my family! What the hell was I supposed to do?"

"You were supposed to tell *me*," Jesse growled. "I could have protected you and your family. Now it's too late."

The deputies pulled him down the hall while Jesse pushed Colt back into his office, and Noah closed the door after them.

"So Chester and Roman drugged my mother at the party, probably bribed a nurse to tell them which room she'd be in, and freed Gordon so he could take her," Colt said, trying to piece together their plan.

"Why?" Jesse asked. "That's so much effort for people who were just after Gordon for money he owed."

"Because Gordon doesn't just owe them money…he works for them." It was the only thing that made sense. "He told them about my mother's wealth. This is a job to them."

"If that's true," Noah said quietly, "then you're about to get a call."

"I've already contacted one of our technology specialists." Jesse lifted his cell and called someone. "Claudia, you ready?" A short pause. "Good."

Colt frowned when he hung up. "You think you can trace the call without a warrant?"

"She's bringing a portable trace unit and a frequency scanner. They won't give us a GPS, but they'll tell us which tower Gordon's hitting, and it will narrow the location down a bit over one square mile."

"That's nothing," Noah said.

Colt nodded. "With Becket and Holden's help, plus the deputies, we'll cover that easily."

A female deputy stepped into the room, laptop bag in one hand, map in the other.

"Colt, Noah, this is Claudia. Claud, we're expecting the call to come to Colt's phone," Jesse said.

"Got it. I've already circled the local cell towers." She handed the map to Jesse before taking out her laptop. "I'm going to connect the call-monitoring software to your phone, Colt, using Bluetooth."

Colt didn't question the woman, just handed it over.

She hit a few keys on her laptop before fiddling with his cell.

"Connected." She handed it back. "I'll log the call's number and try to see the cell tower it came through using my mobile signal analyzer."

Colt didn't have time to try and understand anything she was saying before his phone rang. His spine stiffened as he saw an unknown number.

This was it.

He hit answer and put the call on speaker. "Where is she?"

The deputy silently started hitting keys on her laptop and the machine next to it.

A deep chuckle sounded, and it made Colt's skin crawl. "You'll find out when you get me what I need."

"How much?"

"Ten million wired to an account. I'm going to give you thirty minutes, or I start shooting holes into your pretty wife."

Ten million? Jesus Christ.

His back teeth ground together. "I want to know that she's safe first."

"You don't believe me?"

"Not even a little bit."

Another laugh from his father, then a shuffling noise.

"Colt?"

His eyes shuttered at her voice. The relief it brought him almost sent him to his knees. "You're okay."

"I'm okay. But I'm really wishing we were back at the party. Or close to it at least. Somewhere big enough for just the two of us."

He frowned at her odd statement. "I'm going to get you back, Cricket. I promise."

Another shuffling noise, then Gordon came back on. "There, she's alive. *Now* you ready to get me my money?"

"Give me the damn details. My mother and I will give you everything we own. Just don't hurt her."

"That's the cooperation I was looking for." Gordon relayed the bank details. "Remember, within the half hour or your woman's going to get hurt."

His father hung up, making Colt want to reach into the phone and tear out his fucking heart.

"Got it," Claudia said quickly. She looked up and pointed to one of the circled cell towers. "He's closest to this one."

Colt frowned. That was within three miles of their park.

Indie's words came back to him. "She wished we were back at the party…or close to it."

"And somewhere just big enough for the two of you," Noah finished.

"I thought that was strange too," Jesse added.

"It was a hint." Noah frowned. "She was telling us that they're near the cabins."

"But where?" Jesse asked.

Suddenly, it hit Colt. "Somewhere just big enough for the two of us… The old toolshed!"

"Shit, you're right," Noah finished. "He's probably been sleeping there."

Colt started running, sprinting out of the office and into the cool evening air. They were right about this. The shed wasn't too far. He just had to pray he wasn't too late.

CHAPTER 32

*S*ilence. It surrounded Indie, and God, it felt heavy in the small toolshed. Heavy and dangerous and a bit like a ticking bomb.

Gordon rubbed his eyes. Eyes that were still red and raw from the repellent spray. Then his gaze returned to the cell in his hand. His attention had barely left that thing since he'd ended the call with Colt.

She tugged at the rope around her wrists, trying to loosen the knot or at least give herself a bit of space to pull a hand out. He'd forced her onto a wooden chair and bound her hands behind her but had left her feet untied. Probably because just tying her hands had been such an effort. That spray had really affected him.

Good. She needed him weak. Because Colt would work out the hint she'd given him and figure out where she was, or she'd save herself. Either way, a weakened Gordon was a good thing.

"Are you waiting for the money to hit the account?" she asked, needing to distract him so he didn't realize what she was doing.

"I'm waiting for Chester to confirm he got the transfer."

"Then what?" She wasn't sure she really wanted to know the answer to that, but keeping him talking felt smart right now.

He rubbed his eyes again. "You'll find out when I have the money."

He wouldn't just let her go. There was no way. "Do you ever feel even a little bit of remorse for everything you've done to your ex-wife and son?"

"No." The answer was instant, obviously requiring no deep thought from him. "I've never understood those kinds of emotions. I feel anger. I feel resentment. I've learned to imitate everything else."

That's how he'd convinced Sylvia to marry him? By imitating love?

Jesus. He was so open about his inability to feel anything close to empathy. That was the definition of a psychopath, wasn't it?

Another tug at her bonds. Almost there. A little more and she'd get her hand all the way out.

She eyed the knife on the small table nearby. It was closer to her than it was to him. And if she moved fast enough, she could grab it. She'd prefer the gun, but it was on the other side of him. There was no way she'd get it.

Either he didn't think she'd escape, or he just hadn't been thinking when he'd put it there. Whatever the reason, it was a mistake he'd regret.

"Will this pay your debt to Chester?" she asked quietly.

He scoffed. "That asshole will never let me go. Once you get into bed with Chester, the only way out is in the ground. I was always gonna use the money to run."

"And now?"

"Now I survive until I can come up with another plan."

Indie wiggled her hands in the rope again. Another tiny bit of her hand out. So close.

"Why hasn't he transferred the money yet?" Gordon growled. "He's fucking obsessed with you. He should have transferred it already."

"He doesn't have the amount you're asking for. He'd need to

access Sylvia's money, and she's probably still unconscious from whatever your friends gave her." And they *did* give her something. This entire thing was too well orchestrated.

"Colt would have her bank details. Sylvia always loved that boy too much. He would have access to everything."

One more tug—

Air froze in her lungs. Separated. Her hands were *separated*. She was free.

Gordon's head shot up. "What are you doing?"

Shit. Had she moved? Had she given herself away? "Nothing."

"You're lying. Are you trying to get out of the bindings?"

Now. She had to move now.

He rose.

And she lunged, grabbing the knife and plunging it into his gut.

Shock cut across his face.

She pulled out the knife and kicked him between the legs.

He growled and dropped. Then she was running, shoving outside into the darkened evening and sprinting through the trees.

Branches snapped beneath her feet.

She didn't know where she was going, maybe to a road or toward the park. Maybe to the middle of nowhere. A part of her didn't want to run too far in case Colt worked out where she was, only to find her gone. But she also had to put distance between herself and Gordon.

Her foot hit a tree root, and she fell, hitting the dirt with a thud.

She groaned, the pounding in her head from earlier intensifying as she pushed up, forcing her arms to function.

Something rustled behind her.

A buzzing started between her ears.

Run. She had to run!

She scrambled up. Sprinting through the forest, desperate for a way out. A person who could help her. A hiding spot. *Anything*.

The trees thinned ahead, and she recognized where she was— the edge of the park where the granite cliffs were located, used for rock climbing and bouldering.

Not good. This was not good.

She spun around, scanning the forest.

Bang!

A bullet hit the dirt near her feet. She cried out and ran to the right before diving behind a tree. Then she breathed. Forced the air in and out of her lungs even though the oxygen felt too thin. Trying to silence her fear, which felt like it was going to explode out of her.

She closed her eyes and gripped the knife, listening for any movement, ready to lunge if he got close.

She wasn't sure how much time passed, but there was only silence. Complete silence. The kind where you only heard the wind through the trees.

Had he given up? Gone the other way?

God, please say he had.

A footstep crunched immediately to her right.

She turned and swung the knife.

* * *

BLOOD ROARED between Colt's ears as he sat in the passenger seat of Noah's car. Technically, he and Noah shouldn't even be going to the location. It was the sheriff's job. But nothing and no one could have kept him away. This involved his wife and his father. He *needed* to be there. He needed to make sure she was safe, and that his father paid for his crimes.

He checked his watch. Five minutes until the thirty was up. They had the money, but that wouldn't save Indie. Probably the opposite. The second Gordon got what he wanted, he'd have no use for her. She'd become a loose end.

"If he's hurt her—"

"Then we'll *both* murder him," Noah said under his breath, deadly anger in his voice.

Colt swallowed, the fury spiraling through every limb. Making it hard to move. To breathe.

When they reached the outskirts of the forest, Noah didn't pull into their usual parking spot. Instead, he cut into the trees and drove as far as he could toward the toolshed.

That's when he saw it...a car. Jesse had received a call to say that a Toyota Camry had been stolen from the hospital parking lot. That was it.

"She's here."

Colt shot a glance behind him, seeing Jesse and his deputy Claudia in the passenger seat.

He lifted his Glock, and the second Noah parked the car, he was out.

"We approach the toolshed from different directions," Jesse said, once he and Claudia joined them. "Claudia and I will go from the east and you two go from the west."

They all nodded.

Jesse met Colt's gaze. "We only shoot to save Indie's life. Understood?"

Noah nodded.

Colt's jaw clenched; he didn't want to promise anything. He wanted the asshole dead. He wanted to make sure, with absolute certainty, that the man could never hurt a member of Colt's family again.

But he nodded anyway. They didn't have time to argue.

"Good." Jesse stepped back. "See you in a few minutes."

Colt turned and ran, sprinting through the trees. He'd already studied the map. He knew exactly where to go.

His feet sank into the dirt, the moon casting a dim glow over the path ahead. He pushed himself to move fast, feeling the air whip across his skin.

He let his mind go blank from everything except reaching her. Saving her. Getting her home.

When the shed came into view, he forced himself to slow. He crept through the trees, and when he saw the entrance...he frowned.

The door was open. Why? Had they left?

He crouched low and inched forward, Glock firmly in his hold and close to his body. Noah moved behind him, his steps just as silent as Colt's.

When they reached the shed, Colt stood beside the door and listened. Silence. Then he spun around, Glock pointed.

But there was no one inside. It was empty. Indie wasn't here. Gordon wasn't either.

His eyes narrowed when he spotted blood on the floor. Hers or his?

Noah stepped in behind him. "She escaped."

It sure as hell looked like it. But where had she gone?

They stepped out.

"She's not inside?" Jesse asked, as he and Claudia jogged toward them.

Colt shook his head. "Someone was hurt. I'm hoping Indie broke free and hurt him. But if she did, Gordon will be angry. Probably angry enough to kill."

"So we find them fast," Jesse said. "We split up and we search every inch of this forest until we find them."

"Blood looked fresh," Noah said. "They can't have gone far."

"Good."

Colt scanned the trees closest to the shed. She would have wanted the shelter of those trees as fast as possible. "I'm going this way." He didn't wait for a response, just started moving. Running. Sprinted through the forest to search for her.

A gunshot cracked through the air. His heart jumped into his fucking throat.

Indie.

He sped up, closing the distance between him and where that noise had come from. When he reached the cliffs, he frowned. Where was she? He looked over the edge.

Clear. Thank God.

He turned, eyes narrowing on a single footprint in the dirt. It was barely visible. He inched toward it, Glock close to his body. A thick tree stood a few yards away. It was a good hiding spot.

Two more steps before he darted around it.

A knife flew toward him.

He grabbed Indie's wrist before the blade could make contact.

Her eyes widened. "Colt!" She dropped the knife and flung herself into his arms.

Relief hit him so hard his knees wanted to cave, like the earth was tugging him down. He forced himself to remain where he was, for his arms to lock around her. "You're okay."

"I'm okay. But he's still out here."

The words had barely left her lips when a flicker of movement from the right had his gaze shooting around. Colt flung himself on top of Indie just as a bullet hit the tree beside them.

He rolled them so that Indie was protected by the tree.

"You're not hurt?" he asked, scanning her body.

She shook her head.

"Get the fuck out here, son," Gordon shouted. "Let's end this once and for all."

"You're still holding on to this 'son' shit?" Colt yelled, slowly rising while making sure the tree covered both of them.

"Sorry, kid. You may not like it, but you will *always* have my DNA in you."

"Yet I'll always be better than you. Stronger. Smarter. Tougher." Colt threw a rock at a nearby tree.

"The fuck you will," his father growled, firing a shot.

Colt rounded the tree and pulled the trigger, getting his father in the temple.

Jesse, Noah, and Claudia appeared just as his father dropped.

Dead. The asshole was finally dead.

"Colt," Indie whispered.

He lowered beside her. "Hey."

"You shot him?"

"I did."

She searched his eyes. "Are you okay?"

"That man was not my father. A bit of DNA doesn't make a dad."

Tears filled her eyes. "I'm sorry."

"Why?"

"I heard a sound in the bathroom at the hospital. He was behind the door and hit me. I should have gotten you the second I heard something. I was stupid. I—"

"*No.* You thought you were safe. You *should* have been safe in that room. *I'm* so sorry. Nothing that happened tonight is your fault."

She looked at his father and back to him. "I'm still sorry you had to shoot him."

"I'm not." There was not a single part of him that felt anything but relief. "The world will be a better place without him in it." Then he ran his gaze over her again. To take her in. To remind himself that she was alive. "You're okay."

"I'm okay."

He tugged her into his chest again and breathed her in. Let the feel of her in his arms heal every part of him that had felt broken since she was taken.

CHAPTER 33

"*H*ow are you feeling? And tell me the truth. If you feel like crap, say 'I feel like crap.'"

Indie ran her finger around the rim of her chai spiced latte. She was finally over the coffee-induced nausea and could have kissed Clara's feet when she'd opened the door and seen it in her cousin's hand. "I'm doing good. Colt's been making sure I'm on strict bed rest. And this morning, he told me they're tearing the old toolshed down, which made me feel even better."

She couldn't believe it had already been a week since the kidnapping. A week since she'd stabbed Gordon and run for her life. A week since Colt shot his father. But he seemed to be telling the truth, that killing Gordon really hadn't affected him.

Clara tilted her head. "Are you sure? You went through a lot."

"Positive. It's actually been kind of nice to be waited on hand and foot." Indie chuckled. "Not to mention the daily chai lattes everyone's bringing me." She should actually text Colt to let him know she already had one, because she was ninety percent certain he'd show up with one when he got back from the park.

Usually, she wouldn't say no to two lattes in one day, but

being pregnant, she was trying to limit herself to one or less. It was hard.

"I was more worried about Colt than me," she said quietly. "He shot his dad."

"He had to. If he hadn't, his father would have shot him or you. Or both of you."

"I know. I still hate that it was him who did it."

Clara looked down at her drink. "I think we got really lucky with our parents. Then really *unlucky* when I lost my dad and you lost both of your parents. They were good people. Not everyone has that. And unfortunately, I don't think love's a given."

"Gordon missed out on a great son."

"He really did." There was a small pause before Clara said, "What about your sister? Have you spoken to her since answering her call on Noah's phone?"

"No. I want to reach out, but I'm scared she won't want to talk to me. And maybe I'm a little scared that she'll tell me *I'm* the reason she won't come home."

"Why would you be the reason?"

"I was always so angry at her because she made our parents' lives so hard. She would never do what they asked. Then her boyfriend died and everyone blamed her, and she rebelled further. Then our *parents* died. It was hard for everyone. She didn't need to leave."

"You should tell her."

"I did. After she took off, when I left messages trying to get her to come home. She never responded."

Clara tilted her head. "I'm sorry."

"Me too."

Clara sipped her tea. "Hey, did you ever find your wedding rings?"

"No. I have no idea what happened to them. Colt says we'll replace them, but they were family heirlooms." She straightened. "This has softened the blow though." She leaned down and opened the drawer on the coffee table before lifting out the sono-gram and holding it to Clara.

Clara gasped as she took it. "Peanut!"

The smile on Indie's face grew. "They gave us the printout at the scan. I can't stop looking at it."

Tears gathered in Clara's eyes before she looked at Indie. "I'm so happy for you."

"I was so worried about the baby after the kidnapping—whether the fear, the stress, or the trauma had somehow hurt them. I was terrified I'd lose them before I got a chance to hold them." Her heart raced just thinking about it. "But they're obviously a fighter."

"They're resilient. Just like their mama."

"Thank God, because if something had happened—"

"*Nothing* happened, and nothing *will* happen." Clara leaned forward. "Your baby is happy and healthy. They're perfect."

This time, Indie got teary. She nodded.

A knock on the door had Indie's head jerking up.

Clara frowned. "Expecting someone?"

"Colt should be home soon, but he wouldn't knock." When she looked through the peephole, she stopped breathing for a moment.

Sylvia. She held two containers in her hands.

Colt's mother had dropped by a couple of times in the last week, but he'd always been home. And he'd kept the visits short, thanking Sylvia for the food she'd brought and sending her on her way.

She opened the door. "Sylvia. Hi."

"Hi, dear. Can I come in?"

"Colt's not here."

"That's okay. I'd like to talk to you."

She tried to hide the shock, not sure if this was a good thing or a bad thing. In any case, she stepped back and let Sylvia enter her home. "Sure."

Clara cleared her throat as she rose. "Hello, Sylvia."

"Hi, Clara."

Her cousin crossed the room, and when she hugged Indie, she whispered, "Do you want me to stay?"

"No, I'm okay." If she could handle a kidnapping, she should be able to handle her mother-in-law...

Should.

Clara pulled back and studied her closely, like she was trying to figure out whether to believe it. Eventually, she nodded. "I'll text later."

"Thanks for the latte."

"You've got another coming tomorrow."

When Clara left, the awkward silence in the house made Indie want to squirm.

"Would you like some coffee?" Yes, coffee, that was a good idea. It would keep her hands busy. Indie took a step toward the kitchen.

"No, thank you."

She stopped. Dammit.

"I made you some lasagna and some corn soup," Sylvia said, as she set the dishes onto the kitchen counter.

"Thank you."

Sylvia's gaze landed on something in the living room. Slowly, she walked toward the coffee table and lifted the sonogram. She swallowed hard before setting the print down.

Then, she pulled something out of her pocket and held it out. "I believe these are yours."

It took Indie a moment to realize what she was looking at.

Then she gasped. "My rings."

"Back when you first bought the house, Colt gave me a key. You may not remember, but six months ago, I ran into you and asked about your wedding rings. You said you put them into storage in the spare room." She lifted a shoulder. "I got angry. I felt like they belonged to my family and you weren't with Colt anymore. So I came and I took them when you weren't home."

Unbelievable. She'd stolen them. Not just stolen them. Broken into her house and searched through her things to steal them.

"Take them," Sylvia said gently. "They're yours."

Indie took the rings from her palm, and when she looked at Sylvia again, there were tears in the older woman's eyes before she said, "I'm sorry."

Indie blinked. The two words sounded genuine. "You're sorry?"

"Yes. For everything. For years, I haven't treated you well. I should have welcomed you into my family. When you were going through the hardest battle of your life to become a mother, I should have asked what I could do to help. I should have asked you if you needed support during your medical appointments and brought you meals."

Indie almost wanted to press a hand to her chest to stem the ache. She'd craved those words for so long. So many times, she'd wondered what *she'd* done wrong. What *she* could have done differently.

Sylvia stepped forward. "I told myself that it was because you were weak, but it was the opposite. You were strong and brave in ways that I've never been, and you loved my son. Really loved him. I got scared."

"Scared of what?"

"That you were going to take my boy from me. That he would stop visiting. Stop calling. Stop wanting to be a part of my life because he was building his own with you. I was scared that he'd see all your strengths, and they would accentuate my weaknesses. I saw you as a threat when I should have seen and treated you like the daughter I never had. You deserved more from me."

Now tears gathered in Indie's eyes. Everything Sylvia said was so late but also so validating. "I needed to hear that."

"I'm going to do better. I've told my friends that the rumors I started about you were lies. I'm going to do better for my son, for you, and for my grandchild." Her gaze flicked to Indie's stomach. "I promise."

Indie inhaled deeply. "It will take time, Sylvia. A lot of time." And even then, she wasn't sure they'd get there. But for Colt, she wanted to.

The front door opened, and Colt stepped in. His expression was hard, probably because he'd seen his mother's car on the street. His eyes narrowed when they landed on Sylvia. "What's going on?"

She blinked the tears away and straightened. "I just brought some meals and had a conversation with Indie."

Concern was etched into his features as he turned to Indie. "Are you all right?"

She nodded, so many emotions swirling inside her that she didn't know *what* to feel.

Sylvia crossed the room and gripped Colt's shoulders before pressing a kiss to his cheek. Then she turned to Indie. There was genuine warmth in her eyes before she leaned forward and hugged her. *Really* hugged her, like she'd never done before. It wasn't cold or tentative or quick. It was the hug of a mother.

When she leaned back, she smiled warmly. "Ben and I would love to have you both over for dinner on Sunday. Please let me know."

"Ben and you?" Colt asked.

Her smile softened. "Yes...we would be hosting together."

Then she walked out.

Colt immediately stepped in front of Indie. "What was that?"

"I think it was a new beginning." Hopefully, one where she and her mother-in-law weren't at war. Where she was pregnant with her baby. And she and Colt were married and in love and at peace.

Life was pretty good.

* * *

COLT LOOKED at the now-closed door before shifting his focus back to Indie. Then his gaze lowered to her fisted hand. "What are you holding?"

She opened her hand, and there in her palm was her wedding and engagement ring.

"You found them?"

Her gaze flashed to the door.

No...no fucking way. "My mother *stole* them?"

"Yes, but—"

"I'm going to talk to her." He wasn't just going to talk. He was going to yell and rage. He spun, but Indie grabbed his arm.

"Colt, no."

"Yes! What did she do? Search the house?" Indie didn't have to answer—the look on her face told him he was right.

"But," Indie added, "she gave them back. And she apologized. And not just about the rings. She apologized for everything. I think she meant it. I don't know if we can recover from everything that's happened, but I'd like to try."

The only thing stopping Colt from going out there and confronting his mother was the look on Indie's face. The hope. She wanted things to be better with his mother.

He gripped her hips. "I hope for *her* sake she means it."

Indie lifted her shoulder. "Only time will tell."

He'd actually started to wonder if his mother was capable of loving anyone other than him and Ben. But then, this last week, she'd been different. Softer. She'd asked about Indie's health and sounded like she honestly cared.

Indie's hands curved around his neck. "So...she wants to have us over for a meal on Sunday."

"Do you want to go?"

"How else am I going to find out if she and Ben are dating?"

NYSSA KATHRYN

Colt laughed. "It wouldn't surprise me. I think my mother has loved Ben for a long time."

Indie suddenly gasped. "Wait! She shouldn't even have walked from her car to the house while Wade and Chester are still out there!"

"Actually—" Right on cue, his cell rang, interrupting him. He pulled it out to see that it was the call he'd been waiting for. "Jesse, do you have good news for me?"

"We have Chester Vane and Roman Korr at the station. We have a long list of reasons to keep them locked up, so they won't be free men for a very long time."

The very last bit of tension eased from his shoulders.

His father was dead, Chester and Roman were with the authorities, and Wade was no longer a deputy. They'd even found the nurse who'd shared the information about his mother's room number and had charged her.

"Thank you," Colt said.

"Just doing my job. Everything okay for you and Indie?"

He looked down at her perfect face, then over her shoulder at the sonogram on the coffee table. They'd seen their baby yesterday. Heard their heartbeat. Good didn't even begin to describe how everything was. "It's great."

"Glad to hear. We'll talk soon."

"Everything okay?" Indie asked when he hung up.

"They have Chester and Roman."

Her eyes closed, relief fluttering across her face. "Don't pinch me. If I'm dreaming, I don't want to wake up."

"Indie."

"Honestly. Things are too perfect right now. I can't—"

"Indie."

She opened her eyes.

"Things are working out how we deserve," he said. "We've done our bad. It's time for the good."

Her eyes softened, and she leaned into him. "Speaking of good, is everything ready for next week's opening at the park?"

"I just left Addie. She's working out the finer details. Noah was on the bouldering wall. He wants to test everything and make sure the activities are ready to go."

"Things really are perfect."

That was a fucking understatement. "We have each other. We're safe. And we have Peanut on the way."

She laughed, but there was a hint of tears in her eyes. "Maybe we had to go through all the crap, just so we could feel this."

"Maybe." But if he could have taken all that hard stuff away for her and made it a bit easier, he would have. They were here now though, and nothing was going to break them ever again. *She* was his priority. She'd always be his priority. "I love you, Indie Reed."

"I'll always love you."

He lowered his head and kissed her, and there it was, everything he'd come home for, right in that kiss with his wife.

CHAPTER 34

*N*oah dropped from the granite wall with a controlled thud. He'd been bouldering all morning. An attempt to both personally test out another of the park's activities and exhaust his body.

Exhausting his body was the only thing that seemed to quiet his mind some days. But hell, even exhaustion didn't always work. Dark thoughts from his past tried to sneak in too often. Things he needed to *leave* in the past, dead and buried.

He shook his chalky hands before lifting the crash pads from the ground and taking them to the new wooden lockbox they'd installed. It made more sense than carrying the equipment through the mountains every time guests wanted to use the cliff edge for bouldering or rock climbing.

Once everything was packed up, he checked the time on his phone. Ten a.m. Addie would be here and working. They could go over the booking system. Or at least, she could dumb it down enough so he understood the basics. He had no damn clue with that stuff, and Colt wasn't much better. The woman was making herself irreplaceable around here.

He set off on a jog through the forest.

Since he was a kid, every time the world got loud, he got moving. Although, back then, he didn't have much to worry about.

Now? Now there were days when he practically had to destroy his body just to get two seconds of peace.

He shook his head. He needed to stop thinking about it. He'd gotten therapy. He was out. That should be enough.

When he neared the office, he slowed to a walk and took out his phone. He hit his youngest sister's number.

Three rings before Bonnie answered. "Noah. Hi."

Every time he heard her voice, she sounded more relaxed. More willing to talk to him and like the little sister he remembered. "Hey, Bonnie. How are you doing today?"

"I'm good. Just...keeping busy at work."

He frowned. There was hesitation in her voice. "What's wrong?"

"Nothing."

"Not nothing. There's something. I can hear it in your voice."

There was a short pause. "I'm just worried. They've cut funding at the shelter, and I'm afraid my job will be axed."

"Shit."

"Yeah, shit."

"Well, you know, there are plenty of jobs here in Amber Ridge." At least, he was pretty sure there were. He had no idea about jobs at any shelters though. Surely there was a local women's shelter, but whether they had any openings, he didn't know.

There was a heavy pause.

Fuck, too soon.

He quickly changed the subject, telling her a dumb story about a fall he'd had on the bouldering wall. Of course he embellished it. It was worth it to hear her laugh.

When he finally got off the phone, he was smiling.

Bonnie was family, and he wanted her home. But it would

take time. She blamed herself for the passing of her boyfriend. And hell, the guy's parents had blamed her too. Which was bullshit. He just hoped she also wasn't shouldering any of the blame for their parents' deaths. It was a car accident, but they'd been on their way to pick her up. It hadn't been anyone's fault.

He stepped inside the office.

"No, Bernie, you promised me today, so it needs to be today."

At the sound of Addie's firm voice, a smile tugged at Noah's lips.

She sat at the reception desk, phone against her ear. In the small space of time he'd had to get to know her, he'd learned one thing...she was a ball buster. She knew what she wanted, and she went after it.

"I need the power connected before she parks her food truck. You told me it would happen today, so I told her to come on Monday."

Noah moved around the desk, snatching one of her M&M's from beside the computer. She whacked his hand, but there was a hint of a grin on her face.

"No, Bernie, that won't work because I don't believe you anymore. If I agree to let you come Monday morning, and you cancel, it doesn't give me time to replace you before she comes later that day. Then I'm a sucker *and* I'm screwed, and I don't like being either of those things. So you have one hour to either come and do the job you told me you'd do or transfer the deposit back and I will take my business elsewhere—and I mean *all* future business for the park."

There was a small pause before Addie smiled. "I'll see you soon, Bernie."

Noah blew out a long breath. "Remind me never to mess with you."

"That's the third time he's tried to reschedule after he demanded a deposit on the initial booking. Tell me again why you asked me to use him?"

Noah lifted a shoulder. "I like him?"

"Is this another Burt's Pizza thing?"

"What can I say? We're nice people here in Amber Ridge."

She scoffed. "Either that or you have this bizarre need to keep people who are terrible at their jobs in business."

"Hm...definitely the first."

She chuckled, and the sound hit him right in the chest like a freight train. He pushed it down. Just like he pushed down what her scent did to him. The fresh nature-like smell that reminded him of the rain in the mountains.

He ignored it all. He was her employer. He was also thirteen years older, which wasn't a lot for some people, but to him, it felt huge.

She frowned at him. "What's with the frown, Marine?"

"Marine?"

She lifted a shoulder as she turned back to the computer screen. "My dad was a Marine. I think the nickname's fitting."

"He was?"

"Yep. A retired gunny. Still shines his boots every Sunday like he's got inspection Monday morning."

Noah chuckled. "Old habits die hard."

"Your habits wouldn't be old though. You only just got out." She turned and looked at him. Closer than anyone else had looked at him since getting home. "How are you doing since being out?"

Shit. Why did her question make him want to flinch? Because her gaze was so intense? Or because if he answered that honestly, he'd be telling her something that he tried not to think about?

"Why?"

"Well, my dad still has PTSD from a lot that happened. Mom has to wake him from these loud, explosive nightmares sometimes." She shivered. "It's awful. I'm not saying you have PTSD or anything, just that I know you have to go through a lot as a

Marine. And fitting back into civilian life afterward can be very hard."

It wasn't just hard. Some days it felt impossible. "I'm doing great." A damn lie. There were moments when he felt fine. And moments when he couldn't breathe.

The memories tried to push to the surface, and his heart rate jumped up.

Not now.

Her brows rose, like she saw right through the lie. "Okay. But if that changes, I'm a great listener."

"Thanks, Addison."

She gave him a small smile. "Now, I have a couple forms for you to sign."

She rose and stepped around him toward the printer. He was still breathing too quickly.

What the hell was wrong with him?

He closed his eyes—but realized his mistake immediately when he saw those fucking chains.

A shoulder bumped his.

The chains around his wrists were like steel. Still, he fought them. He didn't even feel the ache of his bloody wrists anymore. The sharp pain from his broken ribs.

All he could focus on was Boone. His teammate was fighting too, but instead of chains, he was fighting men. Men who'd captured them. Tortured them. The fucking scum of the earth.

A hand suddenly touched his shoulder, and the chains disappeared as he flung the asshole to the floor and wrapped his fingers around his neck.

Noah blinked.

Addie. She was beneath him on the floor, eyes wide, no color in her face. But it was his fingers that he couldn't look away from.

They circled her neck.

Too tight. Too fucking tight.

286

He yanked his hands away like her skin burned him. He wanted to ask how she'd gotten there, how they'd *both* gotten to this position, but he already knew. And the reality made acid churn in his gut.

"Did I hurt you?" Disgust coated each word. Disgust in himself. That he'd touched a woman like that. *Scared* her like that.

She opened and closed her mouth. "I'm okay." Barely a whisper. "Are you?"

No. He was far from okay.

He shot to his feet. He wanted to help her up too, but she was already pushing to her feet and stepping away.

Why the hell would she want him to touch her anyway? She wouldn't. She probably wanted to be as far from him as possible.

"I'm sorry." Sorry? He was fucking *sorry*? That wasn't enough. He'd just *assaulted* her. He could almost see his fucking fingerprints on her neck.

"It's okay," she whispered. "You didn't mean to."

His brows drew together. Did she know that because of her dad? Did *he* have flashbacks like that?

"Do you want to press charges?" He wouldn't blame her. Hell, he'd welcome it. It was what he deserved.

Her brows rose. "Charges?"

"I assaulted you, Addison. I can call Jesse—"

"No. I'm all right. Really. It's you I'm worried about."

He didn't respond. He just stood there feeling like he was suspended in time. Like if he moved or spoke it would make the last five minutes real.

She stepped toward him, but he rushed around the desk. "I should go."

"Wait!"

He stopped mid-turn, when really all he wanted to do was run. Get the hell out. Scared that he'd lose his fucking mind a second time.

"It's really okay," she pushed. "*I'm* okay."

Did she repeat those words because she knew he hadn't believed her the first time?

Air. He needed fresh fucking air and a million miles between him and anyone else—especially her.

"I'll see you tomorrow, Addison."

He turned and walked outside, the same question repeating in his head over and over again.

What the fuck just happened?

He'd never hurt a woman in his life.

One thing he was certain of…he never wanted that to happen again. Which meant he needed to stay the hell away from Addison.

Order book five, Noah and Addie's story, UNCHAINED, now!

ALSO BY NYSSA KATHRYN

Declan

Cole

Ryker

BEAUTIFUL PIECES

Erik's Salvation

Erik's Redemption

Erik's Refuge

SHORT CHRISTMAS STORY

Hidden Shadows

RECKLESS SERIES

Reckless Hope

Reckless Trust

Reckless Fall

Reckless Faith

Reckless Love

AMBER RIDGE SERIES

(Series ongoing)

Unafraid

Unraveled

Untouched

Unbroken

Unchained

JOIN my newsletter and be the first to find out about sales and new releases! CLICK HERE

ABOUT THE AUTHOR

Nyssa Kathryn is a romantic suspense author. She lives in South Australia with hubby and two daughters and takes every chance she can to be plotting and writing. Always an avid reader of romance novels, she considers alpha males and happily-ever-afters to be her jam.

Don't forget to follow Nyssa and never miss another release.

Facebook | Instagram | Amazon | Goodreads